Penguin Books
The Raining Tree War

David Pownall was born in Liverpool in 1938 and educated at Lord Wandsworth College and the University of Keele, from which he graduated in 1960 in English and History. Between 1960 and 1963 he worked as a personnel officer for Fords at Dagenham and Halewood, and then went to Northern Rhodesia (now Zambia) to work in mining on the Copperbelt. He started to write plays for the mining town theatres and after six years in Africa returned to England to take up writing as a profession.

For two years he worked with the Century Mobile Theatre as a publicity officer and resident playwright, and then with the Duke's Playhouse, Lancaster, with which he continues a close writing association. In 1975 he started his own touring company, 'Paines Plough', which specializes in new plays. He has also written another African comic novel, *African Horse* (to be published simultaneously with this volume); *God Perkins*, a novel about the theatre; *My Organic Uncle*, a collection of short stories; *The Dream of Chief Crazy Horse*, a play for children; and *Another Country*, a collection of poems. He also writes for radio and television.

David Pownall now lives in Lancaster.

David Pownall

The Raining Tree War

Penguin Books

Penguin Books Ltd, Harmondsworth,
Middlesex, England
Penguin Books, 625 Madison Avenue,
New York, New York 10022, U.S.A.
Penguin Books Australia Ltd, Ringwood,
Victoria, Australia
Penguin Books Canada Ltd, 2801 John Street,
Markham, Ontario, Canada L3R 1B4
Penguin Books (N.Z.) Ltd, 182–190 Wairau Road,
Auckland 10, New Zealand

First published by Faber & Faber Ltd 1974
Published in Penguin Books 1977

Made and printed in Great Britain by
Hazell Watson & Viney Ltd,
Aylesbury, Bucks
Set in Linotype Pilgrim

For Mary Ellen
and the Summer of 1972

I

Maud

She stood on the steps of the mud-brick and corrugated-iron cathedral which her followers had built for her, a babe at each colossal breast, her awesome body gleaming with oil, Maud Mamuntu, Wife of God, Spouse of the Almighty, six foot nine and a half inches of magnificent, mammalian prophetess.

'Who tells you that I am old?' she thundered. 'Who has seen a grey hair on my head or anywhere else for that matter? All my husbands, stand up and bear witness!'

Forty-seven men of various ages rose to their feet out of the seated crowd.

'All your hairs are as black as night, Wife!' they chanted together. 'You are as bountiful as the maize-field, as young as the first bean-plants coming through the red earth! You bear us children even though you are well into your seventies! You are as strong as the buffalo, as sweet as the fresh beer in the gourd!'

'All right! All right!' Maud held up a massive hand. 'Now hear me now any that do not believe!'

She paused, her mouth opened, a huge red cave.

'Who is God's woman?' she roared tremendously.

'*Wena!*' the congregation responded.

'Who is God's wife?'

'*Wena!*'

(The forty-seven men sat down again at this point in the ceremony.)

Maud plucked the sucking mouths of the babes from her nipples, handed the infants to an assistant, and rubbed her breasts over with the palms of her hands. Before her sat five thousand Muntu, swatting flies, squinting sideways at the sun or holding broad leaves over their heads for shade. Maud had called her people to Myanis Kupela to hear her speak, to give them encouragement to keep on loving God, her heavenly Husband. The Muntu had woken early, left their fires cold outside their huts, and gone with empty bellies to listen to their spiritual leader. She was breakfast enough for any man. As her people had crossed the ponds, islands and sedges of the Bengweulu Swamp towards the cathedral, Maud had sung to them from the top of the tower, the eastern sun flashing about her gigantic frame.

> God has only just gone!
> *Yena hambile konamanje!*
> He has left my side
> And left his Seed! *Hlebela!*

As the Muntu came nearer they had raised their voices in one of Maud's original hymns, written especially for her holy Husband.

> We are where Life started,
> In the mire! *Molo! Molo!*
> We are at the beginning of Time
> In the ooze! *Molo! Molo!*
> *Ehe!* God is good! God is good!

Settling down to life in the swamps had not been an easy adjustment for the Muntu sect. Most of them were from tribes which traditionally inhabited the high plateau-land of central Africa, a country of dry earth, bush, well fed by broad rivers. There the ground was firm, crops of mealies, cassava and beans could be grown; and every village had its shop where Persil could be bought, tins of Portuguese sardines, Park Drive cigarettes, wire coat-hangers and Basildon Bond writing-paper. No man went short on the great table-land, the world was on his doorstep with its wealth crowding for admittance. All of these things had to be sacrificed when Maud decided to take her people into the great swamp to escape the persecution of Doctor Mulombe. The sweets of Life were left behind and the vast Bengweulu Swamp swallowed the Muntu up, hugging them to its muddy and malarial bosom.

After six months in the feverish bogs the Muntu were exhausted and on the verge of starvation. All their residual energy had been used up in the building of their capital, Myanis Kupela, and Maud's great cathedral. Their plight was not unnoticed and when the news that Maud and the Muntu had clashed with Doctor Mulombe and his Progress Party – the future rulers of Zonkendawo – a number of secret legations had set out from various parts of Africa, hoping to contact the rebels. The American C.I.A. helpfully suggested that the Muntu use the waters of the swamp as a fish-farm and promptly flew in five thousand spawning salmon by helicopter. A date was fixed for a ceremonial hand-over and the Muntu gathered at the end of the main pond selected for the experiment. As Maud and her people watched the big, silver fish being tossed into the black waters, an invasion fleet of crocodiles appeared and ate them up, then hung around on the sand- and mud-banks, staring at the disappointed Muntu with cold, hungry eyes. The Canadians wanted to start a timber industry and sent out a forestry expert with a large consignment of Scots Fir. While he was looking for suitable soil to make a plantation, a renegade Muntu youth stole his lorry and the trees and drove up to the Copperbelt where he sold them off for Christmas. The only government which had been successful in attaching an agent to the Muntu was the People's Republic of China. They had sent an expert in rice-cultivation, convinced that the nature of the terrain was suited to the growing of this staple crop. Now he lived at Myanis Kupela with the Muntu, conducting experiments with various types of rice-seed.

On the morning of the Wife of God's address to her people, Bwana Cat's-Eyes (as the agronomist was called by the Muntu) was sitting just inside the door of his hut recording Maud's speech on a tiny tape-recorder hidden in a ping-pong ball.

'My sons, my daughters, my friends, my people,' Maud boomed, her enormous rib-cage heaving grandly, 'God came to me last night. *Ehe! Tina hlanganile!* The earth shook! After our passion had abated He talked to me of you, His Muntu. He loves you as His true children, as His own. He says we are right to throw away Zonkendawo and Mulombe [here the crowd hissed and dug their heels into the ground] because they have turned their backs on Him! Here, He says, is Paradise. The flies, the mosquitoes, the fevers, the bad water, what are these things? *Aiziko!* Nothing at all! Remember, even that eunuch Mulombe would go to the garden of Eden if he could find it! What man turns away from true happiness? Who rejects the Truth when it is staring him in the face? Here we have perfection!'

An old man got to his feet holding a branch of *mupapa* leaves over his ashy head.

'Maud, I would speak with you.'

'Go ahead, *madala*,' Maud folded her arms. 'Speak and be heard!'

'Maud, Wife of God, Woman of our Friend, I seek comfort as one who knows that his death is coming. I am a sensitive person and can feel that I will die before many days have passed.'

'*Ukufa!*' groaned the crowd. '*Muhle wena hamba! Muhle wena hamba!*'

The old man nodded his head, conscious of their sympathetic understanding of his poor situation.

'When you sink me in the swamp with stones on my breast, I will be no more and will not be able to ask you questions, so I am asking now before it is too late.'

'*Ukufa!*' the crowd tetched softly. 'It is a bitter thing to die.'

'Like all men with any sense,' the old man quavered on, 'I fear death because I like it here, but I know that even you, Maud, who is the Woman of the great God Himself, cannot turn the clock back. Hm!' he summoned up a rusty laugh, then spoke bravely, his head a little higher. 'You will mourn me for a while and talk of my good nature, my misdeeds, some of my laughable mistakes which I have made, then I will be forgotten. It is not fair but that is how it goes.'

Maud held up a shovel-sized hand.

'It is the same for all of us, *madala*. Do not blame us for death.'

'Ah!' the old man cried with sudden vehemence, 'but I might blame God!'

'Why blame Him? Blame your old mother,' Maud grumbled sonorously. 'She's the one who bore you in flesh and blood. If she had wanted you to live for ever then she would have born you in stone.'

'If I had been born in stone then I would have been already dead before I started!' the old man replied crossly.

'So what are you moaning about?' The prophetess leaned back, her vast belly swimming with sunlight. 'And be thankful that you were born to die.'

Sitting down, the old man put his head in his hands. The crowd around him touched his shoulder, tapped him on the head with their shade-leaves, tugged his shirt and tried to make him feel better.

But he was inconsolable.

'*Madala!*' Maud called, a smile rising in her face like the eastern morn. 'Listen to me.'

'I hear you,' the old man sniffed, 'but there is nothing to be done. When you have got to go, you have got to go. I was only talking for the sake of it.'

'We are your friends, *madala*, your *chamwares*, God is your best friend. For a man to die amongst friends is not a bad death. Have you not been happy with us?'

Maud left the cathedral steps and picked her way through the crowd until she stood by the old man, his grey head placed in her shadow.

Her voice was soft.

'I could paint pictures in your head, *madala*, steal your last pinch of salt. I could say that you will live forever, but you won't. The burial-pond is full of we Muntu. It is floored with babies. Its foundations are not of earth and rock, old man, but of mothers and fathers. We are the food of the crocodile. We all wear the hood of black water one day. That is Truth. What my Husband says is that death is an end, and that is all He can afford. His purse does not stretch to everlasting life. Perhaps He is poor? If we do not give ourselves back to God then there can be no more planting. The seeds in your head, the seeds in your knuckles, the seeds in your navel, the seeds of your heart, God needs them all in His sowing-basket.'

Maud bent down, slipped a hand under the old man's armpit, and heaved him to her breast, both his feet leaving the ground.

'*Madala*,' she whispered in his ear as she gave him a bearlike embrace, 'if the dance does not end then it cannot begin again.'

'But I will die!' the old man gnashed at the air in frustration, his face half-buried in Maud's cleavage. 'Just when I'm really enjoying myself!'

Maud hugged him close, then gave him an affectionate shake which rattled the old man's teeth in his head, and put him back amongst his companions. Turning on her heel she stalked back to the steps, her mighty feet kicking up clouds of red dust.

'Life is here!' she pounded the heaped splendour of her belly. 'Here! Here! Where is death then? It is not in me! It is not in you! It is Time and the outside, that is where death is. Death is Mulombe. He stops a man being alive when he is full of breath. He makes him die while he still walks and lies with his wife, making more death. Mulombe ties the knot of death in the cord, he ties it up with Freedom, ah, he knows nothing of the word! All of you have seen Truth on this island, you have seen real Freedom. You have seen me!'

Maud pointed a finger at the old man.

'Oh *madala*, oh ungrateful old man. You were with me in the early days when I was mocked. You believed in me when the people pelted me with stones and drove me from village to village like a dog. You were there when they took away my children, murdered some of my husbands, broke my cooking-pot and tore off my apron. We have been together a long time and I love you, my Husband loves you, Life loves you. Go gladly into the swamp when the time comes. You have walked the road on the right side!'

The Muntu applauded vociferously, showering themselves with dust. While they cheered their sweating leader, Bwana Cat's-Eyes wrinkled up his nose in disgust. He was an ascetic by nature and this type of subjective, fecund philosophy appalled him. The giant size of Maud in her blooming black mountain of flesh, her gargantuan lusts and ideas, the rivers of perspiration that ran from her arm-pits, the pot-hole of her navel, the bulge and gleam of her herculean thews, the sheer power of her body-odour which surrounded her much as an atmosphere encloses a planet, the musky wind of her breath and the white and brown roll of her terrible eye, all these natural advantages which Maud enjoyed served only to repel the fastidious Chinaman.

Although he would never have confessed the fact, even under torture, Bwana Cat's-Eyes found the Muntu difficult to live with. He preferred people to be delicately sophisticated, have a nimble and graceful wit within the confines of the only true and practical political creed. The Muntu had none of these virtues to their credit. They were irrational, uncivilized, chronically afflicted with intellectual blindness, brutishly sensual, hopelessly inefficient and they couldn't play ping-pong.

Around the edge of the cathedral square stood twelve ping-pong tables which had been painstakingly dragged overland from Dar-Es-Salaam. Many of the wooden trestles had been eaten away by white ants. All the nets had been taken for fishing. The screw-clamps had been purloined by young girls for ear-rings. Then the bats themselves had been spirited away to appear shortly afterwards as genital-coverings. The final blow had been the use to which the tables had been put by the ingenious Muntu. Leaving them in position round the square they had moved in underneath, building walls of reeds around the sides, and had started using them as homes. From his hut, Bwana Cat's-Eyes was forced to look across at the failure of a great experiment.

'Why must we do this thing?' the Muntu had asked in wonderment as Bwana Cat's-Eyes ran from one end of a table to another, playing ping-pong with himself because nobody would take an interest. 'What are you trying to prove?'

'It is a substantial fight against my own weakness!' Bwana Cat's-Eyes had panted. 'And to sharpen up my reflexes. Ping-pong was invented by the Chinese people at the same time as chess, gunpowder and individual liberty!'

'I am a living testament!' Maud thumped her chest. 'I am not paper or thick books! I am here! I live! Look at me! Is this what you find in a gospel?' she thrust out a strong, powerfully-muscled leg. 'Is this a pulpit?' she banged her skull with her knuckles. 'The women's magazines of the West say I am overweight, that I should be dead!' Here she roared with laughter, pounding her loins with clenched fists. Had they ever heard such nonsense as the women's magazines of the West went on about? To be fat was to be prosperous. To be big was to be at an advantage. To be as huge as Maud was worthy of the wife of God.

'I have seen it!' Maud chanted. 'Oh I have seen it!'

'*Yena bona!*' her followers murmured.

'It was as it was! As the book says, God came down unto a woman! What man is widowed in youth, God is always young, and does not take a second wife? We are all the children of

God. The missionaries tell us the same but say that there was one child more of a child of God than the other children. How can that be? A child is a child. He is from womb and seed. You cannot make a child outside yourself with wood and nails. *Ikona!* We are all children of God and I am His woman!'

High on the cathedral tower Stanley Firbank listened to Maud's speech. He had offered to take the watch that morning, keeping an eye on the humid fens that stretched out from the island on which Myanis Kupela had been built. As he did so, his eye often strayed to the hut where Bwana Cat's-Eyes lived. He knew that the Chinaman was in there. They were rivals but in different spheres. As a man of God himself, Firbank's relationship with Maud was that of acolyte. Their friendship was sustained through religion only. Bwana Cat's-Eyes was a practical man whose only interest was to make paddy-fields in the swamps and gather information about the strength of Maud's potential resistance to Doctor Mulombe.

Firbank had come to Africa after a two-year spell of service as chaplain to the Second Air Cavalry of the United States Army in Vietnam. He had gone to Vietnam as a holy-roller Baptist and come out as a man with a god of his own whom he carried around in his head. No one else had seen this god. He was a primitive deity, a curious flame burning in a lamp of bloody oil. When Maud spoke of her husband, Firbank saw something of his god in hers. It was never quite the same because Firbank's god manifested himself in blood while Maud's came in lust. But there was enough of a connection for Firbank to feel at home with the Muntu and stop his wanderings. He stifled the sincere expression of his faith and participated in Maud's vision as far as his conscience would permit. From the cathedral tower he could see across a land that his god could easily have inhabited, his strange barbaric spirit swimming in the blue film of marsh-oil, whining with the mosquitoes, writhing through the light-less waters like a snake.

'Let us worship that thing we can touch!' Maud bawled below. 'The one who will let us hold Him in our hands. Forget the smoke! Forget the high places that we cannot reach!'

Firbank had reached up to his Baptist god. He had kept his eyes fixed upwards as he followed the troops into combat. As he had tramped along, head held back, he had kept tripping over the dead and dying. After a while he had kept his eyes down while still thinking that he was looking up. It was the only pragmatical approach to the problem of moving forward without breaking his neck. Soon his god changed from radiant white to satin red, wings for spread-eagled lungs, blazing eyes for staring pupils that fixed the sky where his old god had lived with a disbelieving stare. God was not up there any more. He was under the feet. He appeared in a new guise.

Firbank had always accepted the premise that Death was part of his old god's bag of tricks. If there was no death then there would be no god because nobody would need one. It was a matter of survival for his old god to keep people aware of the fact that they would surely die. As his Vietnam career entered its second year he saw that the real god was Death. Life had only been invented by him in order to get some recognition in a desolate universe. He had listened to the old man's plaint with interest as he argued with Maud. There was half a convert but the time was not yet ripe. If he moved in on Maud's territory and started his own movement there would be unpleasant repercussions for Firbank that might ruin his apostolic mission.

'How can we take any notice of a man like Mulombe? What inspiration has he ever had? What is the source of his power? Can we be told that God rules all things one day and Mulombe another? His people, the ones who came to try and interfere with us, said that we must render unto Caesar the things that are Caesar's. That may be all right, but we certainly are not giving them to Doctor Mulombe! We have eyes, we have ears, we know, we people here! We have a good friend to take care of us, to advise us. He is my man and me His woman. We talk a lot about you all. Better to keep that which is close and you can check on than stretch yourself to ruptures!'

This rhetoric brought shouts of approval from the Muntu. It was not only good sense, it was good economics.

'Mulombe says we must pay to join his Party! Do we have to pay to join God's party? Mulombe says we must pay taxes! Does my husband ask us for taxes? Is Mulombe any better than the British who knew we never used money and demanded hut-tax so we would have to go to the Copperbelt and work on their mines? Is he? We still use no money. Who has money here? They are all far from God, the true God my man. Between Mulombe and the British you could not slip a blade of grass!'

'*Yenazonke silwanyana!*' the crowd roared angrily. 'They are vermin!'

Maud paused, a finger held upwards to the tower.

'If we pay anything, we pay in love. If we hand over the fruit of our hours then it is in the acts of love. My man sees this great thing we did for Him. It is His hut on earth and I lie there to wait for Him each night for all of you. We Muntu are not fools. Can God's best friends and the friends of His woman be fools?'

Laughter greeted her unbeatable logic. All eyes rested on the great tower of mud-bricks, 300 feet high. It was an achievement that every man, woman and child had contributed to and was enormously proud of; it was a fitting home for their indomitable, titanic prophetess and the God who was her husband. When the Muntu had been in the open without the protection of the swamps, every church that they had tried to build for Maud had been destroyed before it had got beyond the foundations. The Party watched them as closely as they did the opposition or the Jehovah's Witnesses, the other sect which refused to accept government authority. Whenever Maud had held a meeting in the urban areas it had been broken up by Party hoodlums, whenever she had tried to approtch Mulombe himself she had been chased away and beaten. No matter what she did the Party was waiting for her.

People still came to her even at that time, and that had been her strength. Avoiding the towns she had wandered the bush with a few disciples, living off what she could beg. One day she had arrived at a village by a tributary of the Luangwa and felt at home. Most of the villagers were in a state of religious suspense, neither one thing nor the other. Christ had been and gone, the old paganism had decayed long before. When Maud told them that she was the Wife of God the villagers flocked to her and pleaded with her to stay. When she had agreed they had built her a hut. That had been the time of the great tree-bed. Instead of God coming to her at night in the hut, which was crowded, the villagers had erected a platform of branches in a *mululu* tree just outside the village. This was for God and His woman to love in and be nearer the stars.

One man had not believed that Maud Mamuntu was the true Wife of God. He had approached the prophetess one evening and invited her to his hut to try and lay her. Whether it was the sparkles that danced in his evil, crafty eye or the gnarled hand on her powerful buttocks that warned her off will never be known, but she wasn't having any. He was the hoofed Devil and there was no love in his heart.

The man had got the hump and ridden his bicycle twenty miles to the nearest office of the Progress Party where he had informed the regional secretary of what was going on in his village. Assembling a gang of Party supporters, the regional secretary had borrowed a truck and driven through the night, guided by the informer. By the light of the truck's headlamps every inhabitant had been asked for his Party card after being dragged out of bed, then beaten. None of them had ever heard of the Party except the informer. No one had ever bothered with them before, the village being so far off the beaten track.

Maud had heard the truck arrive, her senses sharpened by her experiences with the Party, while up the tree with God. Shinning down she had watched her hut burning with her husbands in it, then set off on her wanderings again.

It was this, and a thousand other acts of persecution, which made Myanis Kupela a miracle of faith and security to Maud. It was the tower of her life, the citadel of her great body. To her and her followers it was the place of God who went on into her each night. Once darkness fell on Myanis Kupela there was a total curfew. No one stirred outside their huts or raised their voice above a whisper. Maud had not imposed the curfew on her followers, it had developed naturally. The Muntu were listening for God.

Some had heard His footsteps, others had not. Some had heard Him whistling as He strolled, dry-shod, over the swamps. Some had heard Him pass through the high grasses around the island, crashing like a herd of elephants. One boy had heard Him urinating among the *mufumbe* trees; the sound, he said, was like a waterfall. Almost everyone had heard God at one time or another, even if it was only His hair growing.

Others had seen Him (never completely for that was too much to hope for and perhaps Maud was the only one to be so privileged), and their testimony was cherished in the sect's lore. His eyes, blazing like monsoon lightning, had been sighted many times as He came across the swamp to His woman. Blue, filmy with flame were His garments as they drifted over the marsh-gas lying on the water. Rough, thorny and tangled was His great head of hair as He peered over the reed island to see if everything was ready for His coming. The bats turned away from His presence as they did from a hill, the night-birds shrieked at the flapping of His robe, the bullfrogs boomed beneath His feet with joy, glad to be the living sole of His exquisite feet. At night God made his way to Myanis Kupela. There was no doubt of that in any Muntu's mind.

If there had been, there was one sign that he could not have avoided. It was in his ears, and an undeniable proof of God's presence in their midst. When Maud, from the cathedral, began her nightly groanings, sighings and gurglings at the top of her stentorian registers, then the whole world knew that God was having His will of her.

When God had come and gone there would be a further silence maintained until Maud's voice, happy and revitalized, was heard calling out the name of one of her earthly husbands.

There had been a time in the early days of the sect's existence when Doubting Thomases had disputed with Maud on the fatherhood of her many children. Were they the offspring of God or man? Was it fair on a child not to know who his father was? If a child was the son or daughter of God should it not have special treatment?

Maud had reasoned them out of their doubts.

'God is a man,' she had argued, 'so what is the difference? If He was not as other men are then He would not be able to enter me. He does not ask that His children should erect barriers between themselves. He does not agree with any kind of separation. What is His is yours, what is yours is His.'

'But Maud, Wife of God,' the suspicious disciples had insisted, 'why should God let other men tamper with His woman? We would not endure it. If a husband finds another man with his wife then he fights him. If God is a man then He should do the same if He is to remain honourable.'

'You are asking that God should be jealous? Jealousy is a sin, yet you ask that God should be sinful. God shares all He has with us. That includes me.'

'But if you are the Wife of God, and these men [they had pointed to the husbands, not so numerous then as the Muntu was not the mass-movement that it later developed into] are your husbands, then they are the husbands of the Wife of God and therefore are God themselves because He is your husband. Is God one person or many?'

Maud had asked for time to think about this poser and gone into the shade of her hut to work on it. Two days later she had summoned a meeting.

'You asked me a hard question,' she had admitted, 'and I had to discuss it with my Husband.'

'Which one?' a wit piped up.

'Do you wish to know His answer or is this a time for jokes in poor taste?' she rumbled aggressively. 'I have spent much time thinking about what has been said. God has helped me.'

While the wit was told to shut up and hustled to the edge of the crowd where he could be watched, Maud had explained.

'Would you expect God's woman to be as other women?'

'*Cha!*' had come the reply. 'Never!'

'How do we see God? We see God through appetite and desire. It is the senses that tell us we are alive. God is life and it is through these same senses that we see Him. I can see God better than anyone else because He comes to me. He comes to me because I can appreciate Him better than any other woman could. Why? Because I have more desire.'

The disputants had sat on their haunches, rocking backwards and forwards as they tried to follow her argument.

'Are you saying that God cannot satisfy you?' the wit yelled from where he was standing pinioned by two angry disciples.

Maud was nonplussed and ordered them not to beat the man. He was a small, undernourished fellow with a long scrubby face and bald patches on his head. When Maud stepped through the crowd and picked him up, putting him under her arm, and returned to her place at the head of the congregation, the man had confidently expected to be battered to death as an example to other disbelievers. He had made no complaint as he was tired of life and was only baiting Maud for something to do.

'What are you going to say now?' the wit had tittered hysterically from under her forested armpit. 'You'll never convince me.'

'I am not going to try and convince you with words,' Maud had replied sternly. 'The only way to get through to cynics like you is to marry you.'

And so the number of her husbands grew, each steamrollered into a state of grace.

2
Friendship and the Fokker

Pyper disliked flying over Africa. There was always a chance that he was missing something. Leaning over the side of the cockpit he hunched his slender frame against the buffets of the wind and looked down at the long road to Mufunsi.

From the illicit shebeens and friendly whorehouses of Myakajunji, Zonkendawo's capital on the southern plain, all the way due north across the vast plateau of bush and river to the Copperbelt, he had a string of working contacts. Along that straight African highway there ran a juicy grapevine, its branches penetrating every hidden corner of the enormous territory. Nothing stirred down there; no birth, death, liaison, scandal, upset or triumph but that John Pyper heard about it. The stories that rose from his typewriter did not come from the hacked syndication of the world's horrors but from the thin distance between a Zonkendawon's foot and the red ground he walked on. Now these authenticated tales were being acted out far beneath him, lost to his eyes and ears as the aircraft made its deafening way towards Mufunsi.

He sat back in his bucket-seat and tried to shrink into a ball. Ahead, perched above the howling wind-deflector of the pilot's cockpit, was the wispy dome of Desaix's head, his thick wreath of brown curls flattened against the sides of his skull while his bald patch reflected the sun. As Pyper concentrated his gaze through the polaroid sun-glasses that were perched on his dainty nose, staring at the lumpy hemisphere that was the middle-aged French aviator's nerve-box of responses and reactions, he became aware that Desaix L'Ace was not looking forward through the thundering propeller of the ancient triplane but was grinning back over his shoulder. Pyper did not grin back.

Instead, he sighed.

In his white cotton jacket with stitched lapels, black silk shirt and dove-grey slacks, orange neck-scarf and two-tone moccasins, Pyper cut a flamboyant though slightly girlish figure. Blond, with the surpassing fairness of the north, a downy tenderness around mouth and cheek, he could have been an effete youth overly conscious of cutting a dazzling figure. What kept him way outside this classification was his eyes. They burned with a hard, icy blue. Even the morning had not dampened the freezing arctic temper, a blue so cold that it was hot. The filigree network of surface blood from his persistent drinking had only served to decorate his astounding pupils.

John Pyper was flying due north to Mufunsi, a mining town on the Copperbelt of Zonkendawo on the eve of the country's independence. For seventy years Zonkendawo had been a British colony, kept so for its mineral wealth, mainly copper. After ten years of civil insurrection, riots, killings, strikes, commissions, imprisonments, delegations and political horse-trading, the imperial power had decided to hand over the restive colony to Doctor Mulombe and his People's Progress Party, the victors in the internecine struggles between the different Zonkendawon freedom movements. The British were getting out.

Behind them they were leaving a land that was nearly as empty as when they had found it – except for the Copperbelt, a string of mining towns lying close to the pedicle of the Congolese Katanga. Here, living a life that was famous throughout Africa for its extravagance, the British who were getting out elsewhere were staying, as were the South Africans, Rhodesians, Spaniards, Hungarians, Jews, Greeks and everyone else. The Zonkendawons were staying as well. With independence round the corner it was suddenly worth it.

Pyper thought about his recent article in *The Zonkendawon Times* attacking Desaix's small air charter company. The United Nations Commission of 1961 had condemned the exploitation of Zonkendawo's mineral resources by foreign dividend-exporting companies which had parent directoral boards in South Africa. Also they had hammered the European Mine-workers Union for negotiating agreements with those companies which used racial differences as the basis for a closed shop and selective job-allocation. Pyper had taken to heart his editor's invitation to expose this terrible state of affairs. Ignoring the copper-mining companies, who had shrugged off the commission's verdict with monolithic indifference, he had turned his burning ice-blue eyes on the little contracting organizations.

Desaix was number one on the list. He might have been gearing himself to make a fortune out of the tenderfoot incompetence of Doctor Mulombe and his new African government when they assumed power. At the stroke of midnight all authority over the enormous tracts of upland bush, river, desert and swamp, plus three and a half million people, would pass to men whose only knowledge of power was feeling the brunt of it. They would need protection from men like Desaix L'Ace, veteran of three wars.

Pyper had carved up the struggling, debt-ridden air charter company of his friend with ruthless candour. It was inefficient, had only one aircraft, a German 1914–18 Fokker that was obsolete, and was managed by a drunken, whoring 'high-altitude hobo'. There had been a photograph of the Fokker in pieces, surrounded by a crowd of grinning African youths. Desaix had been in the foreground, an African girl tucked under his arm like a crutch. With a nice sense of symbolism she was holding a bottle against Desaix's inner thigh. Pyper had captioned the pic: 'IS THIS THE FUTURE OF ZONKENDAWON AVIATION?'

Pyper had stolen the picture off Desaix's mantelpiece. It was a reminder of a very happy occasion for the Frenchman, the refit party for the Fokker when all the apprentices of Mufunsi mine had given up their leisure-time to help Desaix put the old plane back together, having overhauled the engine, balanced the new wing-sections and repaired the wear and tear on the fuselage. The bottle was Fanta Orange, the girl an innocent virgin who had been unaware of the poetry inherent in her stance.

But using the picture had been justified.

Doctor Mulombe was an old freedom-fighter, ignorant of Science, Finance, Economics or Democracy. He knew a lot about fighting for freedom but not much about sharing it around afterwards. Government was a mystery to the old hoodlum and his scarred gang of Party supporters. They had survived a long, nasty war. In and out of prison, hounded, persecuted, vilified, slandered, they had managed to cudgel the gigantic country of Zonkendawo into some kind of unity against the British. Desaix was on their wavelength, he was spiritually allied with such men. The Fokker was as much a part of Zonkendawo's aerial landscape as the baobab tree was a feature of the bush. Mulombe could see all the problems of handling Western technocracy writ small when he looked closely at Desaix L'Ace – he was a miniature of the face that neo-colonialism wore in Africa.

The *coup de grâce* had been the misprint which Pyper had ordered the boys on the compositors' bench to make. Instead of using the pilot's dignified *nom de guerre* in its proper form, he had changed it from L'Ace to L'Arse. It had been a masterstroke. The whole of Zonkendawo had laughed.

Had he been fair to Desaix?

Pyper's eyes wandered over the land below. Desaix was a close friend, he loved the man. He was tough, rugged, indestructible. Zonkendawo wasn't. The product of some diplomatic cartographer in London, its frontiers straight-lined with negotiated international backstairs deals, it contained in its treatified box a host of tribes, nations and races. Most of them did not realize that they were about to become citizens of the same sovereign state. When the British were there they had a point of common antipathy – the same taxman. With Doctor Mulombe this focus of dislike would even disappear. The old man could not count.

Tomorrow everyone in Zonkendawo would wake up with a similar taste in their mouths. Independence eve was to be dry. Doctor Mulombe's draconian edict had closed all bars, beerhalls and illicit shebeens and banned any kind of celebration of independence. His out-going colonial advisers had recommended this course of action to prevent any backlash against the white population – the miners would still be needed, they had pointed out, copper does not dig itself.

The other reason why Pyper was going to Mufunsi was connected with this savage and unthinking decision. In Field-Marshal Montgomery Crescent in the outskirts of Mufunsi, there would be a party. He was sure of that.

Yes, he had hurt his friend Desaix for the common good. Pyper believed that a journalist should write about what he knows best and in this case this meant his friends. The people who weren't his friends were unknown quantities, mysteries; how could he honestly attribute motives, analyse their actions and draw significant conclusions? All over Zonkendawo there were people who understood and despaired of the well-known convention whereby Pyper wrecked the lives of his friends by publicizing their innermost secrets, frailties and errors. Throughout the country Pyper's enemies enjoyed the blessings of anonymity.

Yet Desaix had not tried to divest himself of Pyper's friendship, even at the height of the scandal. He had taken the blow on all the chins that descended from just below his generous mouth to the collar of his flying-overalls and never flinched. He had never mentioned the summons from the aviation ministry, the checking of his licence, the midnight visit from four Progress Party hatchet-men, the drop in business, the humiliation, the jeers of people in the street. He had acted towards Pyper as he had always done. It was as if the article had never appeared. The Ace of the Air had soared to a stratosphere of astronomical forgiveness.

Desaix jabbed a forefinger at the horizon. A column of dark smoke stood against the sky, the top of it melting away into the encompassing blue, its source invisible in the hazy earth. It was the smelter stack of Mufunsi mine. They were not far from their destination.

Glancing down again he saw the road going towards the smoke, slicing through the weathered baize of dambo and bush, flying across the Kafue River and its shallow valley. Running parallel were the ponderous steps of the pylon line bringing electric power up from Kariba Dam in the south, and the railway. There was a train heading for Myakajunji, loaded with copper wirebars. He could see them lying cross-piled in the waggons, dull and red. From Myakajunji the train would turn south-west to Livingstone, cross the Zambesi at the Victoria Falls then into Rhodesia and down into South Africa or Mozambique. Some time in the future the copper would end up on the London Metal Market and a price would be quoted per ton. That figure was Zonkendawo's economic identity.

Death was at the end of the Mufunsi road as well. It was at the end of every journey which Pyper had taken since his medical examination the previous month. The doctor had told him that unless he changed his life-style he would be dead before he was thirty-five. Pyper had thought that was generous. He didn't think that he could take another seven years of feeling like he did before the British Empire Service League opened for breakfast at half-past eight. All he could afford to hope for was that the offal inside him would keep up with his crusading mind; that it would run on the same fuel that his brain fired on until the whole system blew up. Two kidneys and a liver was not much to found a new humanist society on, but it would have to do. Like Doctor Mulombe had often said in his speeches, Zonkendawo was going to be the first sincere experiment in multiracial togetherness and Pyper was completely in sympathy with the old blackguard's sentiments. After Pyper was dead, the rest would be up to his friends.

So Death scuttled along the road to Mufunsi after the frail New Zealander, hallooing as he leaped the Kafue, hurdling the pylons, grinning up at the fair-complexioned hopeful lad who was looking down at the dreadful vision wondering whether he should puke and be done with it.

'Why?' Pyper cried out at Death's gruesome gambols. 'Why?'

Desaix heard the shout and strapped himself in with a satisfied chuckle. He had not seen Death that day, but he knew what Pyper was questioning. While Pyper had been thinking about his premature demise, Desaix had been thinking about the Fokker. There was seldom an hour passed without Desaix occupying his thoughts with the old triplane's future. Many of the rough women whom the Frenchman knocked around with, their laboured, encoarsened wit being that of working girls, thought that the pilot would be better off if he fucked the Fokker and got the relationship on a proper footing. They had heard him calling out in his sleep using technical terms of its great German engine. They had heard him mutter about landing-gear shimmy and airframe-shudder until sex was no fun any more. It was his love of the old warplane (he had bought it at an auction of the estate of an English lord who had kept it in his tobacco-barn since its capture during the 1914–18 war when the Germans were in Tanganyika) that kept him in one piece. It was the same love that guided him towards the smelter-stack.

Desaix liked Mufunsi. Below him he saw the African townships with children waving up at him from the school playgrounds. To the far right, just below the slimes-dam and overburden dumps was the apprentice school where the photograph had been taken. Anyone who helped with the Fokker had an instant entrée to Desaix's heart. For ten years he had kept the plane in the air by taking help from anyone who was prepared to give it. There was no handicrafts class, no tinker, carpenter, boilermaker, fitter, garage mechanic or model-aeroplane maker in the country who had not put some hours in on the Fokker. It was kept up by love.

'Why?' Pyper shrieked again.

Now he was not questioning his fate but asking why Desaix had flown straight into the smoke from the smelter-stack. As the Fokker hurtled up the thermal of choking, stinging fumes, Pyper's unsettled stomach clawed up in a spiral, the journalist's burning eyes were on the maw of the stack. Although he was coughing, cursing, his silk shirt dragged over his heaving mouth while red-hot particles stung his milk-white skin, he was by no means angry with Desaix. The Frenchman had come down off his Olympic height and taken his revenge. He had forsworn the dignity of his magnificent, charitable forgiveness and proved, yet again, one of Pyper's main articles of belief. All Man is undignified and it was the greedy and cheerless ambition of those who wanted to get away from this unifying bond of brotherhood and be dignified that was ruining the world. In Zonkendawo very few people were dignified because they couldn't afford it. The British civil servants were, but they were leaving and their dignity was so obsolete that it was inimitable; the managements of the mining companies tried to be but with such comic-opera results that no one ever took them seriously – so here was a great opportunity to create a completely undignified society. That gaping chimney was a funnel of Man's essential nature, a plunging shaft that shot downwards to the smelting of all men together. Even though it was killing him by suffocation and the breathing of toxic fumes, it was a wonderful thing, that smoke. It was the burnt offering of Dignity rising in the clear African sky, the sweetest smoke of sacrifice.

At the top of the Fokker's climb the fumes petered out. Pyper breathed the pure air, his blue eyes gummed together with sticky tears. His shirt was smouldering with sparks and his blond hair stank with singeing. Gasping as he looked down at Mufunsi, he just had time to store the brilliant image of the stack in his mind before being shot back into his seat as Desaix dived the plane back into the smoke. As the Fokker roared down the column of choking gases Pyper was sick all over himself but this did not prevent him from wondering why Desaix was about to commit suicide after all his years of struggle.

Or would the French bastard parachute out at the last moment and leave him to go down the stack alone?

3
T.C.G., F.C. and Unity

Fines Chingola sidled into Field-Marshal Montgomery Crescent, checked the address written in biro on the palm of his hand, then slipped along the shadow of the bougainvillaea hedge towards his objective. Upon his narrow shoulders, in the honeycombed brain borne by his long vulpine skull, in the thickets of his unnatural thoughts, lies the guilt for what happened to the Black and White Minstrel Show in the Muntu War. He was the cause of their peril, the disruption of their day-to-day lives, and maybe the mover of a miracle.

To Fines Chingola, apprentice African politician and manipulator of human destinies, guilt was an old mattress to be thrown away, a pile of unread newspapers littering the corner of his reeking mind. He had gone out with sacks of guilt at night and dumped them over fences, in sewage-tanks and down disused bottomless mine-shafts where spirits were reputed to have their homes. Fines could murder guilt, cut it up into little pieces and scatter it up and down his enormous country. Miracles? Now they were a different *mulandu*. Fines would never have recognized a miracle if he'd tripped over one on his front doorstep or found it smiling warmly up at him from his pillow. It was outside his talent and function to perceive the extraordinary.

As he padded along the drive of the house he heard Tarzan Cool Guy's voice. He was inside, talking to someone. It was not the voice which Fines remembered from their schooldays together when the handsome wrestler had been the toast of the night-shift widows, the women left at home while their husbands toiled 3,000 feet under the earth mining copper. In those days Tarzan Cool Guy had been known as Sixpenny Cassava Root and he had been something of a joke, a mere perambulating *umtondo*. Now things were different. Tarzan Cool Guy had authority, strength and a reputation. He had a place in society. Fines was full of envy as he knocked on the door and prepared himself for the dog-attack.

His eyes explored every bush, tree and flower-bed. There were *maningi* dogs in this part of town, all of them trained to bite Africans on sight. Fines had been brutally mauled by alsatians, doberman pinschers, boxers, poodles, pyrenean mountain dogs, all the pedigrees of the canine world.

The chihuahua streaked along the polished hallway, skidded up to the door, leapt vertically in the air and tried to tear its way through the mosquito-gauze.

Marge strolled out of the kitchen and shouted at the dog to be quiet. Fines held his breath. So this was Tarzan Cool Guy's *umfazi*. She wasn't bad for forty, well-built, strong legs, Fines opined to himself as Marge picked up the chihuahua and threw it into a side room.

'Yes?' she said politely through the mosquito-gauze.

'I want T.C.G.,' Fines declared.

Marge studied the long, flat face of the caller. It was the visage of a man not at ease, a suspicious, anxious set of features that were oddly at war with each other. Without his nose his eyes might have passed muster; without his lips his teeth would have been superb. As it was, Fines was ugly.

'What do you want it for?'

Fines paused. So it was the old story. Tarzan Cool Guy was being patronized by this woman. She would not even give the wrestler the right to be human.

'You should keep that dog under control,' Fines complained, 'I know your sort. You probably put it in a sack when it was just a puppy, left its head out so it could see what was going on, and got your African house-servant to kick it around the yard until the poor creature hated all black people.'

'What is it, Marge?' Tarzan Cool Guy called from the kitchen.

'It is me, not it!' Fines shouted back.

Marge lifted one eyebrow and leaned against the wall.

'I think he's from the R.S.P.C.A.,' she said over her shoulder, 'and he wants to borrow some T.C.P.'

'T.C.G.!' Fines hissed, waving his arms about. 'That's him!'

'What?' Marge uncovered her ear and bent forward.

'We are old school chums from way back!'

Tarzan Cool Guy came out of the kitchen, immediately recognized Fines and invited him in. After giving him a cold beer he asked the politician what he wanted.

'Well, it's been a long time, T.C.G.,' Fines said through the cool foam, 'and you're looking as powerful as ever, old fellow. Really in tip-top shape.'

There was a long pause as Tarzan Cool Guy examined his visitor with curious compassion. He had not remembered this speech impediment. With the stresses of political life falling daily on his puny soul, perhaps Fines had developed it as a nervous reaction like twitching the eyelid or hugging the crutch, two common features of neurotic behaviour which the African wrestler had noticed in others.

'Yes, Fines, it has been a long time,' he mused, carefully choosing his words. 'I'd say you've changed quite a lot.'

'T.C.G., I'd have come to see you anyway out of friendship's sake, but I must admit that I do have a problem that I'd like to discuss with you,' Fines said confidingly, leaning over sideways in an effort to exclude Marge who was listening with interest.

Tarzan Cool Guy spread his hands.

'If you like. We haven't seen each other for ages, but if it's me you want to discuss it with, go right ahead. None of us are perfect.'

Fines was confused. He looked across at Marge, took in her buxom creaminess and the little lines of determination around her mouth and eyes, and noticed that she was confused as well. The only people who were not confused were Tarzan Cool Guy and the chihuahua which was trying to gnaw its way through the side-room door in order to rip the visitor's throat out.

'Why does he need to be perfect?' Marge asked gently. 'People who love animals have got a lot going for them. He must be fairly perfect.'

'He keeps making that singing noise.' The wrestler grinned apologetically and got to his feet to get Fines another beer. 'And he didn't used to.'

'What singing noise?' Fines demanded. 'Me?'

'Teeceegee teeceegee teeceegee,' Tarzan Cool Guy chuckled understandingly. 'That's a new one on me, Fines. You must have a hard life working for the Party.'

'That's you!' Fines slapped his bony knee and laughed aloud. 'Christ, man, that's you! In the Party it's all initials in readiness for tomorrow when Doctor Mulombe becomes His Excellency the President of Zonkendawo – get it? He'll be H.E. – you'll be T.C.G. and I'll be F.C.'

Tarzan Cool Guy was bewildered and it showed in his usually calm countenance.

'Why can't I just stay Tarzan Cool Guy?'

Fines patted his old friend's massive shoulder and pushed him towards the refrigerator in the kitchen where the beer was kept.

'Two factors broo ... I may call you brother, eh? Just like I used to in Standard Four?'

'Call me what you like,' Tarzan Cool Guy grumbled unhappily. 'I'm out of touch.'

Fines followed Tarzan Cool Guy into the kitchen and waited until his friend had taken out a cold Lion Lager.

'Open it for me, T.C.G., in the old way ... you remember?'

Marge peered round the corner just in time to see her lover taking the top off the bottle with his teeth.

'Stop that, you idiot! You'll take all the enamel off them!' she commanded. 'You'll regret doing that kind of thing when you're older!'

Tarzan Cool Guy spat the top into the waste-bin.

'Thanks, T.C.G.,' Fines said smugly, aware that Marge was developing a tangible hostility towards his presence. 'That always knocked the girls sideways when you did that. He was always popular with the girls.'

Marge watched the young politician go past her back into the sitting-room and listened to the chihuahua's snarls, gulps and frettings. It had always been her belief that instinct was the best guide to people. She had an instinct about Fines.

'Now to get back to this initials business,' Fines sat down and crossed his legs. 'It really is very simple. Now you'll remember that the British governor was always called H.E. – His Excellency – well, he still is until midnight when Zonkendawo becomes independent, I suppose...'

'I never met the governor,' Tarzan Cool Guy said. 'He never came to see my fights.'

'Well, I met him, not a bad sort as the *musungus* go ... he's called H.E. and that gives him a lot of status in Myakajunji in diplomatic circles.'

'Diplomatic circles?'

'Yes, it gives him authority, strength. We want Doctor Mulombe to take all that over so the people of Zonkendawo will look up to him in exactly the same way as they did the British governor.'

'What's a diplomatic circle?' Tarzan Cool Guy asked, dumbfounded. 'Christ Almighty, Fines, we've been living in different worlds for too long.'

'The representatives of other governments, T.C.G. We're not going to be an isolationist state, oh no. We've got to build up a name for ourselves. Do you know that we're the biggest copper-producer in the Commonwealth?'

'I don't go round in diplomatic circles so why call me T.C.G.?'

Fines paused, conscious of the fact that Tarzan Cool Guy was lagging way behind. It was true that their roads had parted. While Fines was learning statecraft and the basic structure of international relations, Tarzan Cool Guy had been solely interested in the physical side of life; with his low intelligence quotient that was not unusual. Wrestlers were not famed for their intellects. Perhaps that's why she called him 'it'.

Marge looked out of the window and thought about her instinct. It was now becoming a compulsion.

During the next twenty minutes, the gods of Africa, or the one God of all continents if he is interested in the process of cause and effect that shapes human destinies, might have peeped through the window of the sitting-room and tried to assess Fines' position in the hierarchy of Fate. Was he an instrument of Destruction, of Rampant Evil, as he sat drinking Dennis's (Marge's husband) beer? Did he know that his horny foot was raised above a tender though prickly plant in the African earth? Would he have cared if suddenly able to see into the future, and what would happen to the lives that he was trying to manipulate? As he did his job as special political assistant to the commanding officer of the Zonkendawon Territorial Army and tried to persuade the country's only African wrestler to join up, had he anything at the back of his restless mind but his own ambition? As Tarzan Cool Guy brought him his fifth beer, and his mouth opened to enclose the delicious hoppy foam, was not that mouth a trapdoor with the Devil grinning up from the fiery chambers of a fame-lusting heart?

'T.C.G., you can't imagine the boost it would give to their recruitment figures if a celebrity like you was to enrol,' he explained enthusiastically. 'It would set a terrific example to the nation's youth.'

'They don't need an example!' Tarzan Cool Guy protested. 'They'd leave me standing when it came to the army. Those kids in the Youth Brigade are born soldiers. You've seen them at work. I can't compete with kids like that, I'm not in their class at all. They don't need any example from me.'

Fines shook his head and gave the wrestler a friendly but pitying look.

'They're kiddies, T.C.G., kiddies. All right, they can throw a few stones, burn down the Jehovah's Witness meeting-rooms and rough up people who haven't paid their Party dues, but they can't drive a tank, can they?'

'Give them half a chance and they would!'

'Come on, be reasonable.'

'I am being reasonable! They frighten the life out of me.'

Fines drained his glass and sat back stroking his long, flattened nose.

'Look, broo, you know the rotten situation we're in. At midnight we get a mob of old soldiers, all the riff-raff, the scum, the drifters and lay-abouts that the colonial government, the mines and the white unions have been bolstering up for years ... we get them for our army, our people's army. All the clerks, bookies, cagetenders, butcher's boys, chiropodists, joiners, railway guards ... the whole tribe of *musungus* who've been keeping our people out of employment for years, they're the ones who are in the Territorials now. They joined up – d'you know what for? Those *musungu* pigs joined up to help the colonial government keep us in order! They didn't think that one day we'd get our freedom and they'd be working for us! It's ironical, T.C.G., really ironical. The men who signed on so they could keep their feet on our necks will tomorrow be our servants, ready to die in battle for us! That's a laugh! Ha! Our first line of defence, those white bastards! Give them half a chance and they'd stick us all up against a wall and shoot us!'

'That's very sweeping!' Marge turned from the window, her compulsion hardening. 'Very sweeping indeed!'

'Look you, I'm talking to your husband!' Fines snapped.

'He's not my husband!' Marge blushed, more with anger than embarrassment. 'He just lives here.'

Tarzan Cool Guy's meaty black hand seized Fines' knee and cracked it hard against the table-top. Fines ouched and started to sweat.

'Fines, I don't mind you making speeches in my house,' he began.

'Dennis's house,' Marge reminded him, 'and you'll have to find a job soon because you can't expect him to keep you.'

Tarzan Cool Guy paused. He was as conscious of his position as she was. Living off Dennis was humiliating.

'But if you ever speak to my woman like that again I'll beat the living daylights out of you!'

Fines rubbed his tender knee-cap.

'Okay, okay ... I'm sorry ... surely you can see how deeply I feel about this, T.C.G.?' he groaned piteously. 'Jesus Christ that hurt!'

'Forget it, shall we?' Marge suggested amiably. 'But you shouldn't make such sweeping statements.'

Fines managed to flash a glance of pure hatred across to the mature Englishwoman. He knew that she didn't like him, was enjoying his discomfort.

'Yes ... I withdraw unconditionally,' he said stiffly. 'It was a silly thing to generalize like that. But all I'm trying to say is that we must have a real citizen's army. That's logical, isn't it? Zonkendawons are the best people to defend their own homeland.'

'Yes, that's right,' Tarzan Cool Guy agreed.

'Then you'll join?'

'No, I won't join. I wouldn't join anyone's army unless there was a war on and I thought it was worth the trouble.'

Fines covered his head with his hands.

'Come on, T.C.G., for an old school pal.'

'Don't be ridiculous.'

'Not for Mulombe?'

'You're joking.'

'For your country!'

'Who says it's for my country? I haven't got a country until tomorrow morning and the first thing you want me to do is give away some of the freedom you've been going on about. What kind of a Party is this you're running? Are you in the Territorials?'

Fines confessed that he suffered from asthma and would never be considered, much as he would like to offer his services.

'Look, Fines, I've made sacrifices already. After today I'm broke, finished. The wrestling game is over in this country.'

Fines unexpectedly started laughing, his distorted features stretching in a new dimension of ugliness.

'But you're the best there is!' he expostulated. 'There's no one to touch you, you can't go wrong!'

Tarzan Cool Guy grinned bitterly.

'I'm all there is, Fines, you great prick, the only one. They won't give the Mine Club Sporting Promotions Committee any more import permits for the Hairyback *musungu* wrestlers to come from down south once we're independent. And d'you know whose fault that is? Yours! The Party's the one that's stopped it! They say it's racial! What about me? Where does that leave me? There's no one to fight!'

'I'll speak to Customs and Excise, I've got a cousin working there, he's at the Chirundu border post and he'll let all the South African wrestlers you like come through,' Fines gabbled, 'and I can get you a bursary to study if you like, go to England and do a course ... anything, money? Easily fixed. A cushy number in some obscure department? No bother. I can get you on the board of one of the mining companies if you like – they're desperate for some black window-dressing.'

Marge left the window and pressed her hands down on Tarzan Cool Guy's shoulders.

'Now don't get excited, love, he's only doing his job.'

Tarzan Cool Guy glowered across at Fines, his frame trembling with rage under Marge's grip.

'Who does he think I am? I'm a worker, damn you! A worker! I don't want your soft jobs!'

'Yes, T.C.G., yes,' Fines retracted hurriedly. 'I should have appreciated that.'

Fines realized that he had muffed his mission. Back at Party headquarters he would have to report to the Regional Secretary that he had failed and the Youth Brigade would be summoned from the playgrounds of the township to deal with him. But he had one last trump card, a forged letter from Doctor Mulombe which he had spent most of the previous night composing. He had asked the Regional Secretary for such a letter immediately the mission had been dreamed up by the Party Action Committee, but the request had been turned down. The future President was up to his ears in work trying to find a dozen ministers for his cabinet who would not spend their office hours arguing the toss and trying to drop each other in the shit.

'As a last resort, T.C.G...'

'And you can stop calling me that you *mubi* bastard!'

'All right, keep your wool on ... as a last resort I have a letter here, a personal note from Doctor Mulombe himself.'

Reverently, the grubby envelope was brought out of Fines' jacket pocket and handed over to Tarzan Cool Guy who immediately passed it on to Marge.

'It is for your eyes only!' Fines blurted.

'What is for me is for her. We have no secrets. And besides, I'm a slow reader.'

Fines had forgotten what Tarzan Cool Guy had been like at school. If he had done his background research for this project things might have gone more smoothly. He remembered that the wrestler had been the despair of his teachers, only interested in hiring out his sixpenny cassava root.

'Then I'll read it for you!' Fines insisted, making a wild grab for the envelope and hitting Marge across the face by accident. 'It's top secret!'

His knee flew up and beat a tattoo on the table-top, the pain leaving him speechless. Marge thoughtfully rubbed her cheek and ripped open the envelope.

'Fines, this is the last of an old friendship,' Tarzan Cool Guy said grimly, as he let the twitching limb fall back. 'Next time it will be your head.'

Marge put a restraining hand on her lover's arm and spread the letter out on the table.

'Dear T.C.G...' she began reading.

'Is every jumped-up Party hood I know going to go around calling me T.C.G.!' Tarzan Cool Guy yelled threateningly, his face like pitch-black thunder. 'You pass it on to that old thug that I'm Tarzan Cool Guy and I'm staying that way!'

'I will ... I will ... don't worry...' Fines chattered hurriedly. 'It's a damned silly affectation calling people by their initials anyway.'

Marge smoothed the paper out.

'Shall I go on?'

'You might as well.'

Tarzan Cool Guy gave his guest a last warning look and sat back in his chair.

Dear ... (well, we'll leave that aside for the moment as it upsets you) there are many secrets that must lie heavy on a man of destiny such as myself, many visions that enable me to see danger where it really lies ... Zonkendawo will be midwived by enemies (he said that in a speech last week) we are at the cross-roads ... we must go in all directions at once (can't see that happening) the Territorial Army is our first line of defence against the forces of imperialism, neo-colonialism, the People's Democratic Congress Party, the Chinese, the Congolese and the Muntu ... every eye is on you, my boy, and how you will jump. Join up today and prove my faith in thee. Yours sincerely S. Mulombe, M.D.

Tarzan Cool Guy sat silent for a while, scratching his head with a stubby forefinger.

'No,' he said suddenly. 'No. It's beyond me.'

'That was the President speaking directly to you!' Fines exploded in panic, his chance of success fading before his eyes, the Youth Brigade already dousing him with petrol and striking matches. 'The President and the Party leader! He needs you! We all need you! Once you've joined there's no need for you to actually do anything. I can get you off all the camps and parades, get you promoted quickly so you can be an officer.'

Marge knew that her compulsion was shared by her lover.

They often thought alike, could tell what was in the other's mind without asking. When she opened the door of the side room she found that the chihuahua had gnawed its way through to the last millimetres of wood. The tiny canine stood in the hallway, its jaws foully festooned with splinters, paint and saliva, and gave Marge a beady beam of gratitude before it sprang into the air and began the pursuit of the fleet-footed politician.

4
The Black and White Minstrel Show

Tarzan Cool Guy was sitting in the garden, his woolly head abuzz with light from the flowers and the shade of the frangipani. He was dozing in the sun, his splendid torso bared. Equally bare was his mind, from which the inimical figure of Fines Chingola had been successfully banished.

He was not sun-bathing for cosmetic reasons, but because he had heard that the sun is a source of an important vitamin and the only African wrestler in Zonkendawo needed every kind of life-giving substance which he could lay his hands on.

Tarzan Cool Guy was unemployed. Much as he enjoyed the thought of his country being free, it was an emotion spiced with disappointment. He had managed to build himself a future in the wrestling game, a future based on honest toil and expertise, and freedom was taking it away from him. The British had often warned that once they left Zonkendawo economic disaster would follow, then the breakdown of Law and Order and the return to the barbarism of the old days. Tarzan Cool Guy had not expected it to happen so suddenly.

Picking up a glass of cold beer he sank the cool bottom on to the firm flesh round his navel. A track of goose-pimples ran up the central ridge of his abdominal muscles. He looked at himself, flexed all his muscles, and decided that he was in good nick.

Up until independence Tarzan Cool Guy had needed to be so. If he had neglected his physique, slid back from the peak of physical fitness, then he would never have survived the wrestling matches which he had fought in the Mine Club. The white miners were famous for their love of sport and paid handsome contributions to the Sporting Promotions Committee so they could get top-flight white wrestlers to come to Zonkendawo and fight Tarzan Cool Guy.

At the highest pitches of frenzy, when all sports-fans are likely to say things that they don't really mean, the white miners had been heard to encourage the imported wrestlers to go beyond the accepted limits of the game and cripple, maim, wound, castrate, blind the local champion, even to break him in half. If Tarzan Cool Guy had ever let himself go, stopped caring about physical fitness and lost his strength, then he would have perished. Without an African wrestler to pit against the European imports, the whole sport would have suffered from a decline in standards.

There were other people to consider as well. Although the miners kept Africans out of the wrestling matches there were employees of the Mine Club who had managed to snatch a glimpse of the titanic struggles that took place between Tarzan Cool Guy and his opponents. They were Africans of little or no influence; waiters, barmen, cleaners and kitchen-staff, but they carried the news of what they witnessed back into the townships. Their accounts were garbled, highly exaggerated and often delivered when these humble men were under the influence of gallons of millet-beer or hemp – but the people listened. Over the years they had the story of one heroic battle after another. It seemed as though Tarzan Cool Guy was the only African south of the Sahara who was prepared to face the *musungus* on his own. When he fought it was not for any lesser cause than the dignity of his race and the heritage of his people.

He always lost. Was that surprising? Everyone else in the recreation room was white. The referee, the timekeeper, even Tarzan Cool Guy's second was white. Whenever Tarzan Cool Guy had his opponent in the Sumatra Death-Grip the referee always tapped him on the shoulder and made him let go. In the name of Christ the King was that fair? He had no chance against the howling mob of unfriendly wrestling fans and the whole corrupt conspiracy of the Mine Club Sporting Promotions Committee.

As time went on Tarzan Cool Guy became a hero of folklore. When his fights came up there was always a crowd waiting outside the Mine Club for news. The employees slipped out at the end of each round and recounted the struggle, hold for hold, throw for throw. Tarzan Cool Guy became a legend in his own time.

Marge was an English woman of forty, good to look upon,

cheerful, pleasant and intelligent, who had lived in Mufunsi for several years. She was married to a biologist, Dennis, who taught at the local technical college. His main interest in life was beetles. Most of his spare time was spent in the bush, a treasury of insect life, and he had been glad when Marge had started to take positive steps to become involved with things outside the home. She did some charity work, joined a few women's clubs, tried to play tennis, but none of these adventures gave her what she was searching for ... what was she searching for? Marge was becoming bothered by this question and not knowing the answer.

Tarzan Cool Guy was an easy man to admire. Even the miners gave him credit for his magnificent physique and courage. He never played the villain in his matches, was always courteous, never used bad language in the ring or protested to the referee about foul blows or being attacked after the end of the round. He took his punishment like a man, absorbed every forearm smash, flying drop-kick, hair-pull, Boston crab and back-breaker and came in for more until the referee signalled to him that it was time to take a dive. Then he would submit to a hold, or allow his opponent to pin-fold him – but no knock-outs. Tarzan Cool Guy would never contract to be knocked out. Once unconscious he did not know what indignities might be inflicted on his prostrate body.

The match with Willy de Kok had taken place a week after the British government had announced that Zonkendawo would be granted full independence during the following year. Feelings were running high in the Mine Club when 2,000 white miners packed into the recreation room to see Willy de Kok crucify Tarzan Cool Guy. They had been sold out by the colonial power, their livelihoods were in jeopardy, and it was all Tarzan Cool Guy's fault.

Marge had been in the audience, dragged there by a friend. When the African wrestler ran down the aisle ducking a hail of missiles and vaulted into the ring with his arms over his head, Marge had experienced a twinge of anxiety.

What happened then has passed into the annals of Zonkendawon sporting history. After four rounds Tarzan Cool Guy looked meaningfully at the referee. He was ready to take his dive. He could hear the berserk roaring of the crowd and knew that this match was one on its own. They would really like to see him ripped apart. But the referee gave him a blank stare in reply. He was far away, breathing hard, eyes glassy, whispering to Willy de Kok to tear that stinking Kaffir bastard limb from limb. He had joined the miners in their blood-lust. Tarzan Cool Guy was alone. His contract had been torn up.

'I'll take the dive now,' he whispered into Willy de Kok's ear as they crashed to the canvas. Willy throatily informed him that his part of the agreement had not contained any reference to a rigged victory. He was the Good Guy in the bout and he was going to win honestly. As Willy thumbed around Tarzan Cool Guy's neck for pressure-points and the crowd erupted into delighted caperings, screams, droolings and songs of defiance against Doctor Mulombe, the only African wrestler in Zonkendawo realized that he was about to die.

Tarzan Cool Guy was not a brave man. Before becoming a wrestler he had been a loafer, an interferer with impressionable girls and his own aunties, and a gigolo. They had called him Sixpenny Cassava Root in the townships because that was his price and he went anywhere at any time, doing the rounds of the older women whose husbands were on nightshift and who had been able to save up out of the housekeeping for a night with the splendidly-muscled, statuesque youth who wandered around the market with his shirt off. When the mine Welfare Officer had persuaded him to take up wrestling he had dropped Sixpenny Cassava Root for Tarzan Cool Guy – it gave him status in a society of people who had come from the bush and were desperately trying to urbanize themselves.

Now he had fame, reputation and a good job and they were all going down the roaring pit that was in his head as Willy de Kok tightened his throttle-hold. Knowing that he was about to die, Tarzan Cool Guy threshed around, his eyes bulging and tongue sticking out, tried to call out for his mother whom he hadn't seen for years, and beshat himself.

Love has many strange beginnings. Pity is not the best of them. When Marge clambered into the ring and hammered at Willy de Kok's head with the heel of her shoe, it was because she felt sorry for Tarzan Cool Guy. As she stepped back from the slumped body of the South African wrestler, staring at the half-moon indentations which her stiletto heels had made in his shaven skull, she could not hear the thunderous applause of the miners who had never seen anything to match this in all their born days, nor did she note the timekeeper and the referee who were yelling at her that she would shortly be in court for ruining their promotion. All she was aware of was the man at her feet, Tarzan Cool Guy. He was a great babe, his man's stature reduced to infancy by the midden he lay in.

The love of the giver is the kind that cannot be denied. Pity left Marge's heart that instant and she decided that Tarzan Cool Guy was hers for the taking. Recruiting a small crowd of delighted miners to aid her, Marge had him taken down to the house in Field-Marshal Montgomery Crescent and nursed him back to health. At first he was so ashamed of what had happened at the Mine Club that he tried to escape. Marge followed him and brought him back. He pleaded with her – she remained adamant. He belonged to her. There was no way out for the black wrestler. After two weeks of resistance he admitted defeat, fell in love with Marge, collected his few possessions, and moved in permanently.

When Marge's husband Dennis queried the presence of the African athlete in his house, Marge explained that he was her lover and would be staying for ever. Dennis had made no initial comment and drove out of town, parked his car in the bush and, instead of walking around looking for beetles, sat down and thought about Marge. They had been together for fifteen years. They had been good years in which she had given him more than he had given her. Now she wanted something for herself. It might have been a car, a horse, a piece of furniture, a holiday. He had not expected it to be a man but the fact that it was did not alter what Marge deserved.

With his killing-bottle in his hand he set off along a narrow path, searching for beetles. There was ether in the bottle, enough ether to kill him. If he drank it then Marge could have her lover and Dennis could be at peace with the situation. But that would mean that he would never discover the leaf-eating beetles that he was convinced had evolved under the peculiar climatic and soil conditions of the region. When he returned to the house in

Field-Marshal Montgomery Crescent he found Marge and Tarzan Cool Guy sitting in the garden. Opening the fridge he took out three cans of cold beer and walked out into the garden. Sitting cross-legged at their feet he ripped the tops out with a fraction more effort than was needed and started talking about leaf-eating beetles.

Tarzan Cool Guy heard the roar in the sky.

He stood up, shielded his eyes and watched the Fokker doing a victory-roll over the house. In the front cockpit was a familiar white blob, in the second a colourful flutter. He heard a high voice shrieking and saw a yellow head hanging earthwards. Tarzan Cool Guy scratched his chin. Was it the woman from the aviation ministry whom Desaix cultivated in order to get his licence renewed? She was a blonde but Desaix seldom went around with her except just before the licence expired. The screams rose higher. The last time that he had heard a noise like it was some months ago when he had taken John Pyper round the back of the Tonga Bar and thrown him among the dustbins. His reason for this assault had been Pyper's write-up on his wrestling bout with Julius Van Dyck, the Durban Dare-Devil.

Tarzan Cool Guy sat back in his chair and tried to work it out. He had banked on Pyper being in Myakajunji to watch the flag-raising ceremony with all the other world journalists. That would be the proper place for a newshound on the eve of independence.

'Was that Desaix?' Marge called across from the verandah.

The wrestler nodded thoughtfully.

'He was flying upside-down.'

Marge came across the lawn, the sun soft in her fluffy brown hair.

'I thought I heard something else as well.'

Tarzan Cool Guy waited until Marge had curled up at his knee before placing a large black hand on her head and telling her in the gentlest way possible that Pyper had come to ruin their party.

Johnny McSilver blew his whistle and threw himself to the ground as Desaix did his second victory-roll over the Mufunsi

Blackpool football stadium. The team of African youths followed his example and immediately started doing press-ups so as not to waste time while the Fokker buzzed the pitch. Johnny's Glaswegian ire boiled as he glared at the hurtling plane – he would sort Desaix out later in the vegetable garden at Field-Marshal Montgomery Crescent.

'Ya bastard eejit!' he gritted furiously as the African youths dropped with exhaustion around him, their arms reduced to benumbed jelly. 'I'll get ya bollocks in a vice later! Up-two-three! Up-two-three!'

'Hello, Des!' waved the tall, golden-haired Marilyn from the shadows of the stand where she was waiting to serve tea and sandwiches to the footballers after training.

Her call was a pleasantry for Desaix could never have heard her sweet voice above the engine. Most things associated with Marilyn were pleasantries because she was pleasant, her eyes were green and pleasant like pastures, her mouth was always smiling and pleasant as fresh fruit lying in cool water, even her tallness was pleasant because it was the tallness of a tree. The daughter of a gold-prospector in Tanganyika she had been brought up, when her father died of black-water fever, by a German uncle in the Belgian Congo. During her childhood she had seen strange and unnatural horrors, been pursued by the nightmares of the rain-forest and the great Congo itself. Until she met Johnny McSilver in the mine stores where she had been working as a one-finger typist, the world had been an alien place – but she never showed it. Her defence was the defence of the sun, she shone. No matter what hardship faced her, Marilyn beamed. When Johnny arrived in Zonkendawo from Scotland where he had been a professional footballer with Glasgow Rangers, his gritty perception of life told him that the woman was gormless. Sentimental he might be, but he could see the hard practicalities of existence. You just couldn't smile that much and be normal. So Marilyn shone more until Johnny was encased in summer. Often he would lean across her desk and ask her what the hell she was grinning at? He had faced many surreptitious smiles when Glasgow Rangers prematurely terminated his contract. The whole street saw the downfall of Johnny McSilver, from the saloon bar of every pub in the Gorbals to the moment when he tackled one of his own side who was trying to get a cross to the goal-mouth, Johnny's humiliation had been a public spectacle. Africa is full of men who have left a shame behind and gone to hide their heads in the wilderness and Johnny was one of them until he pulled back the drab tenement drapes from his eyes and let Marilyn shine in. She did not change him. His secondary passions (she became his first) were whisky and football and fighting and crying. She often confessed that he bored the pants off her talking about his father who nobody could ascertain was alive or dead. But between her shining and his weeping there appeared a temperate clime that was love.

Like the Church, the Theatre is part of the baggage of any travelling people who have roamed the earth looking for new homes. The land they have rejected and leave behind in the wake of a ship soon becomes forgiven as time and the rigours of the new life begin to disappoint and curdle hope. They look back to times that were grim and make them comic, occasions that were indifferently nice become marvellous milestones of joy. History is tarted up like the Queen of Heaven in a Spanish cathedral, the crumbling plaster glued together with gilded paint and overpowering nostalgia. So it was not surprising that the miners built themselves a theatre in Mufunsi with the profits of the post-war copper boom. In it they produced plays about English life that reminded them of the culture they had left behind to work underground with a gang of half-witted Africans. Shortly after the theatre was built, the scourge of the legitimate stage was introduced into British public life – television invaded the sitting-rooms of the supporters of weekly reps up and down the country and many people employed in the acting profession were put out of work, not for a few weeks 'resting' but for ever. One of these men decided to go to Africa. He took ship, bummed his way north from Capetown, and found himself a job teaching French to African children who couldn't speak English. When he found the theatre lying under the trees in Kantata Street he walked through the swing-doors and took the place over. His name was Humphrey Fluellen and he was Welsh, blackly mischievous, rotund, spiteful, pathetic, warm-hearted and a tragic loss to the English stage.

'That's Desaix,' he grunted across to Kovary, a burly Jewish school-teacher-cum-playwright who was onstage with him at the time. Kovary did not look up but studied the script in his hand.

'Humphrey, how do you feel about this bit?' he asked. 'Do you think it's too predictable?'

The actor paused, his great belly resting on the pudendum of his partner, and cocked his big, blocky cranium to one side.

'And I can hear someone screaming. It sounds like Pyper.'

'Do you think it's too transparent?'

'That's him just gone past,' Humphrey started moving again. 'No matter what we do he'll tear it to pieces. And if he catches us like this we'll be on the front page tomorrow.'

Kovary put down his script, his puggish countenance thoughtful. The coloured nurse beneath him took her arms from under her head.

'Do you watch television like this as well?' she demanded.

While both men resumed the rehearsal of Kovary's new play, the audience stopped chatting among themselves and paid attention. The theatre staff were usually brought in for a couple of days before the last week of rehearsals in order to test public reaction. Afterwards their remarks would be noted and maybe, if Humphrey and Kovary agreed with their criticisms, changes might be made in the script or direction. The stage-carpenter, an African who had often worked on the Fokker in his spare time, called out from his seat in row D that Humphrey seemed to have lost most of his stand after the aeroplane of Bwana Arse had gone overhead.

'If I may say it,' he shouted, 'the bwana is fucking like an arthritic elephant.'

Humphrey snorted angrily and increased his labours, beating his belly against the woman until she was pushed over the end of the bed, her legs raised in the air like the funnels of a sinking ship. The cleaners, tea-boys, barmen, backstage staff and the box-office lady applauded loudly while Humphrey followed her down, giving a burst of intense power that made his buttocks merge into a stroboscopic blurr. Panting, he turned to the audience and looked for the stage-carpenter.

'Ah, bwana,' the craftsman yelled, 'if I was up there that woman would not be silent. Like the gentle nursing-sister from Mufunsi Mine Hospital who is playing the second lead, she would cry out and make an interesting pattern of primitive audial responses.'

Humphrey glared across at Kovary. The nurse was moaning and making agreeable sensual noises. Getting to his feet he stepped over his stunned partner and stormed off to the dressing-room. When Kovary joined him later, having got the audience to their feet with a symphonic crescendo of babbles in Hebrew, Afrikans, English and Fanagolo, Humphrey started complaining about the set.

'Look, I'm not happy with the atmosphere. Get the stage-manager to make an effort for Christ's sake. Pictures on the wall, erotica, some embroidered curtaining. Try to create the right atmosphere.'

Kovary nodded and pulled on his shorts.

'I'm not sure.'

'Not sure about what?'

'Whether this is the right kind of show for Independence Week. You know what Mulombe's like. He's a Methodist, isn't he?'

The Open Pit at Mufunsi is a mile long and 600 feet deep. It lies at the point in the copper-bearing strata where a synclinal fold comes nearest the surface and a man can keep the sun on his back while digging it out with monster power-shovels and 100-ton trucks. It is a cheaper mining method than underground workings because no one has to worry about the roof caving in, no tunnels need to be bored through hard rock, no railway lines laid, no supporting timbers erected, no shafts sunk. The profit per ton of copper sent to the Free World was higher at the Open Pit than at the underground mine and this made Hammerkop, the Open Pit Manager, glad because it put him in a good light with the board of directors in Johannesburg when they reviewed his salary each year. What would have made him happier still would have been the spiriting away of one small unit of his labour force, without whose presence the profit margin would have been measurably greater.

From his viewing platform outside the office Hammerkop watched the Bucket-Wheel Excavator. The gigantic machine was stilled, its scoop-hung wheel poised with its teeth in the red earth. Along the enormous boom no rock was being carried. The conveyer belt that stretched from the huge forest of steel to the dumps at the south of the pit was not running over its rollers, bearing away the useless covering of the copper ore. For the third time that week the insanely expensive machine was out of action, rendered so by the very people charged with its care.

The Bucket-Wheel Excavator Gang.

Under the leadership of Matthias Mvula, their supervisor, the ten Africans in the gang had defeated every move that Hammerkop had made to discharge them from the mine's service. He had proved to the soft-hearted and prevaricating Personnel Department that the whole gang were Communists, Congolese, hemp-smokers, drunks, fornicators, saboteurs and escapees from the nearby leprosarium. He had written reports to the General Manager until his arm ached. He sent anonymous letters to the Progress Party fingering the Bucket-Wheel Excavator Gang as supporters of the People's Democratic Congress Party in the hope that they would be dealt with in the frequent purges. He had telephoned the police when his binoculars had picked up the telltale smoke issuing from the cab of the Bucket-Wheel Excavator. On night-shifts he had lain close to the earth, dust up his nostrils, the trembling Personnel Manager by his side and tried to catch them wandering through the cuts and ditches with the low women they had invited over from the beer-halls. At every turn in their career, the Bucket-Wheel Excavator Gang had outwitted him.

'I'll take a little peek at those Kaffirs,' he growled to himself, concerned that the sloppy blue-overalled figures were not visible around the machine. Going round to his garage he reversed his white Land-Rover out and took the back road behind the dumps, suddenly arriving beside the Bucket-Wheel Excavator in a cloud of dust. From the soft earth beneath the great caterpillar tracks a host of sleepers arose, brushing away the dust Hammerkop had brought with him. As he leapt up the steel ladderway to the cab to catch them playing Liar Dice, reading pornographic magazines or eating pot cookies, the Bucket-Wheel Excavator Gang silently climbed into the Land-Rover, Matthias taking the wheel in two fat hands, and drove away.

As the cab was empty Hammerkop balanced his way along the catwalk of the boom to examine the scoops on the wheel. More than once he had found members of the gang hiding there puffing at a cigarette or fumbling with a pock-marked woman. The accident record of the pit had been hard hit last year when one of the gang had fallen asleep and had been found travelling along the conveyer belt in a mutilated condition, one hand still gripping a copy of *Playboy*. Hammerkop had replaced him with a trusted man, an old servant who knew his place and considered his first responsibility to be towards the company. For three days the man sneaked round to Hammerkop's mansion beside the golf-course and told him what was going on. It was as he had suspected. The Bucket-Wheel Excavator Gang were planning his downfall. They were going to start an uprising against the management, take over the mine, rape the wives and daughters of the officials, burn down their houses, join the Mine Club without paying the membership fee, and bring the whole structure of private enterprise in Africa crashing to the ground. Then the old man had given him the chance that he had been waiting for.

'Bwana Hammerkop, you know me, I am an ignorant Kaffir. But I have standards. What this man Matthias Mvula is doing to the old European Cemetery that lies to the east of the dump is well below my standards.'

'What are you talking about, you stupid coon? Necrophilia?'

The old man shook his head.

'You know that the new university Doctor Mulombe is opening in Myakajunji is to have a medical faculty, not that an ignorant Kaffir like me knows anything about higher education but I read my *Zonkendawo Times*, and there are to be three hundred students enrolled just after independence? Well, the Bucket-Wheel Excavator Gang have worked it out that they will need skeletons for their anatomical studies.'

Hammerkop went pale. It was more than he had hoped for but his elation was mixed with disgust because his own father was buried there, victim of an early rockfall.

'You mean they're going to dig them up? The pioneers?' he gasped.

'Ten pounds apiece they calculate, bwana. Also they are aware of the presence of your venerated father and intend to send him in a parcel to the British Museum as an example of Early Man.'

Hammerkop had been left breathless by the enormity of the planned crime. Giving his spy threepence as his reward he booted him out of the back door, having first extracted from him the date on which the mass exhumation would take place. The ground had been cleared in preparation and Matthias was supposed to be walking the Bucket-Wheel Excavator across to the old European cemetery the following night to start digging. According to the old man he and the rest of the gang were to stand by the conveyer and pick the bones of the pioneers out as they went past, skulls one pile, tibias another, pelvises another. Afterwards they would wire them together in any order and sell them off to the medical students.

'I've got those black bastards this time!' Hammerkop grated as he made a list of people to ring up, starting with the General Manager, then every man of religion in town, the police, the hospital authority, the army. 'They'll swing for this!'

The following night, under a full moon, Matthias stood on top of the dump with the old man and the rest of the Bucket-Wheel Excavator Gang and listened to Hammerkop explaining his mistake to a crowd of men who had driven ambulances, armoured cars, black marias, and clerical bicycles to the old European cemetery. When Hammerkop mentioned the old informer in his speech of apology Matthias shook the wizened hand, pressed the two pounds that they had collected in a whip-round for the aged liar, put him on his Vespa scooter and sent him on his way home to his village 800 miles away in Malawi.

'*Hamba lapa madala*,' Matthias whispered, 'I will get the union to extract your pension fund contributions from the soft-hearted and prevaricating Personnel Department and send them to you. Go well.'

'Stay well, Matthias, and keep fighting,' the old man grinned as he kick-started the scooter. 'The people will thank you one day. Death to Hammerkop *mukwai*!'

'Death to Hammerkop!' the Bucket-Wheel Excavator Gang

hummed as they headed for the beer-hall through the darkness. 'It will not be long.'

It was these men, with this calibre of spirit and manhood, who were driving Hammerkop's Land-Rover away when Desaix's Fokker appeared over the southern lip of the Open Pit and began its third and final victory-roll. Desaix waved as he crossed the Bucket-Wheel Excavator, imagining his friends to be in the vicinity, then, as he came out of the victory-roll, sighted the Land-Rover ahead.

'It is Bwana Arse,' a member of the gang said quietly. 'He will think we are Hammerkop.'

The road that Matthias was driving along went down to the bottom of the pit through a series of hairpin bends. If he had stopped and turned round it would have given Desaix all the time in the world to catch the Land-Rover in open ground and try to pitch it over with his landing-gear. They had seen him attempt this manoeuvre before and nearly succeed. Slithering through the bends Matthias tore towards the pit bottom while Desaix banked and came in for his first attack. Watching through the rear window the Bucket-Wheel Excavator Gang tried to shout up to Desaix that they were not Hammerkop but friends, the ones who arranged with the Open Pit Workshops to have his engine rebored. As he came nearer they shouted even louder and thrust their hands upwards but they could not rise above the engine and the other noise.

'That sounds familiar,' Matthias mused, as he skidded through 360 degrees. 'What's he doing up here?'

The Bucket-Wheel Excavator Gang covered their eyes and ears as Desaix zoomed in, tipped the Land-Rover with one wheel and sent it crashing to its side, then turned over and flew towards the drainage sump with a colourful figure trailing from the second cockpit by one hand. At the exact moment, his timing perfect, he rapped Pyper's knuckles with a spanner and the howling journalist plummeted into the sump.

When the Bucket-Wheel Excavator Gang had extricated themselves from the back of the Land-Rover, out of common humanity, they trooped over and watched Pyper swim to the side of the sump. As he flopped on the ground at their feet it was noticed that a half-empty bottle with a sailing ship being struck by lightning on the label was in his jacket pocket. Relieving him of this Matthias sat down beside the bedraggled New Zealander and opened the conversation.

'What have you come to Mufunsi for this time, John? None of your friends have been up to much lately.'

Pyper waited until the cane-for-pain had been passed round all the Bucket-Wheel Excavator Gang and raised himself on one elbow, snatching the last drop for himself.

'I've come up for Tarzan Cool Guy's Independence party,' he sniffed. 'They've shut all the bars in Myakajunji.'

'But if you go to this party the rest of us won't,' Matthias teased Pyper's backside with his boot. 'If we go to the party with you there then we must all go to prison.'

'That's a chance you'll have to take,' Pyper replied sternly, 'because I'm not prepared to bend my principles for subversives like you. What's news is news. Just don't make any and you'll be all right.'

And while they sat by the still waters and talked of Truth and its place in a changing world, Desaix L'Ace made a perfect one-point landing at the airfield.

5
Party to Freedom

Matthias Mvula and Desaix L'Ace were the same shape. When they leaned over a bar together there was no way of telling them apart except by their colour. Anyone sitting at the tables in the Tonga Bar that evening would not have been able to tell the two friends apart because they had their heads together, leaning well forward, and were trying to look up the well-worn stairs to Margaret from the Tonga Bar's room where she was having a *kwela* with Pyper. He had beaten the Frenchman by a short head. Margaret from the Tonga Bar was an old companion of the New Zealander and her name had often appeared in the paper but she didn't mind. The publicity was good for trade.

Matthias cupped his chin in his hands and brooded. He was the man responsible for Margaret from the Tonga Bar's state of mind. Many people thought that she was so good-natured, happy-go-lucky and well-balanced that she was stupid. The cause of that equilibrium was the supervisor of the Bucket-Wheel Excavator Gang. He was guilty of creating the perfect, all-round, golden-hearted whore.

Two years ago Matthias had gone up those well-worn stairs with a book in his pocket called *Variations On A Sexual Theme*, a marker in page 57. He had showed the explicit photograph to Margaret from the Tonga Bar who had readily agreed to try out the new position. In it, she had to face the wall standing up, lean forward on both hands, and be penetrated from the rear. Everything had worked smoothly until Margaret from the Tonga Bar had experimented further. Taking one hand off the wall she had reached between her legs and tickled Matthias's swinging balls. This aroused him to such a state of voluble ecstasy that she wanted to take him to the utmost point of bliss and took her other hand off the wall. As she groped between her legs she fell forward and knocked herself unconscious, leaving Matthias fucking fresh air.

She had never been the same since. As the days went by she became even more generous, sympathetic and amenable. She stopped lifting her clients' wallets and valuables and charging higher prices at week-ends and on bank holidays. She became a push-over.

And it was all Matthias's fault.

Behind the two men at the bar sat the Bucket-Wheel Excavator Gang who were trying to tell Matthias and Desaix apart.

'Bwana Arse is the one wearing aertex drawers that we can see above the waist-band of his baggy trousers.'

'Matthias is the one wearing the fashionable drain-pipe boiler-suit with "Mufunsi Open Pit" across the back in yellow luminous paint...'

'Bwana Arse is as a sundered pumpkin in the rear, a cleft *tanga*!'

'Matthias is pigeon-toed from his childhood attack of rickets.'

'Bwana Arse stands at ten-to-three and has fallen arches.'

'Matthias is the one not paying for the drinks.'

'When Hammerkop pays, who can afford to love his friends? *Au! Au!* What can you do with one and ninepence an hour?'

They continued with their simple game until Matthias and Desaix had finished discussing what they could do with Pyper. As the journalist came down the stairs, his blue eyes momentarily softer as he watched Margaret jogging down before him, they beckoned him to come and join them for a drink.

'Are you hungry?' Matthias asked casually.

'Starving sport. Old Margaret has got a draw like wind-tunnel, Christ she gets better every time. Ever get that empty feeling?'

Matthias raised his troubled, moody eyes and smiled winsomely at Margaret who was washing up some glasses. She smiled back, then winked.

'How's things, Margaret?' Matthias asked solicitously. 'This little prick treat you right?'

Margaret resumed her chore, her eyes full of guilt.

'She didn't charge you, did she?' Matthias said tiredly. 'She can't go on like this. Everybody will take advantage of her.'

'That's what old Margaret wants, isn't it?' Pyper quipped cheerfully. 'She can't help it if that bang on the head you gave her has stopped her becoming a materialist. What's money, anyway? Zonkendawo is going to be more than a money-orientated society, isn't it? The old Doctor has promised us that much.'

'You're still hungry, aren't you?' Matthias grabbed Pyper's hand. 'Come on, I'll take you home and give you a bite to eat.'

Matthias took Pyper to his house, made him a cheese and tomato sandwich and locked him in a wall-cupboard. When he returned to the Tonga Bar he gave Margaret a brief lecture on how to curb her open-hearted spirit, gave her three pounds in conscience money, and went down to Field-Marshal Montgomery Crescent with Desaix and the Bucket-Wheel Excavator Gang on foot. Tarzan Cool Guy had asked all his guests not to bring cars as it might excite the attention of the police. When they arrived the Bucket-Wheel Excavator Gang spent a few minutes drop-kicking the chihuahua from one end of the lawn to the other to teach it some manners, then went round to the vegetable garden to watch Johnny McSilver beating up Desaix. Sitting on a pile of rotting banana leaves was Pyper, writing a blow-by-blow account of the fight for the morning edition of the *Zonkendawon Times*.

'Ya bloody eejit!' Johnny spat, as he punched the pilot in the eye. 'Ya could have killed us all! Ya daft French cunt! When are you going to grow up! Stand up!' Then he hit him under the heart. 'My boys are highly strung! Jesus ya make me mad! What good does it do them being dive-bombed by a dead-beat, washed-up has-been like you? Find your fun somewhere else!'

A right cross caught Desaix full on the nose and he sat down between two rows of pumpkins. Blood streamed from his nose and he was breathing wheezily from the blow under the heart.

'Get up! Get up, ya fucking high-altitude hobo!' Johnny screamed.

'I knew that phrase would catch on,' Pyper muttered to himself with satisfaction, 'I thought it would stick.'

Desaix knew the rules and managed to get to his feet. Swaying in the moonlight he took the final blow on his many chins and nose-dived into the soft earth, glad that it was all over.

'Get me a drink!' he mouthed through the soil. 'For God's sake I can't go on!'

Johnny stiffened, staring down at his stricken friend.

'Are you all right, Des?'

'Get me a drink, you merciless sod!' Desaix grunted. 'You've nearly killed me!'

Johnny whirled round and yelled at the Bucket-Wheel Excavator Gang to get Desaix a drink, then fell to his knees by the stricken pilot, pillowing his head on his lap. Tears streamed from his eyes on to the bloody countenance. With the hem of his shirt he wiped away the dirt and gore. Desaix looked just like his father lying there helpless in his arms.

'That's the way he used to look at me too,' he bubbled through his tears. 'Wouldn't ya think he'd let me forget. Ay, he had a look of you.'

'What about your brothers?' Desaix mumbled crossly. 'Don't forget the rest of the family.'

Johnny's keening was interrupted by the Bucket-Wheel Excavator Gang bringing Desaix's glass of cane-for-pain. They also carried a canvas chair and a bottle of whisky, while leading the golden Marilyn into the vegetable garden by the hand. Unfolding the chair, they held it ready as Marilyn eased Johnny McSilver to his feet and led him across to the little crowd gathered around the chair.

'Thanks, boys, he'll be all right now.'

'We know, *mukwai*,' they sang softly.

'Crying is good for a man sometimes,' Marilyn said pleasantly. 'It's a safety-valve.'

'Then Johnny McSilver is truly safe,' they replied.

Johnny's hand came out and the bottle of Bell's whisky was placed in it. Blubbering still, he forced his shaking lips together and took a long pull.

'Livingstone cried a lot,' Marilyn continued reflectively, 'when his wife died of fever, when his wayward son was killed fighting for the Union in the American Civil War.'

A man held up his hand.

'O Marilyn,' he called out above the heads of his colleagues, 'I would fight for the union.'

'No, not a trade union,' Marilyn's beam brightened into a golden noon. 'This is another kind of union.'

'O Marilyn, so is mine!' the man's eyes were burning with adoration. 'I would fight for even the most *piccanin* chance of a union with thee!'

Marilyn hurried on with her lecture, two spots of colour in her cheeks.

'Doctor Livingstone had a lot to put up with. He came here to Zonkendawo to tell your people the Word of God and many of the tribes would not listen to his sermons. He tells in his books about men, woman and children lying around smoking that awful stuff when he was actually telling them about Jesus and the virgin birth. When you think that if it was not for Doctor Livingstone, Zonkendawo would never have been discovered...'

The Bucket-Wheel Excavator Gang sat close around her chair. Listening to Marilyn was the greatest pleasure they knew of – the only greater pleasure would have been screwing her and that she would never allow. For the working-men gathered at her feet, Marilyn was like the sun hanging around in this one garden, a sun that had forgotten to set and had decided to stay the night. They did not believe that Marilyn really existed.

'O Marilyn,' another man ventured hoarsely, 'if Doctor Livingstone did in truth discover Zonkendawo then why did he give it to us?'

'Because it was yours,' she glowed goldenly, 'you were here already.'

'But then we might have discovered him. If he had not found us then he might never have found himself.'

Marilyn shook her beautiful head.

'Oh, no, he discovered you. You weren't looking for anyone.'

'So until Doctor Livingstone found our people they were not really here at all?'

'That's it exactly.'

There was a long, dreamy, thoughtful silence.

'Being discovered is a wonderful thing,' her questioner murmured, as he stroked Marilyn's toes through a gap between his companions' backs. 'Where would we be without it?'

While Marilyn continued with her lecture about Doctor Livingstone and how he had brought football and God from Glasgow, Desaix was entering the bathroom to patch up his face. He found Pyper kneeling at the pedestal of the lavatory, the lid closed, writing in his notebook.

'How many people would you say there were here?' he asked the bruised pilot. 'Just a rough estimate?'

Desaix did not answer. He wiped his bloody face with a flannel and ran out to find Tarzan Cool Guy. He could not trust himself not to murder Pyper this time. He saw the wrestler in conversation with Humphrey Fluellen who was smoking a joint in an ivory cigarette-holder. As Desaix joined them Humphrey ruffled the Frenchman's hair with the glowing end.

'Tomatoes are good for you. *Oui ou non?*' Humphrey cooed, his eyes strangely glazed. 'What animal can tell the time? Why, the clockodile! Who punched you in the face? You look different tonight. All night long I danced the Shadow Waltz with you. Holy God, look at that rainbow.'

Desaix swatted the tip of the cigarette away and tried to explain about the dangerous situation concerning Pyper. Humphrey shuffled forward, sweet smoke held deep in his lungs.

'I know what you're upset about. Pyper got to the Tonga Bar before you, didn't you? He's faster than light when he's after *hlanganana*.'

'Will you shut up?' Desaix shouted and drove his elbow into Humphrey's belly. Smoke poured out of the Welshman's mouth as from the funnel of a steam locomotive and he sank to his knees. Tarzan Cool Guy frowned reprovingly at the angry pilot and helped Humphrey to his feet.

'He doesn't know what he's saying when he's high,' the wrestler said. 'You've got to be patient with artistic people.'

'Christ, what a trip!' Humphrey beamed, while sucking on his cigarette-holder. 'This must be elephant-grass!' Tarzan Cool Guy put his arm round the Welshman's shoulders and held him steady while Desaix raved on about the menace in the lavatory.

'It's your house, *mon ami*, you do what you think's best, but I know what I'm going to do – I'm going to kill him this time! This afternoon I played games with the treacherous *salot*. Now that is over. He is not going to ruin my life a second time.'

Humphrey preened his great belly as if it was the splendid

breast of a swan and smiled through the silvery haze of smoke which surrounded his head.

'It's not his house, it's Dennis's house! Raus! Louse! Mouse!'

Humphrey covered his ears and roared with manic laughter.

'He's right, Desaix, for God's sake don't let Marge hear you saying it's my house or I'll really get into trouble. Dennis is getting a bit touchy about me staying here without paying anything towards the upkeep of the place.'

'Why don't you go and get Pyper out of there and throw him around for a while like you did before? That broken collarbone had him wanking left-handed for two months after you chucked him into the dustbins behind the Tonga Bar. Give him another Flying Mare and he'll keep quiet,' Desaix muttered wrathfully, 'because if you won't, I will!'

Humphrey uncovered his ears and wheezed as he gulped down more sweet smoke. Tears poured from his eyes and he coughed explosively.

'Bwana Arse! Farce! Ha-hee! Bwana Farce-Arse! About-Farce! Arse-about-farce! Christ, I'm on form tonight! Don't hold me back! Hooo!'

Desaix's features settled into a calm and dangerous mask. He waited until Humphrey's laughter had subsided, then stood chest to chest with the Welshman and stared into the dark tunnels that were his dilated pupils.

'This afternoon I chanced to meet the old stage-carpenter. He was in the Tonga Bar surrounded by people from every walk of life. They were listening to his every word. He was telling them about a *mis-en-scène* that he had witnessed at the theatre this morning. Bwana Humphrey Fluellen, so the craftsman called you, what a performance! What a failure! Certainly he will not get the Best Actor Award this year for this role. Bwana Humphrey Fluellen fucks like an arthritic elephant!' Desaix smiled maliciously and watched Humphrey slide to the floor, his huge round face ghastly with distress. Bending over the collapsed actor Desaix prodded him in the chest with a blunt forefinger.

'Humph can't hump eh? *Humph ne hump pas!* Humph-humph! Humphy-Dumphy sat on a wall! Humphy-Dumphy can't fuck at all!'

Tarzan Cool Guy pulled Desaix away. He could see the signs. A great creative talent was in smithereens, surrounded by smoke. Desaix had blitzed his way through to Humphrey's inner soul and the temple of his pride.

'Remind me never to cross you, Ace,' the wrestler said gravely. 'I'd rather have you as a friend than as an enemy.'

'Just a joke,' Desaix snarled with sudden vehemence. 'Now let's get Pyper before he syndicates his story to the *Washington Post* and *Le Canard Enchâiné*!'

They walked through to the bathroom. It was locked.

'Come out of there!' Desaix shouted.

'No!' piped the response. 'Never!'

'We'll break the door down!' the enraged pilot yelled threateningly.

The tinkling chuckle that greeted this outburst was too much for Desaix. Stepping back he kicked the door down and leapt through into the bathroom.

'What do you want that's so important?' demanded the youngest member of the Bucket-Wheel Excavator Gang whose voice had not yet broken. 'Can't a fellow get any peace?'

Desaix thought of apologizing to the youth sitting on the pedestal who was flicking the red dust out of his turn-ups with Tarzan Cool Guy's toothbrush, but thought better of it. It had been a genuine mistake and his actions had been in everybody's interests.

'Where's Pyper?'

'He's in the airing-cupboard.'

'How did he get in there?' Tarzan Cool Guy inquired.

'When I told him that I wanted to come in here and use the appliances he crawled in there so as not to embarrass me. You know what Europeans are like about their *tabus*.'

Desaix opened the airing-cupboard and found Pyper fast asleep on a pile of folded sheets and pillow-slips. Lying there he looked like a child, his golden hair rumpled, his breath light as a breeze, soft colour in his fair cheeks. Desaix drew back his fist, but then let it fall. The tender vision of the slumbering journalist was too much for him.

'Ah, the Great Writer of Lies is resting,' the youngest member of the Bucket-Wheel Excavator Gang said with a smile as he drew the stiff toilet-brush through his crinkly hair. 'I thought that I did not hear the sound of his typewriter.'

'Look at him, Tarzan,' Desaix blurted, 'look at the bastard! Wouldn't he break your heart?'

Pyper opened one eye and smiled down at the battered features of his forgiving friend.

'*Bonjour* Arse. I was just dreaming about you.'

'God, this is too much,' Desaix screamed. 'Someone give me the strength to kill him!'

Tarzan Cool Guy stepped forward and helped Pyper down out of the airing-cupboard.

'You could have suffocated in there, John,' Tarzan Cool Guy said sternly. 'You're lucky to be all right.'

Pyper stretched his legs, pinned the crease in his dove-grey slacks between thumb and forefinger, then shook his fair head.

'Christ, you're dense, Tarzan. If there's not air in an airing-cupboard where is there air?'

As the party at Field-Marshal Montgomery Crescent got under way Inspector Grutchfield and Inspector Kwango sat under the bougainvillaea hedge outside and discussed who should rightly lead the raid.

'Up until midnight it should be me,' Grutchfield whispered, 'but after then you take over from me and I become just an adviser.'

Kwango took a twig out of his cap-band and thought for a while.

'He's a strong man.'

'There's six of us, Kwango, we're hand-picked men.'

'Perhaps I will let you have this raid as your farewell. You will need the memory of exciting moments when you talk to your grandchildren in your old age,' Kwango laid a hand on Grutchfield's sleeve. 'I hear the *musungus* spend most of their time reminiscing about the good old days in Africa when they get home to Britain.'

'My dear chap, that is a nice thought, but you need the experience. There's no teacher like experience. What's the point in me showing you the ropes if you can't actually do the job when I'm given my advisory post and start taking it easy?'

Further down the hedge four African constables lay on their backs looking at the stars.

'I will never strike a blow against Tarzan Cool Guy.'

'I have brought a plastic container full of *chibuku* beer.'

'Who are we to follow at the charge?'

'If we lie here long enough Margaret from the Tonga Bar is sure to pass and we can look up her skirts to Heaven.'

With such thoughts as these they whiled away the time until the question of command was settled.

By half-past eleven the problem of Pyper had been attended to. He had been released from all restraints and given a table, chair, typewriter, paper and two bottles of cane-for-pain. While the party accelerated around him, the youthful reporter picked out his message to the waiting ears of the nation. He was not a fast writer, the sentences never came without effort. Each word was carefully selected and there were many halts and breaks suitable for refreshment. Standing by his side Dennis, who stood to lose most by the publication of the article, kept his glass topped up while reading an American treatise on sand-beetles of the Badlands. After an hour's work Pyper could not carry on because his fingers kept getting jammed between the typewriter keys and he had twice set fire to the paper with his cigarette.

'There's nothing personal in this, Dennis,' Pyper giggled, as he put out the flaming paper by pouring cane-for-pain over it and making the inferno worse, 'but it has to be done.'

'I understand, John. No favouritism.'

'Right, no favouritism. Equal treatment for all.'

Dennis watched the burning of his typewriter with some nostalgia. So many things had changed lately that he found it difficult to keep track. The typewriter had been a twenty-first birthday gift from his mother while he was at university, it had been with him for nearly twenty years. Millions of words about beetles had been hammered against that fiery roller, thousands of perceptions, points, questions, conclusions, tattooed across that flaming vibrator now buckling with the heat. As Pyper took the bottles of cane-for-pain and went hunting for the laughter of Margaret from the Tonga Bar, Dennis wondered if anything would ever be the same again. There was independence and independence. Was he really strong enough to take the sort of freedom that his friends insisted upon? Could he keep up? He had got used to his neighbours being unpleasant to him, to his house being called 'The Black and White Minstrel Show', to Tarzan Cool Guy drinking his beer and sleeping with his wife in the master bedroom, all these difficulties he had surmounted. But what was happening inside himself, to the beetle-hunter?

Picking up the typewriter with a pair of tongs he went outside and threw the blackened machine on to the pile of rotting banana leaves. A muffled cry rose into the night, halting Dennis in his return to the book about sand-beetles.

'Why me?' Johnny McSilver sobbed from the collapsed canvas chair. 'What have I ever done to ya that ya treat me thus?'

'I didn't see you there, Johnny, I'm terribly sorry,' Dennis stammered. 'I couldn't see you.'

'Come over and talk to me, old friend. God, on a night like this there's plenty to talk about, eh?'

Dennis walked round the pile of banana leaves and found Johnny tangled up in the tubular-steel legs of the chair, his bottle of Bell's tucked under his head for a pillow.

'Are you all right?' Dennis took the typewriter off Johnny's chest and placed it on one side. 'Having a quiet moment to yourself?'

''Am just thinking, Dennis, what's ta become of this country? When are the eejits going to get themselves organized? See you, there's not even a national Football Association yet! When d'ya think these Africans are going to wake up to what's urgently needed? We'll all be deed before the first cup final. Ya cannae credit it, can ya? The bastards dinny care!'

As Johnny got broader and broader in his dialect and deeper into his dream of sporting peace and unity, Dennis looked at his watch and saw that it was ten minutes to midnight.

'Well, what shall we do at the stroke of twelve?' he mused. 'We'll all become free men as the flag goes up the pole. What would be appropriate?'

Johnny sat up, his eyes shining.

'Auld Lang Syne o' course! What else?'

*

Dennis went across to where Tarzan Cool Guy and Marge were watching the Bucket-Wheel Excavator Gang as they sat at Marilyn's feet and listened to her lecture on Doctor Livingstone. She was a beautiful, radiant picture, the moon in her hair, her tall body still golden in the silvery light, her smile shining through the lime and avocado trees.

'Those boys certainly look up to her, don't they?' Tarzan Cool Guy said wistfully. 'It's a great gift she has. They're spellbound!'

They were certainly under her sunny influence. Framed in the dark trees they saw her stripped of all pretence, inhibitions, class-barriers, racial overtones and clothes, a warm golden dream that enfolded each man like a long summer squeezed into an hour.

'Doctor Livingstone thought that football was God in the same way as all his fellow Glaswegians. All the rules are the same as those of God. Would God allow us to be off-side? Of course not. To molest the unprotected goalkeeper? Never. If we play together then that means we must be at peace with one another.'

'Marilyn,' a member of the gang spoke up gruffly, 'is it not true that peace and relief are the same thing?'

'Yes, I suppose so,' she answered gently.

'Marilyn, will you give me peace?'

Marilyn laughed and bowed her shining head until her hair swung forward in a glittering curtain.

'If I can.'

'Then come into the spare bedroom with me now,' the man pleaded.

Marilyn laughed again but there was a hint of strain in her voice.

'I've spent the last hour trying to explain about that. I'm married to Johnny and he's your friend.'

'He's also asleep,' the member of the Bucket-Wheel Excavator Gang pointed out insistently. 'He wouldn't know.'

Dennis broke up the lecture by shouting from the middle of the lawn that they were all going to dance Auld Lang Syne as Zonkendawo became independent. The Bucket-Wheel Excavator Gang complained that they would rather listen to Marilyn talking about God because the longer she went on the more chance they had of getting her on her back. Matthias came out of the house and walked among the gang clipping their ears, rapping their skulls with a pair of steel nutcrackers.

'From midnight you become responsible citizens of a free country,' he growled, 'and any bastard who tries to take advantage of it will be in trouble.'

'Then what is this freedom,' someone asked, 'if a man cannot pursue the object of his desire? Are we not free to look for perfect happiness?'

'Oh, yes, they must be free to do that, Matthias!' Marilyn dazzled a lovely smile at her audience. 'Everyone has that right.'

'Do you know what they want to be free to do?' Matthias dragged a man to his feet and forcibly buttoned up his overalls. 'You mustn't trust them.'

Marilyn smacked at the grubby hands that were reaching up her thighs and shook her head.

'It must be because of the breakdown in traditional tribal values.'

Everyone assembled on the lawn. Pyper brought out Margaret from the Tonga Bar who was telling him about her hallucination. She had seen a squad of prone whistling lawmen looking up her skirt. It was time that she stopped drinking the stock, Pyper advised.

'Where's Humphrey?' Marge asked.

In the sitting-room Kovary was trying to persuade his friend to join in the dance.

'Come on, man, don't be such a misery. It's only a bit of fun.'

Humphrey tucked his chin into his bull neck and shook his head.

'I'm not glad that the Kaffirs are taking over, not after what that stage-carpenter has been saying about me.'

'No one out there can dance like you, Humphrey. We'll all be looking to you for a lead. You've got the best singing voice, the best timing, stage-presence, the best sense of rhythm, you're a natural focus of attention.'

Kovary held out his hand.

Humphrey paused, chuckled, took the offered help and got to his feet.

'Can't argue with that, can we?'

Out on the lawn they made a big circle and waited for Dennis to give the signal. As the Bucket-Wheel Excavator Gang jostled among themselves to be the one holding Marilyn's free hand (the other was holding Johnny up), Tarzan Cool Guy looked round the circle of his friends. Indeed, he was a lucky man. They were the salt of the earth, the best that could be found. Nothing could touch them.

But as Dennis clapped and the Scottish dance began, waveringly at first as they tried for the tune and rhythm with Humphrey showing the way, his rich baritone booming, somebody was coming to touch them. From under the bougainvillaea hedge came creeping Inspectors Grutchfield and Kwango, and they were holding hands. Behind them skulked the squad of mystified constables.

'Stop!' Inspectors Kwango and Grutchfield shouted with one voice. 'In the name of the Law!'

In the pregnant silence that followed, the constables kept their distance from their commanders, trying to look as though they weren't with them. They looked round the circle of dancers, their eyes fearful, ashamed and pleading for sympathy. They had not been consulted over the vexed leadership question, nor had they been warned of its compromising solution.

'Why are you holding hands like a couple of queers?'

Pyper's sharp unlovely accents pricked the silence and the dancers started to laugh.

'What did you say?' Grutchfield shrilled.

'I said that I thought you looked like a couple of old fairies standing there in the moonlight,' Pyper continued meanly.

Kwango cleared his throat importantly.

'This is an illegal gathering! Disperse! I will give you one minute before we charge.' Here he gave the cringing constables a meaningful glance. 'How am I doing?'

'You're messing it up!' Grutchfield hissed. 'You've got to read the Riot Act first.'

'I haven't got the Riot Act!' Kwango protested. 'I've left it at home with my examination revision papers.'

'I thought I'd told you to learn it by heart, you silly fool!' Grutchfield raged. 'You're impossible to teach anything to! What's the force coming to when they're promoting idiots like you?'

Kwango wrenched his hand free. He was suddenly aware of the audience that was surveying them with moon-twinkling eyes, their mouths curved into winning smiles.

'You're all under arrest.'

'We're all under the stars,' chanted the Bucket-Wheel Excavator Gang.

'You have broken the Law!' Kwango shouted.

'You are breaking our hearts,' came the melodic answer.

'I am taking you to prison!' thundered Kwango.

'We are taking you apart,' the Bucket-Wheel Excavator Gang chanted while moving forward as a man.

Inspector Grutchfield and the constables dropped any pretence at courage in the face of this organized opposition and looked sheepishly at the ground. Inspector Kwango was alone, but at a critical point in his career.

'The President ordered that there should be no parties!' he announced boldly. 'All bars were to be closed, all dance-halls and illicit shebeens. Everything was to be quiet on this night. You have been having a party and so you are guilty of a crime and must be punished.' He nudged Grutchfield and whispered at the humiliated policeman, 'Got that bit right anyway, didn't I?'

'You're going to get us all killed!' Grutchfield replied tremulously. 'I know this lot.'

'They'll climb down when they see I mean business,' Kwango asserted stoutly.

'But this isn't a party,' a woman's voice chirped.

Marge stepped out of the ring and looked Kwango straight in the eye. She knew what the young man's problem was. He needed to bow out gracefully, not to go back to the station with his tail between his legs.

'What is it if not a party?' Kwango sneered heavily. 'What are the ingredients of a party then? Booze? Yes, there's *maningi* booze here all right ... *dagga*? I smell it! Women? Yes?'

'All right, what did you see?' Marge asked evenly. 'You tell us.'

'Dancing ... you have all been drinking,' Kwango said with confidence. 'Look at yourselves. You are all drunk.'

Marge folded her arms beneath her ample breast and tapped her foot, her fine grey eyes alive with mockery.

'Is the Scottish Country Dance Society outlawed in Zonkendawo?'

Kwango gnawed his lip and looked at Grutchfield.

'Is it?' he whispered.

'Of course not, you moron!'

'No, madam, it is not.'

'Well, that's who we are. We meet here every week, practise a bit, then have some refreshments. We're just about to have a breather. Won't you join us?'

Kwango looked round him. Anticipation was on every face, the joy of Life, human companionship, the sweet lulling song of the crickets conspiring with the moment to woo him away from ambition. The game was up.

'I'd love to,' he said humbly.

Joining hands again, linking in the six policemen, they went through Auld Lang Syne properly, surging together at the repeat of the refrain, pounding wildly over the grass as they back-pedalled to the perimeter and took up the rhythm with their crossed arms, their voices together as one as they heralded the birth of a unique nation on the face of the earth.

Whether it was the dancing, the emotion of the great moment when a people broke off the last manacle of slavery, or the drink, is difficult to say. Whether it was the information from Kwango that Fines Chingola had ordered the raid through the Regional Secretary of the Party, or the easy manner with which the police contingent settled into the swing of things and spent most of their time going backwards and forwards to the refrigerator until the door was so often open that the beer couldn't get cold, or whether he just got the Blue Meanies is another difficult thing to say. What is easy to say is that at half-past three that night, Tarzan Cool Guy was assaulted by a fit of patriotic conscience. He sat in a chair, his chest heaving, and thought deeply about his country.

'I'm a Zonkendawon, aren't I?' he choked, as Marge stroked his cheek. 'What can they expect off a bum like me? I have no contribution to make. I live here, don't I? I was born in the Northern Province, way up there in the bush where a man knows the earth like he knows his own mother.'

'Where is your mother?' Marge asked. 'You've never mentioned her before.'

'I haven't seen her for years,' Tarzan replied unhappily, his eyes grim with self-criticism. 'You see what a fine son I've been to her? I'm such a parasite!'

Everyone tutted and shook their head. One thing that Tarzan Cool Guy was not was a parasite. The only person who didn't tut or shake his head was Dennis who was beginning to think that he was.

'Things will get better,' Marge whispered soothingly, while she stroked the wrestler's forehead with the tips of her fingers. 'We'll find you something to do.'

'What can I do? I'm a fighter! I only know my own business. Tell me to put on a good show for the fans, plenty of noise and agonized expressions, all the trimmings – I'd even wear a mask if they wanted me to – and I'm all right. But I can't just turn round and adapt myself to another profession. I'm too long in the tooth for that!' Tarzan Cool Guy protested. 'Can't you see that I'm facing a crisis? All I can see ahead is years of being unemployed.'

Kwango suggested that he could join the police.

'There's still plenty of vacancies for people like you. Anyone who can give satisfactory service in the cells on a Saturday night is welcome. If we didn't keep up with the old quick-fire corporal punishment for minor offenders the courts would grind to a halt.'

'Shut up!' hissed Grutchfield. 'You're not supposed to talk about that.'

Tarzan Cool Guy shook his head.

'That's not my line at all. Basically I'm an athlete, a gymnast. I'm not a mauler,' he explained. 'I've already been offered a job as a bouncer at the Tonga but I turned that down for the same reason. I've got my public to think of.'

'That is right!' a member of the Bucket-Wheel Excavator Gang said indignantly. 'What a poor situation would it be if we, his old friends, were to be ejected from the Tonga Bar by a man we loved and respected? It would be intolerable.'

'When we kill Hammerkop, rape his wife, Gladys, burn down his house and plunder all his personal effects, you could take over his job as Open Pit Manager. The only thing I would like to keep for myself is his big green Dodge. I could get all my kids into that,' said Matthias, his eyes half-closed and a dreamy smile on his face. 'Oh, that would be nice.'

'You could always be our garden-boy,' Dennis suggested timidly, his mind locked on to the hope that he might get some participation or return from his omnivorous lodger. 'The grass needs cutting at the moment.'

'Don't be ridiculous, Dennis!' Marge said hotly. 'What a horrible idea! He's not going to be your servant, certainly not! Who do you think you are?'

'I'm not at all sure lately,' Dennis replied sincerely.

Marge paused, then brushed Dennis's self-pity aside.

'God, what a thought! Haven't you got any sympathy for anyone? You can see the predicament he's in. You keep your silly ideas to yourself in future!'

Dennis shrugged and turned away. To his mind the idea of the wrestler helping in the garden was at least a practical proposition. It would keep him busy and use up some of the time that he normally spent in the kitchen with his head in the refrigerator looking for beers or steering Marge into the master bedroom. As he looked towards the door he saw Pyper entering with a carton of bottles, a wicker basket full of lemons and a canister of salt. While the discussion about Tarzan Cool Guy's future continued, Dennis observed the New Zealander closely. Sitting in a corner by the window Pyper took out a bottle and smiled affectionately at the label which was of a sailing-ship being struck by lightning. He then cut a lemon into quarters and held one quarter between his thumb and forefinger. On the back of the same hand he poured a little mound of salt. Taking the bottle of cane-for-pain by the neck he braced himself against the wall, sighed, drew up his knees, licked the salt off the back of his hand, took a swig of cane-for-pain, then bit the lemon and sucked out the juice. When he had finished this sequence of actions he proceeded to do it again and again and again.

One of the features of Man that separates him from the beasts is his insatiable curiosity. No giraffe, butterfly or lizard would have given Pyper a second glance as they went past about their business; but everyone in the room was human that night and subject to the passionate nosiness of the species.

'What are you up to, O Great Writer of Lies?' the Bucket-Wheel Excavator Gang whispered together. 'It looks very interesting.'

'I'm playing Snakebite, you defective shitheads!' Pyper grinned amiably. 'Jesus Christ, your education wasn't up to much, was it?'

Within five minutes Tarzan Cool Guy's employment problems were forgotten and everyone was crowded into Pyper's corner with piles of salt on the backs of their hands, lemons betwixt thumb and forefinger, and passing round the bottles of cane-for-pain.

It took an hour for all the cane-for-pain to disappear. During this time the Snakebiters suffered from a diminished sense of responsibility and became progressively humorous, pleasant and amenable to the point of idiocy. All except one. His sense of responsibility was increased until it became too much for him to endure. When the guilt and self-recrimination in his troubled soul could be borne no longer he rang the house of Fines Chingola and asked him to come round and make the arrangements for Tarzan Cool Guy to join the Territorial Army. Fines explained that he could not get up and come himself because he was suffering from an attack of migraine but he would ring up the European Recruiting Officer responsible and send him round.

'What's the sense in keeping a dog and barking yourself?' he murmured to the photograph of Doctor Mulombe that was stuck on the wall at the foot of his bed alongside a number of artistic studies from *Health and Efficiency*. 'Let that *musungu* pig get on with that and God help the white bastard if he's late for work in the morning.'

When the Recruiting Officer arrived at Field-Marshal Montgomery Crescent it was ten-past five. The sun was already lightening the sky. He drove into the driveway and parked his car alongside four policemen who were all lying on their backs looking up into a paw-paw tree.

'The paw-paw is as the loins of Margaret from the Tonga Bar,' one said to the mystified official who was standing over them with his brief-case. 'Soon it will be our turn to join her on the floor of the breakfast room.'

'I'm looking for Tarzan Cool Guy,' the Recruiting Officer said crossly. 'What a bloody time to decide to join the Territorial Army!'

When the Recruiting Officer was escorted into the house by the four policemen and Tarzan Cool Guy had been brought from his corner, his conscience now corrosive with self-hatred, the Snakebiters took a democratic decision.

'You mean that you all want to join?' the Recruiting Officer said incredulously, one hand already distributing the signing-on papers. 'Every one of you?'

'That is how we want it!' the Bucket-Wheel Excavator Gang confirmed grandly from the queue they were standing in. 'One for all and all for one!'

'This is a binding document you know,' the Recruiting Officer reminded them. 'It won't become invalid in the morning.'

'Leave us to watch for the morning!'

With these words of the Bucket-Wheel Excavator Gang in his ears the Recruiting Officer went round the room, guiding the hands of those who could no longer see far enough to find the dotted line, helping those who could no longer remember what their name was. When it was all over he put all the papers back into his brief-case, stepped over the already dormant celebrants, kicked aside empty bottles, articles of clothing, lemon peel and salt-canisters, and went home to his bed.

6
Maud's Funeral Oration over The Man Who Wanted To Live For Ever

On the first day of his country's independence the old man who had complained to Maud about death died. Freedom struck him in the night and he was finished. In the morning his relatives and friends straightened him out, put a full packet of tipped cigarettes in his hands, wrapped him up in a coffin of bark, placed flat stones upon his chest, and lashed him up with vines. Waiting until the sun had climbed out of the east they sat around the entrance of the dead man's hut sharing round the last of his mealies and cassava and drinking what was left in his beer calabash. As the shadows crept away from the hut entrance, the widow began her mourning, rolling in the sunny dust, beating her breast, tearing at her hair and shrieking out goodbyes to her life-long companion who lay trussed up and propped against the wall of the hut. As the widow went through all the accepted stages of the mourning ritual and began tearing at the vines round the coffin with her teeth and burrowing for her husband's hand through the overlapping bark, more of the Muntu gathered round the hut and they started to sing a mourning-song which Maud had composed long before she ever came to Myanis Kupela, a song from the old days when it had been a risky business to follow the Wife of God in her wanderings across the great African plateau.

Bani lo muntu? Bani lo muntu?
Who is this man? Who is this man?
Lo mgwagwa ena lungile pambili!
The road is good ahead!
Hayikona saba! Don't be afraid!
This one must sleep in the earth
Or dream in the river!
Basopo mazinyo ga lo-ngwenyane!
Beware of the teeth of the crocodile!
Look out for the lies of the Worm!

When the widow had exhausted herself and lay covered in dust, the Muntu took the bark coffin up on their shoulders and carried it over to the cathedral steps, the widow dragging herself along behind. The Muntu then began shouting and hallooing for Maud until she came to the door, her big red-freckled eyes rolling.

'*Tulabo! Tulabo!* You know I'm not at my best in the morning!' she bawled irritably. 'God kept me up half the night listening to his spiritual problems.'

The Muntu held the corpse aloft, shaking it like a solitary arrow in a quiver.

'He spoke true! He is dead!' they cried.

Maud paused, rubbed the sleep out of her eyes and advanced down the steps towards the coffin.

'Ah,' she nodded sadly, 'the man who wanted to live for ever.'

The widow crawled through the mourners and clasped Maud around her magnificently muscled knees, her grey head pressed against the strength of the musing prophetess.

'He was always a child,' the widow sniffed. 'He would never grow up. Do not blame him for his stupidity.'

Maud leaned down and massaged the widow's scraggy neck.

'He was a child of God. Do not mistake stupidity for innocence. Any man who wants to die is truly stupid. Any man who can see no reason why he should die is only innocent,' she said softly.

Tucking the widow under her arm Maud walked across to the old man's hut. Inside she found it all as it should be. The plates were empty. The knife was licked clean. The calabash stood up-ended in the corner, the last drops of sweet white beer spilled on to the ground. Maud picked up the blanket which lay folded near the entrance and put it round the widow's skinny shoulders.

'There, sit in the sun with the smell of him until we have sunk him in the swamp. Remember the good in him. Curse the bad. Hope that he loved you as well as he might have loved another and hope that you were fair to him in his life. If you ever cheated him, be sorry now. If he ever cheated you, forgive him because it is all over between you now. Eat nothing today but in the morning cook a breakfast and eat it alone outside your hut.

While you are sitting there remember to look around you. We, the Muntu, will all be eating breakfast at the same time.'

Sitting the widow down so her back was supported by the hut and the sun struck warmth into her bones, Maud returned to the crowd in front of the cathedral and summoned them to follow her.

It is necessary at this stage to provide some background to Maud's funeral oration over The Man Who Wanted To Live For Ever. As it represents an important milestone in African freedom-fighting history it is worth spending a few moments trying to analyse her reasons for making the death of this garrulous old man the cause of such a significant and far-reaching statement on the human condition. Did she deliberately choose the first morning of Zonkendawo's independence as a propitious time to clarify her political position? Did she have powers of prophecy induced by her frequent intimacies with God and had she been telepathically informed of what was being planned by Doctor Mulombe in terms of the destruction of her people? Had she been tipped off about the formation of that military Leviathan, the National Territorial Emergency Force? Maud took no newspapers. There was no radio in Myanis Kupela except the one hidden in Bwana Cat's-Eyes' hut. Could she subconsciously feel the lifting of the British yoke off the necks of the African people of her country? Was the wave of relief that was felt in every hut, house, hole-in-the-ground, oil-barrel, shanty and shack occupied by Zonkendawons, so great that it created a seismic tremor that could be felt even through the swamps of Bengweulu? It is doubtful whether Maud was deliberately trying to counterbalance the tide of optimism that was sweeping the nation outside the stockades of Myanis Kupela as a result of the flag-raising ceremony on the lawns of State House. No Muntu was affected by this historic event. It did not touch his life. His future was bound up with Maud and whether she would succeed in maintaining her freedom in the face of Mulombe's freedom to do as he liked. What her followers did not know was that an incident that had occurred nine months ago had had profound political repercussions – for Maud had rejected an overture of peace from the Party. What she had done at that time had made

Mulombe determined to exterminate Maud and the Muntu as soon as the British had invested supreme authority for domestic affairs in him and the Party caucus. It was the first act under the official policy of the New Humanism and it was in revenge for the treatment meted out to Ruben Katundu, martyr of the Struggle.

Nine months before Independence Mulombe had been anxious to try and bring the Muntu movement into the Party fold without having to resort to traditional means. Maud and her followers had settled in the Bengweulu Swamps by then and Mulombe's ace-bombers, hoodlums and card-sellers were too tied up with the problem of purging the mine-townships of the Democratic Congress Party to think of a campaign against such a distant enemy. Contrary to the warnings of his advisers – mainly those of his mother Mrs Renfrew Mulombe – the old ruffian had decided to try diplomacy as a means of obtaining his objective. He had sent a Party officer who had recently returned from England where he had been studying politics at the University of Hull – Ruben Katundu – on this vital mission. Ruben had gladly accepted the job as it gave him a chance to establish himself as a suitable candidate for the Foreign Service and also because it would give him an opportunity to do some field-work for his proposed Ph.D. thesis, 'The Influence of the European Missionaries on the Political Infrastructures of Independent Africa'.

Ruben had set out from Myakajunji on his brand-new Raleigh bicycle with the full authority of the Progress Party behind him – his remit, to explore the possibility of integrating the Muntu movement into the ranks of Party membership and leave no trace of their previous values and loyalties. For three weeks he had cycled northwards along the bumpy dirt-roads, his bony shanks pounded into insensitivity by the corrugations. On the handlebars he had carried a pig-skin briefcase containing five books – Plato's *Republic*; *The Holy Bible* (King James edition); Doctor Mulombe's pamphlet, *Towards a New Humanism*, which had been ghost-written by his brother Eustace (450 copies); Machiavelli's *The Prince* and Kenneth Graham's *The Wind in the Willows*.

Skirting the Katanga he had first called at the village of Kapo to pick up two helpers, members of the Bisa tribe who had been wounded in the Copperbelt riots and were convalescing before they returned to the fray. They were both experienced men with first-class records, able to establish a meaningful dialogue with any political opponent or dissenter.

With these companions trotting along by his side Ruben had entered the vast swampland and directed his now-battered bicycle towards Maud's capital. Fifteen miles south of Myanis Kupela he had been forced to exchange his machine for a dug-out canoe. After a day's paddling his craft had made a landing on the shore of the island. Maud had been waiting for him, surrounded by her followers. With a hefty kick of one foot she had sent the canoe away from its mooring.

'That is far enough!' Maud had shouted. 'I know of men with briefcases.'

One of the Party hoods had been a brave man. He had fought against many foes in many guises. The police held no terrors for him, or the army, or any man or woman. He sized Maud up, chose his moment to strike and leapt agilely out of the canoe, with an eight-inch lead pipe stuffed down one leg of his trousers, a sharpened bicycle-chain round his neck, a brass knuckle-duster in his jacket pocket, four copies of *Towards a New Humanism* in his shirt and a pick-axe handle up his sleeve, he sank straight to the bottom of twenty feet of water and drowned.

Above him the debate continued.

'What are you afraid of?' Ruben asked, the sun glittering on his gold-rimmed spectacles. 'If you sincerely believe in your creed then you should have nothing to fear. In the Middle Ages in western Europe theologians and philosophers often disputed their principles and belief in public.'

'I am not middle-aged!' Maud thundered angrily. 'And let's have more respect from you, you little runt! Who sent you here?'

The other hood was watching the stream of bubbles that had been released by his expiring partner. He heard Maud's question and tried to prop up his waning confidence by using a magic word, a word which usually struck terror into the hearts of Zonkendawons.

'Mulombe!'

The crowd were silent. The hood grinned, braced himself,

gratified with the result. It had worked again. He nudged Ruben in the back.

'We're all right now, son. They won't touch you now they know who we're from.'

Maud shifted forward a few steps into the water.

'So you come from Mulombe?'

Ruben straightened up, took a copy of *Towards a New Humanism* out of his briefcase and held it aloft.

'I come to you from the Messiah of Zonkendawo, from the saviour of our people! He has fought for our freedom but without unity beneath him we can never be truly free. We must work harder, more selflessly, and only think of our country and our leader. Let him enter your minds! Let him drive you to greater efforts! Let him persuade you to greater sacrifice! Let us think of each other more than ourselves and of Mulombe more than each other!'

Maud waded further towards the canoe and held out her hand for the book. Ruben threw it to her, his young face perfervid with zeal. He was about to make a breakthrough. Reason was about to conquer religious hysteria and ignorance. He was on the verge of a mass-conversion.

With an effortless crossing of her immense hands Maud tore the book in half and threw it into the swamp. The remaining hood, a cry of rage on his lips, swung his paddle at the advancing Maud and dealt her a sharp blow on the head. Maud rubbed her ear, grabbed the paddle as it swung towards her a second time, broke it in half across her knee, seized the hood by the ears, lifted him out of the canoe and pounded his head against her own until the man went limp in her grasp.

'Is that how you suppress criticism?' Ruben said with quiet dignity. 'Is that how you argue and dispute truth? Can't you see the futility of violence? Who does it really persuade? Humanism as practised by Doctor Mulombe and the Progress Party does not depend on the iron fist. We impress by example. We set standards. We convince people that they have the best chance of a decent standard of living by joining our organization. If you stuff a philosophy down a man's throat then he will eject it in his own time, won't he? Our people are not fools. Do you know that the Party has established three poultry co-operatives in the Solwezi area? How did we do that? By thuggery? Can't you see that by ruling your followers by force and fear you are acting against their legitimate aspirations, their true interests? This is the operation of malevolent tyranny! Let these people go!'

It had been at this point that Maud had lost her temper. None of her followers had ever seen this happen before and they were amazed at the magnitude of her fury. The black waters had seethed and broken into white foam. Whole reed-islands had been torn apart and whirled into the sky. Marsh birds for miles around rose in screaming, frightened clouds and blocked out the sun. The mud heaved and shuddered around the island, lapping thickly at the stockade walls. At the centre of the tempest had been the huge figure of the raging prophetess, mud and water flying about her like a typhoon, her voice loud with a terrible vengeance.

When the turbulence had died down and the waters had calmed, the Muntu had not been able to see any sign of Ruben or the canoe. The area of devastation was vast and there was so much flotsam and jetsam floating on the surface that no one was able to make out what the pieces were. The Muntu had fallen back from the shore as Maud waded in, her eyes still flashing but with a note of regret creeping into her mighty mutterings.

'When you abuse the mountain,' she had sighed on that fateful day, 'it is best to be sure that you are standing on the plain.'

Since that day there had been no contact between Maud and Mulombe. Maud was not aware that Ruben's body had been found floating in the Congo River 920 miles from Myanis Kupela. It was surmised by the police that Ruben had been murdered in the Bengweulu Swamps and his corpse carried by the Luapula, a tributary of the Congo which rises in the swamps, to the place where it had been found. They were certain that Ruben's death was caused by foul play because seventeen copies of *Towards a New Humanism* were found in the bowels of the body and there was evidence that they had arrived there via the anus.

So for nine months Maud had been given a respite from persecution. To her, the explanation was simple. She had convinced

Mulombe – in his own language – that the Muntu movement was a force to be reckoned with and not a minority group whose views could be absorbed or ignored. If Mulombe wanted Maud to accept his power on earth he would have to use better means than the ingenuous youth whose remains, after a hero's funeral, now lay in Myakajunji cemetery.

Yet to Doctor Mulombe this explanation was unthinkable. When he heard of Ruben's death he was up to his ears in the Copperbelt riots and the Struggle was entering its final phase. Supporters of the Democratic Congress were either altering their allegiance or dying in the nightly purges that swept through the mine-townships – one way or the other they were changing their minds. Mulombe had decided, even in his vengeful rage against Maud, to wait until the British got out of Zonkendawo and then he would send an army against Myanis Kupela, raze it to the ground as a symbol of heresy and treachery, slaughter its inhabitants, publicly execute Maud, and stamp out Muntuism for ever.

Maud arrived at the edge of the burial-pond at the head of the crowd. She stood near the water's edge and pointed at her feet. Gently the Muntu laid down the coffin of The Man Who Wanted To Live For Ever and stood back. There was a silence as Maud looked at the dark cocoon. She sighed. Her eyes closed. In her mind she counted the number of times that she had come to the burial-pond in these days of peace. Myanis Kupela was not the best place to live except in the freedom that it provided. On the debit side it housed malaria, black-water fever, typhus, hookworm, malnutrition and bilharzia and they took their grim toll. But the children kept coming. For as many died, as many were born. No shoes stayed empty. They were surviving as a people, growing closer together, dying together, living together, living with God together. Life came and went and was as enjoyable as The Man Who Wanted To Live For Ever had claimed it to be. The old man had been right and had been wrong. Maud's mind fermented like a huge vat of warm yeast and she was conscious of a power of earth-shaking articulation.

She cleared her throat and squashed a dozen mosquitoes on her black buttress of a brow.

'My people,' she cried, 'gather round me and we will discuss the life of one who lies here bound up like a babe to its mother's back.'

'*Lo ingwa yena tiyile!*' the Muntu sang as they crowded into the space between Maud and the edge of the pond. 'O the leopard he is trapped!'

Maud shushed their response, then put her hands on the huge country of her hips.

'He ran with us when there was running. He sat with us when there was sitting. He shared our dust and our road and the pains of our feet. He took our part, the beatings, the spittings, the houndings and the laughings. When he was feeling sorry for himself he was feeling sorry for us all!'

Maud then looked at the sky, the ragged horizon of the swamps, and bowed her head, a tremor running through her body so her bosom shook like an avalanche of anthracite.

'Ulululululululu!'

The women joined in her sad trilling.

'Ulululululululu!'

Maud spread her hands over the corpse.

'He did not want to die because he knew the one truth! There is nothing better than living!'

She looked up, head cocked to one side.

'Am I making myself clear?'

'Perfectly!' the Muntu answered loudly.

Maud wiped sweat and the bloody blotches of the slaughtered mosquitoes off her forehead, and sighed heavily.

'You see the footprints in the mud? Here and there. There and there. We are often mourning, often dying, often bringing forth and often putting back. We come to the burial pond as many times as we take the knife to the cord. Why do we put up with it? This flesh [Here she grabbed a nipple the size of a dinner-plate and tugged it] What is it but our weakness?'

The Muntu roared with laughter at Maud's witticism. The idea of their leader being weak was not only unthinkable but unbearable. She carried them all on her broad shoulders, the world was in her womb, Hope and Love sat in majesty on the brown thrones of her eyes. Maud was the Atlas of Africa.

She wagged a finger at her listeners.

'Noko wena idhala lo sinkwa kupela wena zo gula mbaimbai! Remember! If you only eat bread you will become ill! By itself this flesh is nothing! Without God's life it is a stink! He knew that,' she nodded at the coffin, 'and he had the sense to stay with me and my Husband! O praise him, praise him! Praise his brains!'

The Muntu started a deep humming, their heads rolling from side to side as they interspersed the tune with light claps.

Oho! Hats off to his Common Sense!
Congratulations to his Brains!
Bonga kakulu! Bonga kakulu!

Maud watched her people as they trudged round the coffin, their feet sinking ankle-deep in the mud. Her heart was big then, bigger than the burial-pond or the blue sky that arched above it. She saw the Muntu as God saw them, millions of drifting seeds, dark, floating personalities, each as small as the sperm that created them. In their grime and sweat, in their rags and ringworm, in their faith and acceptance of Maud's love, they were hers, her children and she could get them all inside the immense hall of her womb again. She could be their wall, put herself between them and the rapacity of the cold-hearted, game-playing state that Mulombe strove towards. She could bear the brunt of his insults and abuse, the stroke of his sharp knife or the bite of his bullets. Much as God was her lover and became a welded part of her flesh each night, so did the Muntu survive through the accessibility of her immense body. To Mulombe she was impregnable. To her people she was a wide and secure gate.

The Muntu finished their song. Maud felt the furnace of words blowing heat against her tongue. Her head was on fire with molten thoughts and they must be hammered out, cast into the air and the mud, given to her people. Bending down she picked up the bark coffin, cradling it in her arms as if it was a child. In front of her the pond was still, black and silent; even the marsh birds had left the sky. Maud was conscious of the world turning beneath her feet and her stature over the swamp, as high as the tower of the cathedral, as humble and lowly as the insects that scudded over the inky surface of the water.

The old man was a light burden in her great embrace and the world he had lived in was immense, so full of room for more like him, that she experienced a moment of strange sadness. He was now a straw, a stick in a bush burned by the dry-season fires. Yesterday he had been a thread in the cloth of her dress, a hair on her head, the nail on her finger. Would the children love God as he had done? With a willing but independent heart? As they had not suffered the persecution of the early days, would they have the strength to criticize yet be a firm friend of her Husband? It was all to be found out in the future.

Clutching the bark coffin closer to her breast she began her renowned Funeral Oration Over The Man Who Wanted To Live For Ever.

Men and women! Sons and daughters! Friends and lovers of God! Here is a cupful from the river and a rock from the desert! Here is one inch of the way to the Whole Truth, one splinter of the bridge across to Myanis Kupela. Here was a bean who would fill the pod and always hang on the tree. Honour his affection for the hours of the day and his relish of night-time. Try to find the sweetness that he sucked up even on the eve of his dying. Hunt for the fruit which he found. Look for the tree where he found it. That tree is my Husband's left leg and His right. Those branches are His arms and the twigs His holy fingers. Those roots are His many toes and the earth is the sole of His foot. In His branches He has leaves and birds. In His leaves He has the small workers, the ant, the fly and the beetle. If you stand in His shade you will want to live for ever like our friend here, but there will be the perpetual growing, flowering and withering over your head to teach you the way of it, the coming and going. When your time comes He will not ask you to move from under His arm. You will fall like one of His leaves, or a seed from His pod. You will die but you will live for ever for having been and having the sense to stand in Love's shadow.

Maud paused, the soft lines around her mouth and eyes hardening into clefts. Her hands clutched the bark coffin until it creaked and twisted in her grasp. The crowd stepped back, conscious of their prophet's sudden change of mood.

He was satisfied to live here where the earth is sour. There must have been times when he sat outside his hut wondering what had made him so foolish as to follow a woman to this place. Outside Myanis Kupela he could farm, fish, hunt, grow mealies and cassava, breathe the sweet air of dry ground and the bush. Why did he come with me? Why follow Maud, the one true Wife of God, when there are gods to be had in plenty and greater comfort? Because he was a free man in his head! The British could never give him freedom! Mulombe could never give him freedom! I could never give him freedom! But I could give him something to DO with his freedom! I gave him the chance to live and love his life in peace!

Such was the passionate indignation in Maud's heart that she crushed the bark coffin until the vines began to break. One of the old man's feet became visible. Mighty shudders travelled along Maud's spine and she stamped her feet in the mud. Her eyes rolled and flashed. Like twin howitzers her nostrils roamed the air as though searching for a target.

The Progress Party have no knowledge of love! I am not innocent of the crime of ending lives before their time, but it is not my way, it is not! It is not! All of us lose our tempers don't we? And we regret it! [Here two tears, brilliant drops, fled down her trembling cheeks] I say to Mulombe as he sits in his big house with his hammer in his hand – leave my people alone! Leave my Husband alone! Leave my living alone and leave my dead alone! Let him sit in his chair with his shrunken nuts on his embroidered cushions and forget us Muntu! Is he the husband of God? Is that what he is saying to us? From what I hear about his sex-life in prison he might give it a try! Ha! Ha! Ha!

With this reference to the scurrilous lies spread by the British government about the proclivities of the new Head of State, Maud gave a loud shout of defiance, hoisted the collapsing coffin over her head, and hurled it into the air. The vines burst asunder, the flat stones fell away, the bark disintegrated as The Man Who Wanted To Live For Ever whirled upwards then plunged in a great arc, landing in the middle of the burial-pond.

7
Mobilization

The geological draughtsmen, planners, mine-captains, engineers, crew-bosses and drivers who were in the vicinity of Hammerkop's office when the Personnel Manager rang him up to tell him that the Bucket-Wheel Excavator Gang had been called to arms, had never heard such a sound. They had heard Hammerkop raise his voice before, many times – in fact his voice occupied a special plateau in their audial memory-banks. As soon as they heard the first note of harsh anger, disgust, rage, frustration or revenge, they could imagine the rest and usually blocked their ears against the major volumes of the outburst. When Hammerkop opened his iron jaws, it was Winter that blew – but here was Summer bellowing.

'Yahoooooo! Yippeeeee! Yerayerayera!'

A crowd gathered in the quadrangle outside Hammerkop's office, including the First Aid Officer. The others pushed him forward until the trembling fellow had his hand on the door-knob.

'Gooooo! Gaaaa! Ooooh, Jesus, that's fantastic! Ha-ha! What a break!'

Encouraged by his colleagues, the First Aid Officer knocked on the door but there was no reply, only the joyous gurglings, screams and desk-bangings of the Open Pit Manager as he threshed around in his executive swivel-chair. The First Aid Officer opened the door and peeped around. He had time to glimpse Hammerkop on the phone, flushed, roaring, panting, eyes sparkling like electrified garnets, before a rock sample flew across the office and crashed into the wall by his head.

'He's laughing, he's really laughing!' the First Aid Officer reported fearfully. 'Hammerkop's laughing.'

'What should we do? Call the Chief Medical Officer? He deals with the top management,' a mine-captain stuck his hard-hat more firmly on his head. 'I'm not going in there with the crazy bastard, not if he's laughing.'

Hammerkop's paroxysms became more convulsive. His harsh, rocky screams clattered in a higher key.

'What? They volunteered! Hoooo! Mother! Glad? What d'you mean, glad? Of course I'm glad you simple-minded Pommy prick! I'm delighted! Haaa! Hooo!'

'Perhaps we should call his wife?' the First Aid Officer retreated from the door and put a few other bodies between himself and the unbelievably happy sound of Hammerkop. 'She might know what to do. It might be fits, something that only crops up now and then. If he starts foaming at the mouth and biting his tongue we'll know it's a fit.'

While the crowd waited for Hammerkop to fall to the ground suffering from an attack of epilepsy, the imagined victim of the disease was quietening down, his cast-iron mind racing. He wanted to know what Muntu were. Was it a trick of Matthias's?

The Personnel Manager relaxed at the other end of the phone. It was the first time he had made Hammerkop happy. He explained that the Muntu were a sect of extremists, politically motivated from Peking, who believed that their founder, a giantess named Maud Mamuntu, was the wife of God.

'This Maud, is she a Kaffir?' Hammerkop rasped.

'Oh yes, sir, she's an African,' the Personnel Manager replied carefully.

'I didn't ask if she was an African, you sycophantic Pom bird-brain! I said is she a Kaffir?' Hammerkop insisted merrily.

'The G.M. has issued instructions for all management to stop using the term now Zonkendawo is independent,' the Personnel Manager quavered. 'I think you were at the meeting when he made the announcement.'

'What's this G.M. business?' Hammerkop cackled. 'Christ, you're a fawning little bastard. D'you think he's God? He can't stop a Kaffir being a Kaffir by just standing up on his hind-legs and saying so. That's what they are, they can't help it.'

'I don't think you should say things like that over the telephone,' the Personnel Manager whispered, 'not now they're running the Post Office.'

Hammerkop wiped some of the tears from his eyes and

crushed a cigar tip between his paving-stone teeth. He was really enjoying himself for the first time in years.

'All right, Pommy, all right. Now fill me in about these Muntu. What have they been up to? Are they warlike or are they just the same as all the other cowardly, shiftless, treacherous Kaffirs? Will they really get stuck into the Bucket-Wheel Excavator Gang or fart-arse around like the freedom-fighters in South Africa ... useless Kaffir bastards they are.'

The Personnel Manager explained to the Open Pit Manager that the Muntu refused to accept any temporal authority on earth other than their leader. They had been trying to establish themselves as an autonomous unit within the state of Zonkendawo in order to set up cells of Communist influence.

'Listen, Pom, are these Muntu Communists or lunatics?' Hammerkop rattled. 'One minute they're in cahoots with Peking, the next they're religious fanatics. Make your mind up, man!'

'That's what the radio said. The President himself made a speech. They're up in the Bengweulu Swamps somewhere.'

'Why have I never heard of these Muntu before? I might want to join the bastards. I don't accept Mulombe and his Kaffir assassins any more than they do.' Hammerkop roared with laughter and kicked the waste-paper basket across the office. As he did so he winced at the stiffness in his knee. He had spent all night in his green Dodge with Gladys, his wife, waiting for the Africans to pour out of the township and burn his house, rape his woman and steal his car. In the boot were provisions for the 2,000-mile dash to Johannesburg plus a box of blasting-powder wired to the cigar-lighter. If the Africans had got near him he would have blown himself and his wife sky-high, taking as many Kaffirs as he could along for the ride.

Hammerkop laughed down the phone, a grating cacophony of metallic squeals and groans. At the other end the Personnel Manager winced and took the instrument away from his ear.

'We appear to have a bad line, Frank,' he shouted over the din.

'This is the best line I've ever had! And don't get familiar with me, you grovelling Pommy bastard, or I'll get you the bullet! The name's Hammerkop to you!' Hammerkop lodged his granite jaw in the mouthpiece as if thrusting it into the Personnel Manager's face. 'Now what else can you tell me?'

'I'm sorry, Mr Hammerkop. It was just that we seemed to be getting along so well I presumed ...' the Personnel Manager's voice trembled. 'Sorry.'

'Don't presume anything with me, you nigger-loving graduate redneck!' Hammerkop grated. 'I run this pit with or without useless, unnecessary, non-productive departments like the circus you run.'

'Yes, Mr Hammerkop,' the Personnel Manager held the phone away and looked at his diploma from the Institute of Personnel Management hanging on the office wall. 'I'll remember that. We are a service department.'

'You couldn't serve breakfast you snivelling, devious Kaffir ... ha!' Hammerkop chuckled like a train-load of scrap-iron. 'You white Kaffir!'

Lighting a cigarette while Hammerkop amused himself at the other end of the line, the Personnel Manager thought about returning to England. He had tried with Hammerkop and the General Manager, God knows he had tried. Dumped in Africa, faced by a hostile tribe of warlike reactionary mine managers, he felt like one of the early missionaries. He knew that to go home would be admitting defeat, leaving the heathen unconverted. Modern trends in labour relations had convinced him that the time was fast approaching when autocratic management would be as outmoded as the dinosaur; yet here he was listening to the defensive roar of Hammerkoposaurus Tyrannus like a quivering rabbit.

He put the phone down.

A moment later it rang again.

'Pommy bastard,' Hammerkop said smoothly, 'you ever do that to me again and your feet won't touch ground till you hit Southampton.'

'I don't think we have much to say to each other,' the Personnel Manager flared with sudden courage, 'and I'm tired of your abuse.'

'Never mind that. I know you can't help being like you are, sonny. You welfare-state Poms are all the same. But I want to know more about these Muntu. I don't want to miss this chance of getting shut of the Bucket-Wheel Excavator Gang once and for all. You can help me there, can't you? Sometimes you Poms can be helpful . . . eh?'

In the face of such charm the Personnel Manager had no option but to carry on talking.

Pyper sat in his poky office and started typing his story about the Muntu rebellion. Bernard, his African assistant, had got him out of bed to tell him about the government's announcement on the 6 a.m. news. As his shaking fingers sought the keys, his saturated brain recoiling from the nasty tapping sound which they made, he remembered that he still had two stories to write in addition; the fight in the vegetable garden and the raid by Inspector Kwango and Inspector Grutchfield. He would have to write those on the plane as he flew back south to Myakajunji.

'What's this about the Territorials, Bernard? You say the old President has called the poor bastards up? Most of them have forgotten what a rifle looks like.' Pyper chuckled painfully, his gorge trembling at the entrance to his throat. 'Christ, I must stop laughing before I throw up.'

'Yes, bwana,' the assistant grinned.

'I don't think you should call me bwana any more, Bernard.'

'No, bwana.'

'Most of these Territorials spend their time in the British Empire Service League, the Meritorious Order of the Tin Hat and the British Legion getting arseholes all day. If you tried to drill them on the barrack square they'd die of withdrawal symptoms after half an hour.'

'Yes, bwana,' Bernard giggled.

'These Muntu don't know what a push-over this is going to be for them. All they've got to do is lob a few bricks at the old Territorials and they won't stop running till they get back to the bar. I hope old Doctor Mulombe knows what he's doing.'

'No, bwana,' Bernard laughed aloud.

'You mean he doesn't know what he's doing?'

'Yes, bwana.'

'How's about you and me going down to the British Empire League and interviewing some of these old-timers who are suddenly being sent into battle again? They open at half-past eight and I wouldn't mind some breakfast. It could give us some good material.'

'O.K., bwana!' Bernard pulled his notebook out of his shorts and flicked the pages. 'What a scoop!'

'You'd better behave yourself while you're down there, Bernard, or they might just turn on you. Remember that half the old Boers who were in the British Army thought they were fighting for Hitler.'

'I'll bear that in mind, bwana.'

Pyper strolled through the town to the British Empire League, the sun on his face and Bernard bwanaing along by his side. He knew that he'd be feeling better by ten. The mornings were always rough in Africa. It was something to do with the climate.

The bar at the British Empire Service League was packed with old and middle-aged men. A stunned, aghast expression was on every face. They murmured, passed hands over brows, felt their hearts and pulses, wept in the corner by the one-armed bandit. When they ordered drinks from the African barman they did so with venom, hammering on the counter until all the soda siphons rattled together. Their faces registered amazement, terror, disbelief, bitterness and rage – they had been called up to fight FOR the Kaffirs. Pyper elbowed his way through the lachrymose and indignant crowd with Bernard in tow. As the African cub reporter squeezed through the closely-packed bodies of the white men they gave him rabbit-punches, kicks in the shin and pulled his hair, taking out their frustration with the dynamic decisions of the nation's new President on his person.

'Well now, you gang of piss-artists will have to cut out all the bullshit you've been talking for the last twenty years and really do some fighting.'

Pyper sipped his gin and tonic and watched the lowering, knobbly faces of the assembled bottle-store managers, undertakers, telephone engineers, timbermen and pay clerks who glared at him after his loud and provocative remark.

'Christ, when I think of the times I've had to stand here listening to you white trash beating your gums about what you did in the Western Desert with Monty. How did this spineless scum suddenly find the guts to capture a Tiger tank single-handed? I'd ask myself. Isn't it more likely that they were shitting themselves with fright hiding in a sewer? I'd suggest to myself. Or have they changed since those golden days? What's happened since to change an army of heroes into a mob of dead-beats that couldn't get a job anywhere else in the world but here where the old colonial government gave them a fucking leg-up because their ugly mugs were white? These are the questions, and others associated with this line of thought, that are entertaining my mind as I stand here having my breakfast on this bright and sunny morning.'

Pyper was well known at the British Empire Service League. The number of times that he had been beaten up at the bar were beyond counting. Only two weeks ago a rock-breaker had thrown a concrete bollard through his windscreen for suggesting that Smuts had been the son of a Basuto charcoal-burner. This morning the members were in a mood to wipe the New Zealander out much as they had done the Italians and Afrika Corps, but it was the wrong time of day. Half-past eight in the morning was the time to sit on the verandah and have six or seven Limousin brandies before going to work to hide in a storeroom or disused tunnel until the shift was over. While they slept through the day their passions lay closed up like the blue Morning Glories which covered the trellis round the entrance hall. Evening was the time for tales of derring-do and the reliving of old conquests through physical violence and animated conversation. Angry with Pyper as they were, their sensitivities were more damaged by Doctor Mulombe's call-up. He was sending them to war and they didn't want to go.

'What's so funny, Pyper?' A crawly voice sounded from the back of the crowd. 'You're in it, too. You're in my platoon you Kaffir-loving bastard.'

'What are you drivelling on about, dronky?' Pyper scoffed. 'You're talking out of your arse again.'

'You're on my list here!' The man, a grizzle-headed shift-boss, pushed his way through the crowd and thrust a paper under Pyper's nose. 'Here! Pyper J.!'

Pyper stared at the typewritten list. His name was there.

'This is a mistake,' he began.

The crowd found enough humour in the situation to laugh. Pyper stared into their mocking, bloodshot eyes and the serried ranks of their fillings and false teeth and reeled in the blast of booze-laden wind that roared from their mouths.

'You're the mistake, Anzac! Christ, am I going to crucify you!' The grizzled shift-boss pounded the bar with enthusiasm. 'I'm going to make you wish you'd never been born!'

Pyper sipped at his drink, the ice-fibres in his blue eyes dampened. He watched Bernard scribbling in his notebook.

'What are you doing, you fucking idiot?' he snapped. 'What do you think this is, a press conference?'

Bernard looked up, his brown eyes sparkling.

'I'll get your job if I'm quick. I'm writing out my letter of application.'

'Bwana,' Pyper added for him, 'don't forget the bwana.'

'No, bwana!'

'And another thing, Bernard,' Pyper went on, as vague memories of the party at Field-Marshal Montgomery Crescent percolated up into his brain. 'Never play a game called Snakebite.'

As Pyper rang round his friends to warn them that they were about to be press-ganged into the army, the Bucket-Wheel Excavator Gang were peering over the top of the dump at a large squad of soldiers.

'What have we done today?' they asked Matthias. 'Why bring in the army?'

'You know Hammerkop, he'll go to any extreme to get at us,' Matthias said grimly. 'Just wait till I get down to the union office.'

The soldiers stalked the summit of the dump with infinite caution. Their leader, a young second lieutenant who had been to Sandhurst, was in walkie-talkie contact with Hammerkop in his office.

'We have sighted the men, sir,' he called through the mouthpiece. 'They are hiding at the top of a mound of earth.'

'Well, bring them down you yellow-bellied Kaffir! They're no good to you up there! Get them into the front line before the bastards run away!'

Hammerkop's gaunt, bony face glowed with pleasure as he looked out of the window. When the African lieutenant complained about being called a yellow-bellied Kaffir in his own country Hammerkop switched off the walkie-talkie and went to get his binoculars. Ringing up the Territorial's commander and telling him that the Bucket-Wheel Excavator Gang were going to desert on their first day of military service had been a brilliant idea. Not only was it guaranteed that they would go into the army with a random chance of being killed, but they'd also have to be punished.

'Come on!' Hammerkop clacked his heavy jaw with excitement. 'Scale the ramparts and pull 'em out!'

When the soldiers reached the top of the dump they found the Bucket-Wheel Excavator Gang glaring sourly at them with their hands raised high in the air.

'We surrender!' Matthias shouted. 'We surrender! But we're pretty pissed off with this affair. The first day of independence and there's a military *coup d'état*. What kind of freedom is that?'

The Superintendent fixed Inspectors Grutchfield and Kwango with an accusing eye.

'What do you mean by signing up for the Territorial Army when you're already in the police force?'

Kwango looked at Grutchfield for a lead. On his colleague's features were inscribed fear, mortification and disgrace. He would get no help from him, his training programme for Kwango didn't stretch that far.

'Well? Speak up one of you. Whose idea was it?'

Both men tried to give the Superintendent the nod that it was the other who had started the rot. Their eyes met and slid away again in a blur of filmy red.

Outside the window the four constables stood rigidly to attention under the fierce eye of their sergeant who had been bollocking them up and down the station all morning for trying to run out on him. Their eyes were held to the front, but they could see their superiors through the window of the Superintendent's office as they failed to answer the simple questions being put to them.

'Perhaps you feel you're not doing enough for the public by knocking off petty thieves, homosexuals and pot-smokers? Perhaps you feel that the army gives a man more opportunity for self-sacrifice and public service? If it's self-sacrifice you want I can arrange it next time we have a beer-hall riot.' The Superintendent's sarcasm ripped a breach in Grutchfield's terrified reserve and he watched the young European inspector wilt. 'Well, Grutchfield? Speak up!'

'We weren't ourselves, sir,' he whimpered.

'Who were you then?'

'I mean we were acting on irrational impulses.'

'No, you weren't. You were acting under orders. I told you to go out and arrest Tarzan Cool Guy and his decadent liberal friends for having a party and you join the Territorial Army. It doesn't make sense.'

Grutchfield hesitated. Would it be best to make a clean breast of it and throw himself on the Superintendent's mercy. But the Superintendent never had any mercy.

'You were drunk, both of you. You stink. Your eyes are red. Kwango, you look pale. What am I going to do with a couple of traitors who protect mealy-mouthed racial mixers and don't preserve the *status quo*?'

'We're dreadfully sorry, sir. It was the heat of the moment,' Grutchfield's lip trembled. 'It's the first thing I've ever done like this in ten years with the force, sir, can't you overlook it this once?'

'Grutchfield!' the Superintendent snarled.

'Yes, sir?'

'Let go of Kwango's hand!'

Desaix L'Ace had signed on enough times in his life to be able to have immediate recall of the event as soon as he awoke. Climbing over Margaret from the Tonga Bar he dressed and ran outside, caught a taxi and went to the airfield.

When he arrived at the Fokker he found two Africans painting green, black and copper roundels on the wings and fuselage.

'Who said you could do that?' he demanded. 'That's mine.'

'Squadron-Leader Skidmore.'

Mounted on the bracket in front of the second cockpit was a rusty machine-gun. The last time he had used the bracket had been for a telescope during the days of his wild-life safari package holidays.

'Look, *mes braves*, you're reasonable men. I'll give you ten pounds on the nail if you'll pick up your bits and pieces and tell Skidmore that when you arrived here the Fokker had disappeared.'

As the Africans scrambled to their feet, their hands outstretched for the money, a car pulled up alongside the Fokker. A gross, mustachioed man levered himself out of the back seat. Desaix saw the epaulettes, the cap, the small dark eyes peering nervously in his direction, and promptly sat on the tarmac, his head in his hands.

'Not you, Skidmore. I'm not serving under a lazy blood-sucker like you. You couldn't tell a windsock from a french letter.'

'You've got no choice, Ace, no choice at all. I've been seconded from the aviation ministry. Bit of a leg-up, eh? From chief clerk accounts to S.L. Well, that's war. Now, old son, you'll simply have to do as you're told. Your aircraft has been commandeered for the duration of the emergency.'

'What about me? How will I live?' Desaix banged his temples. 'Oh Christ, I'd like to kill that bastard Pyper. Everything he touches...'

'You've been commandeered as well. We couldn't split up a partnership like yours, certainly not. It would be unthinkable.'

'I'm not playing ball, Skidmore. I'm getting in my plane and flying away, I'm going half-way round the world, anywhere, but I'm not joining your outfit.'

'Ace,' Skidmore smiled oilily, 'I'm your C.O. and you know what that means. I've got admin ability, you know that, you've got the experience. We're a great team, we'll get along fine together, Ace, fine. With you along the whole show will be over in a few weeks.'

'The show's over now,' Desaix said uncompromisingly. 'I'm going.'

'Oh, no, you're not, Ace. You signed up. Last night at that nigger wrestler's place you put it on the old dotted line and you're committed. Don't blame me for your mistakes, I wasn't there guiding your hand.'

Desaix walked over to the Fokker and climbed in to the cockpit.

'I wouldn't serve under you, Skidmore, if you were the last

man on earth. You're a phoney, an arse-licker, a buck-passer and a leech. If I had to fight against anyone, if I had to bomb some poor *salot* it would be you rather than them. I can't stand the sight of you. Good-bye.'

Skidmore remained where he was, leaning against the grille of the Zonkendawon Air Force car, while Desaix tried to find his joystick.

'I don't mind what you think about me, Desaix. Just because I've never had the chance to be on active service like you have it doesn't mean I wouldn't if given the opportunity. You know I've got this glandular trouble that affects my weight. Is that my fault?'

'Where's my joystick?' Desaix roared from the cockpit.

'It's locked up in a safe place,' Skidmore smiled beneath the blanketing fuzz on his face. 'We took it away.'

When Fines Chingola brought the Regional Secretary of the Party, Mr Vapour Mutale, down to congratulate Tarzan Cool Guy personally on his public-spirited gesture in joining the Territorials, they found the wrestler with Dennis on the lawn. Dennis was trying to teach Tarzan Cool Guy how to work the lawn-mower.

'I wouldn't expect too much of you, Tarzan, just keeping things in trim, planting a few seeds, keeping an eye on the fruit trees. Now this is easy to operate.'

Marge was watching from the kitchen window. She had dropped her opposition to the scheme whereby her lover became the garden-boy at Field-Marshal Montgomery Crescent. They could stand there and chat about it if they liked but it would never come about. Although the Snakebite had had its effect on Marge it had not penetrated the fund of love that she had for the African athlete; that had remained clear-thinking and articulate. If she had been able to persuade him against his decision to join the Territorials she would have done but by that time he had escaped her, gone into a dark country of male consciousness where a woman can only get herself lost. Marge had signed on herself, and allowed all her friends to do the same, in order to stay near to Tarzan Cool Guy. It was a mean, selfish, ludicrous, very feminine thing to do.

Now she was waiting. Pyper had rung up to tell her the news about the call-up and the Muntu rebellion in the Northern Province. At some time during the day they would be officially notified. As she washed the dishes Marge found herself singing in spite of the laboured attempts of her common sense to bring home the agonizing predicament that she was in. Her conscience would not rise to the bait. All she could think of was the fact that she had cheated Fate and would stay with the man she loved.

The Party car turned in at the drive flying a brand new pennant. Tarzan Cool Guy and Dennis turned their heads slowly to look at it, their eyes, brains and organs still tingling with cane-for-pain.

'What does that loafer want now?' Tarzan Cool Guy said perplexedly. 'He never learns his lesson.'

Putting two fingers in his mouth he whistled. It was a painful business but the result was gratifying. From out of a bed of snapdragons sprang the chihuahua, ears pricked, nose quivering.

'You didn't have to take over my dog as well,' Dennis muttered under his breath.

'Just watch him go,' Tarzan Cool Guy nudged his companion. 'He's a man-eater.'

But Fines Chingola was not as stupid as he looked. Remaining in the car he wound down an inch of window and called out to Tarzan Cool Guy that he had an important visitor, Mr Vapour Mutale.

When he heard who his important visitor was Tarzan whistled again and the chihuahua took off towards the car, its legs stiff like springs. Reaching the window where Fines was sitting it sprang into the air and tried to enter the inch-wide gap, thrusting its foaming nose forward. Fines hurriedly wound up the window and tried to explain to Mr Vapour Mutale that they were quite safe in the car and that Tarzan Cool Guy would soon call the vicious creature off.

'These dogs are a problem, V.M., we will have to revise the laws affecting European dogs. The present scale of compensation is very much in favour of the owner. There are *musungus* I know who are glad to pay the ten bob fine in order to see their dogs bite an African. Ten bob per perforation of the skin would be a better idea because if a dog bites you it uses all its teeth.'

With his eyes on the leaping dog which was salivating all over the window, Fines felt the perforations in his knee-cap. There was five pounds' worth of bite there if his new system were introduced.

'How can I congratulate anyone if I'm stuck in this vehicle?' Mr Vapour Mutale twitched the heavy-rimmed spectacles up his flattened nose. 'I'm a busy man, F.C.'

'I know, V.M., everyone in the branch appreciates how hard you work.'

'Then get rid of that animal.'

The dog was now doing somersaults of rage, twisting and turning its hideous, hairless, skinned-rabbit body in the air, snapping and snarling with frustration. Tarzan Cool Guy walked over and caught it by the scruff at the high point of a leap.

'What makes you think that you're welcome here?' he boomed at the car window. 'If you don't go away I'll stuff him down the front of your natty *blukwe*, won't I, baby?'

Playfully he shook the chihuahua's face against the glass. Mr Vapour Mutale saw the features of the ferocious mouse distort into even more violent paroxysms, its minute mouth spined with needle-teeth.

'What's T.C.G. saying?' Mr Vapour Mutale was puzzled. 'And why is he showing us his dog?'

Fines wriggled uncomfortably and crossed his legs at the thought of the demented chihuahua gnashing at his genital organs. There were still some things that he was not prepared to sacrifice for the Party.

'You know how temperamental popular idols can be, V.M. Look at Mulombe, for instance.' Fines shrugged expressively and tried to look intelligent and perceptive.

'I'm looking at Doctor Mulombe!' Mr Vapour Mutale's glasses slid down the black ski-run of his shining nose with surprise. 'What about him?'

'Well, he behaves oddly sometimes, doesn't he, like this fellow here?' Fines dipped his head towards the squashed and contorted features of Tarzan Cool Guy and the chihuahua as they pressed up against the glass. 'He has his off-days like they do. It's a natural human failing.'

Mr Vapour Mutale drew in his breath. He was a thin man with not much of a chest but he managed to inflate himself a few inches.

'Does he? The President has his off-days, does he? Are you saying that he is erratic in his performance as Head of State?'

Fines caught the menace in the Regional Secretary's voice and started floundering.

'Well, no ... not exactly ... he's only been doing the job for half a day,' he blathered.

'Perhaps he's had half an off-day?' Mr Vapour Mutale suggested spitefully. 'That would fit better, half an off-day.'

While the basic instruction course for political novices who open their big mouths too much in the presence of their wily and self-preserving superiors continued in the car, Marge came out of the kitchen and called to Dennis and Tarzan Cool Guy. Tarzan Cool Guy was unwilling to leave the car, and the chihuahua was heartbroken at being cheated of its quarry. Entering the house the wrestler flopped down in an armchair and kissed the raving dog between its eyes.

'Patience, *piccanin inja*, we'll try again some time,' he said softly into its ear. 'Stick around and keep your teeth to the grindstone.'

'Neither of you will remember what happened late last night,' Marge began, as she dried her hands on a tea-towel, 'because you're both still drunk.'

'That's what it is?' Dennis smiled out of the window. 'No wonder Tarzan didn't want to push the lawn-mower.'

Marge ignored her husband and concentrated on Tarzan Cool Guy. He was the villain of the piece.

'You joined the Territorial Army last night. At half-past four.'

'I did?'

'We all did,' Marge bored on unmercifully. 'Everyone at the party.'

'I didn't!' Dennis grinned smugly. 'I wouldn't do anything so stupid. It would take me away from my work.'

'We all did, Dennis, me, Margaret from the Tonga Bar, Marilyn, men and women.'

'That was silly of us.'

'Yes, it was as it turns out. But we all wanted to be together.'

Tarzan Cool Guy released the chihuahua. It jumped on to the window-sill and stared longingly at the car that was still parked in the drive, its new green, black and copper pennant fluttering in the morning breeze.

'We can get out of this one. People do some damn foolish things when they're drunk, eh? Fancy joining that shambles. Me! Want a beer, Dennis?' Tarzan Cool Guy stood up and lumbered unsteadily towards the kitchen.

'Pyper rang up while you were talking to those Party men,' Marge followed the wrestler to the refrigerator.

'What did he want at this time of the morning?'

'We've all been called up. There's an emergency in the Northern Province. Some rebellion.'

Five minutes later Tarzan Cool Guy went outside to the car and asked his visitors to come into the house. He sat them down and fed them the last of the cold beer out of the refrigerator. Introducing the subject gently, he asked for consideration to be taken as to the state of his mind when he joined the Territorial Army.

'I was drunk, we were all drunk.'

'What were you doing drunk?' Mr Vapour Mutale stiffened.

'We'd been drinking.'

'Where had you been drinking?'

'Here, we had a party to celebrate Independence,' Tarzan Cool Guy grinned. 'You know what it is.'

Mr Vapour Mutale nodded.

'Yes, I know what it is. You broke the Law. At the stroke of midnight you and your friends became free citizens of a sovereign state and immediately broke its first law. You have a choice therefore – a simple choice, Comrade. Either you can all go to prison or you can keep your word and join the Territorials.'

Tarzan Cool Guy thought for a while then looked questioningly at Marge.

'What do you think?'

'I think I'd rather go to prison for a while,' she grimaced. 'I'm not interested in knocking other people around.'

'Prison for me, too,' Dennis smacked the arm of his chair with unusual vehemence. 'I can get some reading done.'

Mr Vapour Mutale pushed away his beer.

'It seems to me that you are not identifying yourselves with our country's aspirations. We want to build up a society that is based on Humanism and Unity. The Muntu are inhuman and are breaking the natural ties that bind all Africans together. If you will not accept that argument then perhaps you will consider the fact that if you go to prison it will be for a minimum of fifteen years. The magistrate is my uncle.'

Tarzan Cool Guy gasped and turned to Marge. She shook her head. In fifteen years' time she would be fifty-five. The menopause would have been and gone. It was out of the question.

Mr Vapour Mutale read the signs. Standing up he took a pad of Basildon Bond writing-paper out of his jacket pocket and read his brief speech of congratulation to Tarzan Cool Guy on the occasion of his joining the Territorial Army.

Humphrey Fluellen and Kovary managed to get their appeal heard by the Commanding Officer of the Territorial Army, Colonel Vaal Rembrandt, in such double-quick time because he was the vice-president of the Mufunsi Theatre Co-operative. He was a cultured fellow who sometimes took part in musicals when his onerous duties allowed him time. Last year he had been a Highlander in *Brigadoon*, a strawberry-seller in *Oliver*, an American marine in *South Pacific*, and the second dustman in *My Fair Lady*.

Rembrandt was accompanied at the appeal by Major Powderham, a tall, thin, peevish, professional soldier on secondment from the Brigade of Guards, and now appointed as second-in-command of the National Territorial Emergency Force.

'So you wish to appeal against the call-up, eh?' Rembrandt mused. 'That's typical of you, Humphrey.'

'Typical? Typical? What d'you mean, man? I was drunk!'

'Why should I give you a helping hand?' Rembrandt snorted. 'It's your own silly fault!'

'We have a right to retract a foolish decision,' Kovary reasoned. 'The days of the King's shilling and the press-gang are over, Vaal, long gone.'

'Nonsense! If we all had those kind of rights we'd never be held responsible for anything we do. You signed on! Right here!' He waved the papers under their noses. 'An adult, fully-considered, mature decision!'

'I've told you, man, I was pissed out of my mind!' Humphrey glowered.

'Knowing you, Humphrey, I'm not surprised, except that you were probably under a more ... vegetable influence?' Rembrandt sneered. 'Not so?'

Kovary stepped forward and put his shoulders straight.

'Look, Vaal, we have this play opening soon. It's a breakthrough for me, a new dimension. If we have to scrap it my writing career will be put back five years and I'll have to carry on teaching which is breaking me up.'

His tone was that of an honest man speaking his mind. Powderham listened, deeply irritated, and rapped the table with his rattan cane.

'What do you think being in the army out here has done for our careers? Well, we would have been in Whitehall by now if we hadn't been seconded out here with these idiots, yes, don't you know? Why? What special treatment do you deserve that we don't? H'mm? All right, talk your way out of that one!' He glanced sharply at Rembrandt. 'Isn't that so, sir?'

'And another thing,' Rembrandt's eyes hardened, 'while we're talking about it, Humphrey, I've been auditioning for the male romantic lead in the musicals for three years while you've been directing the theatre. In that time you've never given me anything but boring chorus parts, third palm-tree from the left in *The Desert Song* and that kind of deal. Why the hell should I give you a hand?'

Humphrey reddened. He was caught on this one. Rembrandt was a useful man to have on the board because he wasted a lot of time at cocktail and dinner parties wearing his dress uniform and poncing around. When money was needed for a production he often helped to tap the sources of supply. That was why he was given the small parts in musicals. If he had not been useful in getting money out of the wealthy Europeans of Mufunsi he would never have been given a part at all.

'We'll do *The King And I* and you can play the king,' he blurted. 'We'll do it next month and cancel Kovary's new play.'

'You can't do that!' Kovary protested loudly. 'It's in rehearsal now!'

Rembrandt fingered his long silky blond hair.

'Would you want me to cut this off?'

'No, we could get you a skull-cap.'

'My wife has a bathing-hat that she lets me borrow sometimes. If we painted it flesh-colour it could look quite effective and it's tight enough to pull my eyes up at the corner for an oriental effect.'

Humphrey leaned forward across the desk with his hand outstretched.

'It's a deal!'

Major Powderham coughed.

'May I have a word with you, sir?'

'Not now, Powderham, we've nearly got this business settled,' Rembrandt replied cheerfully. 'Just be a good chap and hold on.'

'Sir, I would like a private word in your ear,' Powderham persisted. 'It concerns this appeal.'

Humphrey and Kovary were asked to wait outside for a while. Once the door was closed Powderham turned to his colonel.

'I think you're making a mistake, sir,' he said. 'Yes, a big one.'

Rembrandt got up from his chair and paced the carpet.

'Nonsense, I know every damn tune in that show backwards. If I can get a good female lead for the nanny then we're away.'

'That's not what I mean, sir, not a bit of it. I know you could do the part, you'd be a smash-hit, but what about Doctor Mulombe?'

'What about him?' Rembrandt said with distaste. 'Why bring that awful man into it?'

'You know what he thinks of the Chinese. I heard that deportation orders went out for the Siamese embassy, the Thai embassy, the Laotions, oh yes, the Japanese, the Formosa Nationalists ... and they haven't even arrived in the country yet. He's got a phobia about slant-eyed people. My contacts, hm, in State House, say that he's moving in on the Chinese restaurant in Mufunsi, yes, here shortly and that's run by two old ladies from Bradford... How about that?'

Powderham observed the result of his comment with satisfaction. One thing he was sure of about Colonel Vaal Rembrandt.

He would never throw away his security of office. Another ten years and he was planning to take an early retirement and return to South Africa where he was going to start a music-hall in Potchestroom. For this venture he would need all his pension accrual, leave benefits and severance pay.

'You think he'd take it out on me? For dressing up like one?' Rembrandt was aghast. 'I never thought of that.'

'If I may make a suggestion, sir, yes, come to think of it two suggestions, yes, there's been enough messing around with those two out there, you know the type, draft-dodgers, drop-outs, arty-crafties, let's bung 'em into the ranks quick as damn it and get on with the campaign. The other is, sir, that if they get knocked off, don't be hopeful too much, no, because they're the duckers, sir, they shift when the stuff comes flying over, then you can take over Fluellen's job and give yourself all the best parts in the musicals . . . no, yes?'

Five minutes later Humphrey and Kovary were in an Army Land-Rover being driven home to pack their bags before being taken, under guard, to the base camp at Balyete.

'That's the last walk-on that bastard gets out of me!' Humphrey seethed. 'And I'll tell the bastard what I think of his acting!'

But Kovary was not listening. Inside him a birth was being crushed between the iron jaws of Fate, a babe gobbled up. If he had had the courage it would have been an easy matter to jump out of the speeding Land-Rover and die on the roadside. His play had been coming together, edging into the world. The new experiences that awaited at Balyete and after, did not seem a worthwhile subject for his genius. The Forces clamp down on all originality. Everything has to go through the mangle of routine. These thoughts plagued him as he contemplated the death of his play on the Tiresian dilemma of whores in which the eternal question – who gets more out of it on a hedonistic level, the man or the woman – was explored.

Kovary tapped the knee of the soldier who was guarding him. 'Excuse me, Sergeant, would you tell me something?'

'Depends what it is, bwana,' the man answered wisely.

'You know this place Balyete?'

'If I know it then it is because I live there, bwana,' the soldier sighed. 'With the rest of the world to choose from, that is where I have ended up, Balyete.'

Kovary nodded sympathetically, thrusting his lower lip forward as if in deep perusal of the sergeant's misfortune.

'It must be a tedious place.'

'No, bwana, it is not tedious. It is fucking boring.'

'I understand, Sergeant, nothing to do. No entertainments.'

The sergeant became enmeshed in Kovary's understanding of his problem. Here was a willing audience. Back at Balyete nobody in the sergeants' mess cared any more. They had given up.

'Bwana, you said entertainments. You know Colonel Vaal Rembrandt? He puts on shows for us at Balyete on our stage.'

'Did you say stage? Stage?' Kovary could hardly suppress his delight. 'You've got a stage?'

'Conjuring tricks, songs around the old German upright piano, drag-acts, recitations, extracts from musicals,' the sergeant banged his rifle-butt on the floor with disgust. 'You've never seen such rubbish. We have sent him petitions to have these shows stopped but he pretends that he has never received them. We would rather be bored than watch his "Rembrandt Revels".'

But Kovary wasn't listening. Instead he was exchanging a knowing conspiratorial smile with the best actor in Central Africa.

8
Balyete Camp

'I get painful periods,' the female patient confessed in a low voice.

'So do I,' admitted Doctor James Russell, 'all the time.'

As the woman raised her head, a protest on her lips, the intercom sounded. Pressing the red button the young Irish doctor smiled apologetically.

'Sorry about this,' he said to his patient. 'Never get left alone.'

'I'm not surprised!' the woman headed for the door. 'You should be in a freak show.'

It was the Chief Medical Officer's secretary on the intercom. Doctor Russell was to report to him at once.

'I'm on a very difficult case at the moment,' he complained, 'and I shouldn't be interrupted.'

He released the button and went off in search of his patient. The woman was walking along the corridor trying not to cry.

'Why did you run away? I'm a doctor, I'm used to things like this.'

'You were sending me up!'

'Oh, no, I wasn't. Now come on, let's go back.'

With his hand on her elbow, Doctor Russell managed to get the patient back into the office and sat her down.

'Now we can get started!' he grinned cheerfully, exposing his buck teeth and the gnawed area of his bottom lip and red beard. The woman looked him over suspiciously, took in the man's sympathetic brown eyes, his powerful, craggy hands, listened to his throaty brogue and the earnest tenderness of his speech, and decided to take the risk.

'I suppose you thought I meant depressions?' she shrugged. 'That's a natural mistake. I didn't mean those kind of periods. You know what I meant. You're a doctor.'

Doctor Russell nodded. It was all the fault of his research programme. Before the woman had come in he had been making notes about the *mumpangala* tree. Not only does a chewed and macerated pulp of the roots cure scorpion and snake bites, but it also alleviates bouts of melancholia.

'So what do you suggest?'

The door flew open and a large woman in a tweed skirt, flat shoes and red plastic spectacles stamped in, her eyes red with crying.

'He's shouting at me because of you! Now go and see him at once! I can't stand any more of this!'

'Go away, Mrs Brody,' the young doctor instructed her. 'You can see I'm busy. The C.M.O. can wait.'

'He wants to see you urgently! He'll take it out on me, you know!' Mrs Brody sniffed. 'I can't take it, I really can't!'

Mrs Brody left the consulting-room, slamming the door behind her. Doctor Russell blew the coppery hairs on the back of his hand so they bent like corn in a stiff wind. He also gnawed at his beard.

'Why are you doing that?' the patient asked.

'What?'

'Gnawing your beard. You've made a hole in it.'

Doctor Russell rubbed at the spot and nodded. He had suffered a lot of undue stress lately while waiting for his application for research funds to be considered, and the strain was showing.

'I could use some more sleep, I suppose. If I put the leaves of the *mushikishi* tree in my bed an hour before retiring I'd probably get more rest.'

The Chief Medical Officer of Mufunsi Mine Hospital pressed the button of his intercom to summon his Irish colleague. Outside in the secretary's office he could hear Mrs Brody sobbing.

'Russell!'

'I'm not in!' came the quick reply, then a click.

The Chief Medical Officer pressed the button again.

'If you don't come here at once I'll get your application to the World Health Organization for a research grant withdrawn.'

Doctor Russell pushed back his chair, grabbed his patient's hand and told her to get hold of some roots of the *mufuka* tree, pound them into a powder and mix with fat until a fine paste is formed.

'What good will that do me?' the bewildered patient demanded.

'Well, it's the best cure for haemorrhoids that I know,' Doctor Russell said over his shoulder as he went into the corridor, 'and avoid very hot baths.'

The Chief Medical Officer smiled as the Irishman strode into his office, his complexion as red as his beard.

'You wouldn't do that to me, would you? You know how important it is. Christ Almighty it's my life, my life!'

'Of course I wouldn't, you silly boy,' the Chief Medical Officer chided him. 'Would I stand in the way of such an important piece of research? What do you take me for?'

Mollified, Doctor Russell sank into a green leather chair.

'I must get that grant! I must!'

'I'm right behind you boy, right behind you.'

The C.M.O. was telling the truth. He was right behind Doctor Russell much as Mephistopheles is right behind the Archangel Gabriel. The application for a research grant which had been completed seven months ago was still in the C.M.O.'s drawer. He had deliberately not sent it off to the World Health Organization. His reasons for behaving in this underhand and treacherous manner were connected with the section of the application form titled 'The Subject of Research – please give a detailed description of the project for which the grant is being sought'. On receiving the completed document on his desk one morning, the C.M.O. had turned to this part of the form with interest. He had been a doctor for a long time, had settled down and long forgotten his own ambitions as a young, newly qualified doctor setting out to heal the human race of its ills, but there was the temptation of nostalgia, uncovering old sensations when the brain had blazed with the passion to know more about life.

The blank page was not filled with indecipherable notes, nor was it closely written. Doctor Russell had only used the top of the page. In green ink, the colour of his native land, he had printed:

THE PREVENTION AND CURE OF DEATH

Doctor Russell lifted one long, bony shank and crossed it over the other.

'What did you want me for so urgently?' he said archly. 'I was in the middle of a particularly complicated case.'

'Jim, I wouldn't have disturbed you if it hadn't been necessary. You know that much by now.' The C.M.O. hunched his shoulders and pointed to the intercom. 'It's a nuisance to me as well as you. The General Manager buzzed me not long ago and told me that I had to lose a member of my staff.'

Doctor Russell could hear the sobbing in the outer office.

'She's a mite too pushy for her own good. I suppose she'll get another job quite soon,' he stroked his beard pensively. 'I think there may be some psyche trouble there, self-assertion, frustration.'

Waiting for Jim to finish the Chief Medical Officer had a quiet laugh at the thought of getting rid of Mrs Brody. Anyone who did so would be out of his mind. In spite of her dowdy style of dress Mrs Brody was the best screw he'd had in years.

'Jim, you know that the mining companies out here are in a unique position. They're more than just industries, they're part of the country's administration really. We build towns, schools, railways ... we're a government within a government. We've had to do this because, let's face it, if we hadn't then nobody else would. We get asked for all sorts of help. Well, this morning the General Manager was asked for a very specific kind of help. There's been some kind of uprising in the north – heard about it?'

Doctor Russell nodded.

'I had a patient in this morning who wanted to get a sick certificate so he wouldn't have to go. You know him, McSilver, the football coach ... he's joined the Territorials.'

'Well, so have you,' the Chief Medical Officer smiled benignly, his small round eyes dancing, 'as from today.'

Doctor Russell uncrossed his legs, his buck teeth champing at the red beard.

'What in the name of Christ are you talking about?' he spluttered. 'So have I?'

'You're on lend-lease to the Territorial Army for the campaign. They have no doctor so they asked us for a young, fit, enterprising, well-balanced medical officer who would be able to stand up under the strain of working in field conditions,' he paused, his marble eyes swivelling on to the notebook that Jim was feverishly consulting. 'Are you all right, Jim?'

'No, I'm not all right!' Jim replied, his teeth working on his nether lip like a pestle on a mortar. 'And it wasn't in my contract. I've got you there! It wasn't in my contract! I agreed to go out on trips to geologists and exploratory rigs who were stuck in the bush – we negotiated a rate for that – but there was nothing about conscripting me for the army. No! Forget it! Christ, Mother of God, what do you take me for?'

Changing his tack, the Chief Medical Officer got from behind his desk and went over to the window.

'This is very odd,' he said to himself, though loudly enough for the Irishman to hear, 'very odd indeed.'

Doctor Russell looked up.

'What's so odd about someone not wanting to go in the army?'

'You're odd, yes, maybe even insincere,' the Chief Medical Officer mused. 'I'm not sure I believe in you any more, Jim.'

'Why not? You go out and get the other doctors on the staff to come here and ask for a volunteer. You'll see who's odd!'

'As a doctor it is always presumed that you want to work – isn't that right? You can help in even the worst cases. There's always something you can do. Now when I find a young doctor, full of ideas and the will to pursue them for the benefit of medical science, and I give him a golden opportunity to get some first-hand experience of a subject that he wants to do research in, and he turns it down! Turns it down, boy – what am I supposed to think?'

Doctor Russell sat down on a bench in the examination-room. There was no air-conditioning at Balyete Camp and nearly all the men who had been sent to him that afternoon had been drinking heavily so the room stank of liquor. Of the fifty-seven men he had examined, thirty-nine had failed their medical. Distended livers, alcoholism, collapsed kidneys, uro-genitary complaints, mental instability, delirium tremens, the eleven o'clock horrors, they had all taken their toll of the reluctant Territorials. After drinking all morning in the British Empire Service League, the Meritorious Order of the Tin Hat and the British Legion, they had been rounded up and taken to Balyete for their induction course. Doctor Russell was the first stage and he was holding things up.

'When can we go, Doc?' A pale, distraught face peered round an adjoining door. 'And thanks for getting us off. Fuck me, we were going round the bend thinking about what it would be like with these Kaffirs.'

'You can't go yet. You'll have to wait.'

The head disappeared and a confused murmur rose from the next room. Doctor Russell lit a cigarette in an effort to kill the stench of booze and looked at his watch. It was five o'clock and he still had twenty men to examine.

'Next!' he shouted into the fanlight. 'Come in.'

After a cursory examination of the man Doctor Russell began to gnaw at his beard.

'You know, if you carry on this way you'll be dead before you're thirty-five.'

'I know that already, you buck-toothed prick!' Pyper snapped, as he hoisted up his dove-grey slacks. 'But you're going to fail me, aren't you? Name your price, sport, put a figure to it. This is all a mistake.'

'What's the difference to you? You're on your way out already!' Doctor Russell ran his eye over the pale, fragile youth. 'Years ago you'd have been a consumptive, you know, you've got the figure for it.'

Pyper rubbed at his eyes.

'I can't even see the eye-test board.'

'There isn't one.'

'When I cough my balls don't jump around, sport. All my glands are swollen. I've had clap more times than influenza or the common cold. I get the flaming arsehole the day after I eat curry. I'm a wreck. A week in the army will kill me. I'll drop dead on you.'

Doctor Russell's eyes gleamed beneath his red, shaggy eyebrows.

'Yes, you might. Or we could try and prevent it. You see, if I fail you and you don't get purged of the poisons your system has already absorbed, then I would anticipate the first stages of organ degeneration to start within the next year. If you go into the army and lead a healthy life, and I throw in a little experiment of my own, we might get a better state of affairs. Death can be prevented, you know, with the right treatment.'

Pyper snorted and buttoned up his black shirt.

'You keep to Army medical standards, you bastard quack, and forget the guinea-pig business. I've got a job to do.'

As Pyper finished dressing the door opened and Colonel Vaal Rembrandt, Major Powderham and Sergeant-Major Loudwater marched into the room. They were in full uniform and dazzled the doctor and his patient with their reds, whites and khaki creases, their shining brasses and gleaming boots. All day Doctor Russell had been dealing with old and middle-aged men who were soiled, depressed and drunk. The entry of the soldiers intimidated him with their sharpness, stamping and big-mouthed efficiency.

'Doctor,' Colonel Vaal Rembrandt narrowed his pale eyes, 'you have stripped me of my most valuable asset. Manpower.'

'Failed more than half of them, sir!' Sergeant-Major Loudwater bellowed. 'Failed them on technicalities, sir. He's not adapted to local circumstances, sir! Thinks he's elsewhere, sir!'

Doctor Russell tried to speak but met the fierce unnerving glare of the sergeant-major. He was a short, blocky man with a pointed head that stabbed upwards into his cap like a mountain peak penetrating a cloud. His eyes hung downwards like those of a spaniel, glittering with a drooping malice, while his mouth, a vast grotto of tongue, teeth and lips, seldom seemed to shut.

'That's no good to us, is it? Eh? Hm?' Major Powderham prodded Pyper with his cane. 'I suppose you've failed this young lad too? He's in perfect condition.'

Pyper knocked the cane aside.

'Don't poke me around you parasitic military pooftah. I'm not cannon fodder!' he glowered. 'Within a year they'll abolish the armed forces here.'

Sergeant-Major Loudwater shook with indignation and shuffled his boots over the floor-boards.

'Don't you talk to an officer like that!'

'Listen, Bonzo,' Pyper drawled with deliberate nonchalance, 'if you keep creeping around like that,' he shot a finger at the soldier's shuffling boots, 'people will think you've shit yourself.'

The head reappeared round the door of the room where the

rejectees were waiting to get back to the British Empire Service League and other old soldiers' associations.

'Can we go now?' it croaked. 'The smell in here is terrible. Have you had Kaffirs using this room?'

'You're in!' Sergeant-Major Loudwater shuffled right up to Pyper and bawled in his face. 'On my life you're in! I'll show you who's not been able to keep a tight hold on his ring, that I will! He's passed, Doc!'

'That's my decision,' Doctor Russell said seriously. 'You can't shove me around.'

Sergeant-Major Loudwater shuffled over to the Irishman and thrust out his chest.

'His heart's as good as mine. He's younger!'

'He's not in good shape.'

The man who had stuck his head round the door had heard Sergeant-Major Loudwater shouting, 'You're in!' Returning to his companions he passed on the news. In a mood of self-righteous indignation the rejectees grabbed their few belongings, forced open the paint-jammed window, and stumbled across the barrack square. The sentry at the gate stopped them. They were brought back and paraded with the remaining twenty men while Colonel Vaal Rembrandt addressed them.

'Under the circumstances it has been decided to dispense with the medical examination. It is not that we are not concerned about the physical well-being of our troops but that we know that any man who has lived the outdoor life of Central Africa, with its sporting traditions and emphasis on keeping in good shape, will be a perfect physical specimen, fit to uphold the great traditions of the British Army.'

Here Major Powderham leant forward and whispered in Colonel Vaal Rembrandt's ear.

'Sorry . . . the great traditions of the Zonkendawon Army,' he continued.

'I didn't sign on for no Kaffir's army!' A voice came from the rear rank. 'I signed up for the British Territorials. This is illegal!'

'We will not neglect your need for culture while you are with us,' Rembrandt put his hands behind his back and walked along the front rank. 'There will be plenty of entertainment both here and on the campaign itself. We pride ourselves here on the high standards that we have been able to maintain in our productions.'

Major Powderham leant forward again.

'Ah, yes. Now to introduce you to your army father, ha, ha, Sergeant-Major Loudwater.' Rembrandt patted the quivering non-commissioned officer on the back. 'He is an experienced leader of combat troops, at home on the barrack square or in the thick of the fighting. He is the man who will act as a barrier ... sorry, no, I meant interpreter ... between you and your officers. Powderham, just a word in your ear...'

Colonel Vaal Rembrandt leant over to Major Powderham.

'What do you think of that word "interpreter"?'

'Now, a trifle cold, sir, yes, and not quite the right thing to say. A better word would be liaison, sir. None of them will know what that means,' Powderham whispered, 'and had you noticed that there are three women on parade? I think you should say a special word to them.'

'Scrub that word "interpreter", men,' Rembrandt waved an airy hand. 'What I meant was liaison,' he beamed. 'And a special welcome to the three woman who are with us.'

'Women, sir?' Loudwater exploded. 'Women! I never noticed women, sir!'

The Bucket-Wheel Excavator Gang closed ranks around Marilyn, Marge and Margaret from the Tonga Bar as the sergeant-major shuffled round to the back of the squad.

'And, sir,' Major Powderham listed to one side again, 'you'll remember what the Superintendent of Police asked us, remember, yes? Well, he spoke to me ... yes, it was me, wasn't it? He asked us to give a special mention to his little detachment of volunteers.'

Rembrandt fingered the silky blond hair that hung on his shoulders and looked through the ranks.

'Aha, I can see them. One step forward the police! One step march! Now there's a sense of civic duty if you like!'

Inspectors Grutchfield and Kwango and the four constables listened to the Colonel's short address of praise and welcome with stony faces. They were exhausted with pleading with the Superintendent who, as usual, had been devoid of mercy.

'Those faces look familiar!' Tarzan Cool Guy nudged Johnny McSilver. 'Where have I seen them before?'

'Sir!' Loudwater raised his voice. 'I must protest!'

He stood in the midst of the seething, dissatisfied, unhappy squad of recruits, his downward-slanting eyes fixed on Margaret from the Tonga Bar. 'I have knowledge of this woman, sir!' he ranted.

'Don't we all,' Kovary muttered tiredly. 'Humphrey, why do you think he walks like that, that shuffle of his?'

'What kind of knowledge?' Rembrandt inquired.

'Carnal knowledge!' the Bucket-Wheel Excavator Gang sang in husky unison.

'She's a whore, sir!'

'So?'

'I'm not training whores for war, sir!'

Matthias winked across at Margaret from the Tonga Bar who was thoroughly enjoying the situation. She had never had so much free advertising.

'We can't pick and choose, Sar-major. And she did volunteer.'

'I'd like to know her reasons, sir!' Loudwater shuffled to the front of the squad. 'They're a ropey lot as it is, sir.'

'Their reasons are their own. They volunteered to do the country of their birth or adoption the favour of serving in its armed forces. That is a citizen's right. We have a job to do and these are the people who must do it for us.'

Major Powderham tilted again.

'Sorry, rub that out, what I meant was to do it *with* us, of course that's what I meant. Dismiss them, Sar'major. There's a war on and we must get cracking.'

'One thing, sir, before I dismiss the shower. We have to get ranks sorted out. Lot of them have ranks from the Territorials and I was instructed by you, sir, to honour them.'

Rembrandt paused, then remembered what Loudwater was talking about. He had received instructions from the ministry that all Territorial promotions had to be maintained in his emergency force.

'Best thing is to call them out and check their record, Sar'-major.'

'I'll do that now, sir, with your permission.'

'Carry on,' Rembrandt blinked kindly. 'There may be a few marshals' batons in their knapsacks, ha, ha, ha!'

Loudwater shuffled to a position directly at the head of the squad.

'Right! I want you to listen to me carefully. Some of you have been given ranks in the Territorial Army during the time you were in it under the colonial government. Those ranks are to stand. What I want is a sort out here and now so I know what I'm working with. When I call out a rank then if you hold it in the Terriers then step forward and hold your hand up! Is that understood? Right? On your toes! Lance-corporal!'

Two men stepped forward and raised their hands.

'Corporal!'

Nine men stepped forward and raised their hands.

'Sergeant!'

Twenty-eight men stepped forward and raised their hands.

Loudwater's eyes dragged lower, his vast mouth sagging like the jowls of a bloodhound.

'We can't have this, sir!'

'Hmmm, we do have a problem,' Rembrandt confirmed. 'Difficult.'

'What about the rest of us?' a voice called indignantly. 'What about the sergeant-majors?'

'Sergeant-majors?' Loudwater bawled in disbelief. 'Sergeant-bloody-majors?'

Thirty-four men stepped forward and raised their hands.

An army's rate of march is calculated in steps per minute. There is the average rate of 120 steps per minute, and faster times for light infantry regiments. During funerals a slow rate is used because it looks callous to quick-march the dead to the grave and an army wants to avoid giving that impression.

Sergeant-Major Loudwater had his own rate of marching. It was a unique system of pedestrian locomotion. It was the reason why the British Army had acceded to the persistent requests of the colonel of Loudwater's regiment and transferred Loudwater on loan to the colonial government. From Aldershot to Pirbright it was known as 'The Loudwater Shuffle' and had evolved over the years as Sergeant-Major Loudwater's piles got progressively worse.

'Hup! Hup! Hup! Hup!'

Tarzan Cool Guy and his friends shuffled round the barrack square, their knees touching, boots slithering over the concrete surface. Sparks flew from the steel nails and heel-plates and the noise was that of a steam train climbing a gradient. They were being drilled as a group because they were all privates – the only privates in the force.

'Don't you dare pick your feet up, you bloody gorilla!' Loudwater yelled at Tarzan Cool Guy. 'Keep them skimming over the floor there, that's the way to get along, man, skim across like an hovercraft does, like a bird in the air, son, a swallow on a summer's eve.'

Although the Loudwater Shuffle was the best way for its initiator to get around, it was not fitted to the physical inadequacies of the privates. They got tired in the upper thigh, their crotches smouldered and got chapped, their ankles swelled and the soles of their feet burned. For three days they had been shuffling round the square under the scornful eyes of the Territorial non-commissioned officers.

'Look at that load of rubbish!' one of the sergeant-majors commented as the squad rasped by sweating profusely. 'The bastards must have joined up as a man. Never trust a Kaffir-*boeti* man. All those Black and White Minstrel Show bastards deserve what they get.'

'The Kaffirs will turn on them in the end,' another sergeant-major promised menacingly. 'The bastards know when they're being patronized. Kaffirs respect strength, man, that's all they understand.'

'Fucking subversives,' the first sergeant-major spat into the sun. 'I'll make the bastards jump given the chance.'

The smiling Marilyn, her smile strained to breaking-point by the red-hot traction under her feet, stumbled and fell. Immediately the Bucket-Wheel Excavator Gang gathered around her, misinterpreting her position on the barrack square as being an invitation to libidinous dalliance.

'Ma wee wife!' Johnny gasped. 'Get aff! She's hurt, canna ya see that?'

Sergeant-Major Loudwater pushed his way through the perspiring privates and stood over Marilyn with his pacing-stick over his shoulder.

'You weren't skimming Private McSilver, were you? You were lifting your feet too high.'

'I'm sorry,' Marilyn said feebly. 'I don't seem to be able to get the hang of it.'

'Can we not rest?' Johnny begged. 'We're all bushed. I'm ready to drop and I'm in good condition, God help the others here.'

Any help would have been welcome to Pyper, Humphrey Fluellen and Kovary whose feet were red-raw and blistered. They had grounded themselves as soon as Marilyn had fallen over, grateful for the opportunity. Dennis was tired but still going strong as the Loudwater Shuffle was not dissimilar to his own method of slipping through the bush in search of beetles.

'That's enough for today,' Tarzan Cool Guy squatted next to Marilyn and took her hand. 'You and I are of the same mind.'

Loudwater poked Tarzan Cool Guy with his pacing-stick.

'Since when are you in charge?'

'I'm not in charge, *chamware*, I'm just tired. My woman is tired. All my friends are tired. We've played soldiers for long enough today.'

'Playing soldiers? You're not playing soldiers! This is the real thing. None of you will make a soldier's arsehole, but you're going to take the place of one! Up on your feet, Private McSilver!'

'I think I've done something to my ankle,' Marilyn smiled through the sweat and grime on her sunny face. 'I'm not sure that I can stand up.'

When Loudwater bent down and yanked Marilyn to her feet he found that instead of her weight at the end of his arm he was experiencing a momentary floating sensation. He was not a man who was subject to fainting fits or epilepsy, nor did he approve of those soft drugs that induce hallucinations. His early morning cigarette had long since ceased to make him dizzy, nor did he have vertiginous dreams.

'What is happening to me?' he moaned as Tarzan Cool Guy lifted him into the air and gave him an Aeroplane Spin. 'I do feel queer.'

Kovary, in whom there was a practical streak not present in most of his friends and associates, helped Marge to cool the wrestler down and lower Loudwater to the ground. There was nothing to be gained in busting up the sergeant-major when thirty-four more were sitting under the verandah waiting for a chance to prove themselves.

'He didn't mean that,' Kovary crooned softly, as he straightened Loudwater's red sash out over his shoulder and returned his cap. 'He would like to unreservedly apologize.'

Loudwater tore himself away and stood some distance off, fuming inarticulately.

'Mff . . . gra . . . cou . . . oh, I'll . . . bloo. . .'

'Say you're sorry, love,' Marge pushed Tarzan Cool Guy forward. 'He's quite upset.'

Tarzan Cool Guy stepped over to Loudwater and stuck out his hand.

Mr Vapour Mutale arrived the following morning with written instructions from the President confirming Tarzan Cool Guy's commission as a second lieutenant in the Territorial Army. The adjutant, who was a perspicacious administrator who could see snags when they arose, interrupted the court-martial just as the prisoner was being sentenced for his malicious and unwarranted attack on a superior officer.

'Thought you'd better take a look at this, sir,' he murmured diplomatically.

Colonel Vaal Rembrandt studied the document and passed it to Major Powderham.

Sergeant-Major Loudwater shuffled to attention.

'Prisoner paraded for sentence, sir!'

The wrestler stood with his arms by his side and watched the members of the court-martial conferring. He had spent the night in the camp glasshouse, turning recent events over in his mind. Whereas he was still resentful at the trick that the Party had played on him, and abhorred the idea of being part of a military organization, he had decided to do his best to live with Loudwater and his ilk in peace, complete his Territorial service and return to civilian life as intact as was possible. When Marge had come to him just before midnight, having bribed the sentry with a packet of kinky Japanese condoms, she had told him that the non-commissioned officers were of the opinion that he'd get at least five years in a military gaol for his attack on Loudwater. Having recognized many of the corporals, sergeants and sergeant-majors as members of the audience at his fights, he had discounted this rumour as mere wishful thinking on their part.

'What's the point of training me to be a professional soldier then sticking me in prison for so long? It's wasteful.' He had chuckled as they hugged each other on the narrow bunk. 'They're practical men, Marge, they wouldn't do that.'

He was right. The court-martial had decided not to put him in gaol for five years before Doctor Mulombe's instructions arrived. The sentence agreed upon was ten. Now they were faced with the prospect of upsetting Loudwater who, as the aggrieved party and the principal witness, had naturally been consulted as to the severity of the sentence.

'Stand up straight!' Loudwater snapped at the prisoner who had slouched forward as the officers facing him continued with their hushed debate. As Tarzan Cool Guy stiffened and tucked his chin into his chest, the door opened and Mr Vapour Mutale and Fines Chingola entered.

'Ah, Colonel, you are a fast worker!' Mr Vapour Mutale nodded agreeably. 'H.E. will be pleased to hear that his orders are carried out so promptly. Hello, T.C.G.! You're looking well. Army life must be quite a change, eh? What do you think of your elevation, eh?'

'His feet won't touch the ground!' Loudwater said menacingly.

Colonel Vaal Rembrandt rubbed his forehead and the side of his nose, and teased a lock of blond hair with a beringed finger.

'Mr Mutale, I hope you won't think me discourteous, but we in the army like occasions like this to be kept within ourselves,' he began.

The Regional Secretary folded his hands and flapped his briefcase against his leg.

'Colonel, in this country the military is not a power on its own. It is not autonomous. You will never see a military dictatorship in Zonkendawo. We have seen what has happened elsewhere, the way you soldiers get out of hand and think you can run things better than the politicians. That will never happen here because we are not going to let it! The army is the tool of the Party! Whatever you do concerns the Party! Even if it is a thing like promoting one of your men, then that is of interest to a man like me who has the total responsibility for the enforcement of Party politics in this area!'

'And what about the Law, sir?' Loudwater erupted. 'What about the Law?'

Mr Vapour Mutale regarded the shaking sergeant-major with bland, pitying good humour.

'The Law is the Law of the Party. If it wasn't then there would be no Party. How can the governors govern if there is no Law and if that Law is not theirs? Can a man dig his field if the hoe will not obey his hand? Who can ride a horse if that animal does not obey the rider? If the bird does not control its wings then it falls to the ground.'

Major Powderham leant towards his colonel and whispered. There was a pause while Rembrandt shuffled his papers.

'Sar'major...'

'Sir!'

'Before we ... proceed ... er...'

'Proceed with the sentence, sir?' Loudwater beamed. 'Yes, sir?'

'Sentence?' Fines Chingola's eyes widened. 'What is this sentence?'

Major Powderham jumped in, one hand gripping his colonel's sleeve beneath the table.

'Steady, sir ... no, now what were we talking about was a question of linguistics before you came in. What we were discussing was the comparative appropriateness of using these sentences in promoting a private to a second lieutenant. Now, before we waste any more time, these sentences were:

(a) The King has granted you a commission.

(b) The War Office has invested a rank in you.

(c) You have been promoted.

(d) The Army has found you suitable to hold senior office. Which one would you prefer? Eh? Just a little throwing it back and forth...'

'There is no king here,' Mr Vapour Mutale said coldly, 'so that is out.'

'Shall I remove the prisoner until your discussions with these gentlemen are over, sir?' Loudwater interrupted suddenly. 'It's not right that he should be party to a confab like this.'

'Prisoner? T.C.G. a prisoner?' Fines choked. 'What's going on here?'

'No, that's not what he said, er ... what d'you call it ... yes, he said pensioner. Pensioner. This man is being considered for a special pension.' Major Powderham got up from the table and marched round to where Loudwater had turned apoplectically purple.

'Now I suggest that you go off with Second Lieutenant Tarzan Cool Guy and have a drink with him to celebrate his promotion, Sar'major. Take your time. When politicians and soldiers get together there's always a lot to talk about. Dismiss!'

Tarzan Cool Guy walked out behind Loudwater and managed to catch him as his knees crumbled. Putting the pacing-stick between his teeth he swept the sobbing sergeant-major into his arms and went in search of Pyper and his life-giving cane-for-pain.

The sergeants' mess was full. Everyone was there. Everyone was there by right because the cunning government had solved the problem of having so many non-commissioned officers by promoting everyone to sergeant and down-grading the thirty-four sergeant-majors who were all given an *ex gratia* payment in compensation. Loudwater was the only sergeant-major but he had been promoted as well. Somehow he had been promoted to the human race.

'How's your piles?' Doctor Russell inquired. 'That *muti* I gave you any help?'

Loudwater got to his feet and marched up and down with a free unhindered stride.

'Fifteen years I've been a haemorrhoids sufferer. I've tried everything. Answered every ad in the papers and magazines. There's nothing I haven't used on 'em, nothing. But I meet you with your funny ideas about the trees out here, and bingo! they're gone. Don't tell me how you do it, I don't want to know because it might frighten the daylights out of me, but it works and I'm grateful. You've no idea of the relief!'

Loudwater patted Doctor Russell on the back.

'If there's ever anything I can do for you, Doc, just you mention it. You're an officer and a gentleman.'

The mess was rowdy that night. Humphrey Fluellen had brought his ivory cigarette-holder and was trying out one of Kovary's latest script-ideas on a group of sergeant ex-sergeant-majors.

'Then we all lay them on the bar, side by side, and each man has to think up something to say to it. Yours might be flowery...'

'There's no flowers on mine!' a man cried aloud. 'Who said there's flowers on mine?'

'I mean a flowery speech ... or it might be severely classical. Any man who can't think of something to say is lacking in imagination. Isn't it the source of all inspiration according to Freud?'

Kovary nodded as they tried to edge the group towards the bar where Margaret from the Tonga Bar was handling a bottle-opener that had grown warm with use.

'That's where theatre started, these fertility rites in Greece. All the old shepherds used to lay them side by side on slabs of stone and make up odes, elegies, the old ones it was dirges...'

'We have to get back to the primitive in theatre, the basic fountain of human experience,' Humphrey lilted in his Welsh sing-song voice. 'We have to find our way back to the roots of the human spirit. You're crusted, bottled-up with repressive ideas that have turned you into the defeatists that you are now.'

'Who's a defeatist?' a small, bald-headed man with a cyst on his neck shouted manfully. 'I'm no defeatist!'

'Action not words, boyo,' Humphrey smiled encouragingly. 'Let's see what you're made of. Innovation in the theatre takes courage. If you truly believe in yourself stand up and be counted.'

While the man with the cyst on his neck was looking at the trestle-table and delving inwardly into the full implications of

Humphrey's challenge, Johnny McSilver and Marilyn were trying to find a basis for selecting the football teams.

'Now 'am a great believer in utilizing existing relationships ya know,' he said cannily, 'whatsamarrer with having the Bucket-Wheel Excavator Gang and Matthias as one team? They're a handy unit.'

Marilyn smiled at the hopeful labourers who were gazing at her with their customary steadfastness, their eyes dumbly yearning, their mouths hanging open with the power of their fond imaginings. She knew that the Bucket-Wheel Excavator Gang were a handy unit. She had the finger-marks to prove it.

'Don't count me in with these loafers!' Matthias bent his bullet-head towards the ten lascivious petitioners who were crowded round Marilyn's tall golden presence, each man hugging a plastic bucket containing a gallon of millet-beer. 'I've had enough of the bastards. They're ruining my life. It's about time I got my independence, never mind the country as a whole. They've been on my back all my working life.'

Marilyn edged her way through the Bucket-Wheel Excavator Gang, beating off the seeking hands that immediately darted towards every part of her sunny loveliness. She stood by Matthias's side and took his hand. The Bucket-Wheel Excavator Gang sighed as the imagined bliss of that holy, golden touch communicated itself.

'Poor Matthias,' Marilyn chided him, 'you must try and understand the disadvantages that your men have had to struggle against. They've had none of the opportunities that you have.'

'Oh!' groaned the Bucket-Wheel Excavator Gang. 'What opportunities have you been giving Matthias? Have you allowed our leader into Paradise?'

'No, no!' Marilyn put herself behind Matthias and spoke over his shoulder as the love-sick Africans crept closer. 'I'm talking about his education.'

The Bucket-Wheel Excavator Gang looked on regretfully as Marilyn ran down the length of the sergeants' mess, her long bronzed legs flashing in the dim air of the naked light bulbs. They knew she would be back, but for the time that she was away they would be living in a galaxy that had no sun for its centre. As she went out of the door it was like the swift approach of night, sudden and chilling to the blood.

'Christ, what am I going to do with you?' Matthias moaned and tugged fretfully at his hair. 'I give up! I can't take any more! You're worse than the beasts of the field!'

Sadly the Bucket-Wheel Excavator Gang sat down on the floor, their heads inside their plastic containers.

'You are our only hope!' one man grunted so his voice reverberated within the bucket. 'Without you we are nothing!'

'You got us through basic training!' another muttered through a mouthful of the porridgy beer. 'Oh, *mushi steric* Matthias!'

'Ehe! *Mushi steric* Matthias!' came the responding chorus from the rest of the gang.

'You harnessed the Loud Waters!'

'*Mushi steric* Matthias!' the gang harmonized. 'You are our beloved leader!'

Two of the plastic containers were drained, up-ended and used as drums as the Bucket-Wheel Excavator Gang launched into their songs of praise for their unwilling, desperately unhappy chief.

We have fired the three-oh-three! Ah!
We have used the four-by-four and the pull-through! Ah!
We have tasted the Brasso! Argh!
We have tasted the Blanco! Argh!
You have taught us to endure these things!
O *mushi steric* Matthias!

Matthias examined the faces of his men with dark contempt.

'*Cha!* You don't fool me. Do you think I'm not immune to your flattery by now? Why don't you do something with your lives instead of sitting around all day drinking that bush muck?'

The Bucket-Wheel Excavator Gang were undaunted by their leader's reference to their millet-beer as being an unsophisticated and unclean beverage. Four bottles of dark navy rum had been added to the plastic containers that night and the lumpy gruel had a kick like a frisky rhinoceros.

'Our chief has three Ordinary Level subjects! Ha!'

The drums thundered.

'He is a man of ineffable wisdom! Ha!'

The member of the gang whose voice had not yet broken got to his feet and sang in a pure boy soprano.

'He has Health Science! Eeeoh! Health Science!'

'Health Science!' roared the gang. 'O clean and uncontaminated!'

'He has the Religious Knowledge! Eeeoh! Eeeòh! The Religious Knowledge!'

'Religious Knowledge!' came the joyful shout. 'O wonderful and holy!'

'And our chief has British Constitution into the bargain! Eeeeoh! O he has sucked at the breast of the Mother of Parliaments!'

'O he has the British Constitution and has sucked at the breast of the Mother of Parliaments! O impartial and democratic!'

As the drums carried away the song, rising to a percussive frenzy, Matthias melted. He knew that the gang were exploiting his weak spot, his vanity in his intellectual achievement, but he loved it. Seven years of night-school, seven years in stale-smelling classrooms after a hard day outwitting Hammerkop and keeping the Bucket-Wheel Excavator Gang out of trouble. It had been a hard slog and he deserved some recognition.

Graciously he bowed his head and the gang got to their feet, booming out the final phrases of the song and shaking their Messiah by the hand.

'Let it never be said that we do not appreciate you, Matthias,' a man said stoutly, as he pumped the hand of his glowing, slightly shy leader who had tears in his eyes. 'I can speak for all of us when I say that although we have been a trial to you in the past, it will never happen again in the future.'

This rampant hypocrisy broke the spell. With a violent wrench Matthias tore his hand away and glared at the cowed man who was shielding his face with an upraised arm.

'Trust you to spoil it!' Matthias choked and stumbled away. 'Dear holy God, who will deliver me from this tribe of fornicating alcoholics? Is it my destiny to remain in charge of them for ever?'

Tarzan Cool Guy leaned closer to Doctor Russell and tried to ignore the piteous pleas and howlings of the Bucket-Wheel Excavator Gang as they tried to persuade Matthias of their new resolution to behave themselves and followed him to the trestle-table where Margaret from the Tonga Bar was acting as barmaid.

'How did you get to know about it?' he asked.

Doctor Russell fluffed his beard. After Loudwater's announcement that his piles had been cured by a herbal remedy discovered by the Irishman, all the active hypochondriacs in the mess had gathered round the young doctor in the hope of receiving help for their own ills, real and imagined.

'Well, that was fairly simple,' Doctor Russell replied. 'You'll remember the disastrous Ground-Nut Scheme after the War? We all realize in retrospect that what the British government was trying to do was to keep the human refuse that had been sent abroad between 1940 and 1946 from coming back by dumping them on a desert reservation in Tanganyika, but there were people who genuinely believed in the idea and one of these poor fellows was an uncle of mine. He saw the ground-nut as the source of the world's future and he was badly let down when the scheme flopped. Anyway, he'd got a taste for Africa by then so he came to Zonkendawo and got himself a job on the mines as a cap-lamp-room attendant. There were no Africans available with the right educational qualifications for the job and as Uncle Dan had an Irish School Leaver's Certificate he was a natural choice. Well, the old boy was an amateur botanist – and a good one. He was earning good money because the copper bonus was about 110 per cent in those days and he was getting £200 a month basic and he used this to finance expeditions throughout Central Africa looking for plants and a replacement for the ground-nut. I used to spend hours with him when he came home to Dublin on leave and he really got me interested. I decided to come out here and pursue my studies and try to get a research grant out of the W.H.O. – they're far more sympathetic if you're working in an under-developed country.'

'Is this an under-developed country?' Tarzan Cool Guy asked.

'Oh yes, I'd say so.'

'You mean it's flat?' the wrestler continued, anxious to learn.

Marge squeezed his hand under the table as a signal for him to shut up.

'No, dear, it means we've a long way to go before we're like the countries in the West.'

Tarzan Cool Guy frowned and tugged his ear.

'I thought he meant like Margaret from the Tonga Bar is up front.'

Although a cutting and unkind remark, as it was publicly announced by a man she had always considered as a friend, it was nevertheless true that the hard-working, even-tempered, well-adjusted whore was as flat as a bread-board. Over the years she had endured thousands of coarse suggestions as to the reason for this, the most popular view being that she had been eroded into this condition by her thousands of customers. However, this physical deficiency was more than compensated for by what she carried at hip and thigh, a subject that had occupied countless hours of admiring male conversation the length and breadth of the Copperbelt.

'So you're really going into native remedies on a professional basis? Trying to ascertain whether they have any provable curative powers by biochemical analysis?' Dennis cocked an eyebrow and rubbed a thoughtful finger along the spine of his book about water-beetles of the Mississippi Delta. 'That's very interesting.'

'They work, these old remedies,' Tarzan Cool Guy assured them. 'I can remember my mother going off into the bush collecting roots, bark and leaves when we were sick. When we had coughs she dug up the roots of the *mulama* tree and boiled them ... once I had mumps and she used the *mufilo* tree, *mubanga* for pneumonia, *mulebe* for syphilis.'

'When did you have syphilis!' Marge screeched in terror.

Tarzan Cool Guy patted her hand and grinned.

'Not me, *umfazi*, my father caught a dose in Umtali once. My mum cured it though.'

'Some of these trees have fantastic reputations as healers,' Doctor Russell addressed his remarks to Dennis, in whom he could recognize a fellow-scientist. 'The *mulombwa* tree, for example, is used as a cure for ringworm, corneal ulcers, mouth ulcers, nose-bleeds, malaria, black-water fever, nettle-rash, gonorrhoea and an infusion of the leaves, if rubbed into the breasts, induces lactation.'

'The *mutimbwabusa* tree is used as an aphrodisiac by young girls when they're approaching puberty,' Tarzan Cool Guy added helpfully.

'And the *mupapa* for blepharitis and bilharzia,' Doctor Russell counted them off on his fingers, 'the *munumbenumbe* for rheumatism, and the one that I haven't been able to find yet, for death.'

Dennis chuckled donnishly.

'For death, eh? A cure for death ... that would make the World Health Organization sit up! He! He! He!'

Doctor Russell switched his brown gaze to Marge, having decided that Dennis was a clown.

'One of the indigenous trees of this territory contains, either in its leaves, bark, roots, sap or wood, an extract that will cure, and prevent death.'

'How can you be so sure?' Marge was startled by the young Irishman's passionate conviction. 'Why here?'

'The trees in Africa are capable of curing any disease.'

'Allegedly capable, and the allegation comes from people who aren't world-famous for their scientific pursuits,' Dennis insisted gently. 'Let's not forget that.'

'What d'you mean?' Tarzan Cool Guy retorted defensively. 'We invented the wheel, we even invented people here.'

Doctor Russell started to gnaw at his beard. Dennis was proving to be a difficult case.

'Has cynicism ever proved anything? All the great discoveries of modern medicine have been discredited by reactionaries and people with a vested interest in keeping the old inadequate methods in use.'

'But this theory of yours is archaic in itself!' Dennis banged the table with his book. 'It's going back to the days when medicine was a hit-and-miss affair. You'll be looking for the Elixir of Life next!'

'In the name of Christ what is a cure for Death but the Elixir of Life!' Doctor Russell hooted gleefully. 'You've caught yourself out there! Hoist with your own petard!'

Dennis struggled with the temptation to walk away. The eyes of Sergeant-Major Loudwater were on him, full of dislike for the way Doctor Russell's theories were being scoffed at by a layman. Anyone who could cure his piles could cure Death.

'Listen, mate, there's many things that they used to look for in the old days that we've stopped looking for – and why? Because we haven't got the same guts as the old-timers. They went off after the Holy Grail, the Golden Fleece, the pot of gold at the end of the rainbow, come what may they had a go. And this gentleman has got that same spirit, the fire in his belly. I think it's most presumptuous of you, a simple soldier with lead in his arse, to think of arguing with an expert'

Dennis felt uncomfortable in the wake of Loudwater's ticking-off. The arboreal obsessions of Doctor Russell were only one additional drop in the ocean of incongruities, irrationalities and upsets that he had to endure at Balyete Camp. He decided to withdraw from the discussion and read his book.

'What do you know about this tree?' Tarzan Cool Guy asked with interest. 'Perhaps I can give you some help. I was brought up in the bush.'

'Not a great deal, though I suspect that it's limited to one part of the country – swampy ground I should think – and that there's plenty of tabus and tribal prohibitions attached to it. Livingstone saw it, and I've read everything he's got to say. Great natural observer old Doctor Livingstone was, wonderful eye for the unusual. They say that when he died up in the Bengweulu Swamps, the Africans with him cut out his heart and buried it under a tree.'

'Our tree?' Tarzan Cool Guy breathed. 'The one you're looking for?'

'Could be...' Doctor Russell nodded.

'What's it called this tree?' Loudwater demanded cheerily. 'I'll get all of 'em out looking for it! We can interrogate the locals!'

Doctor Russell smiled enigmatically and stroked the hair on the back of his hand with the tip of his beard.

'Well, all I have is hearsay and guesswork. I've heard that it's called all sorts of things – that's if it's the one I'm looking for. I don't want to start too many hares. But I think we might find it up in the swamps where we're going.'

'Swamps? What swamps?' Loudwater's eye dragged further down.

'Where the Muntu are, in the Bengweulu Swamps.'

'But the Colonel told me personally that it was wonderful fighting country we were heading for,' Loudwater protested in bewilderment. 'Why's he lied to me?'

'Perhaps he was keeping it as a surprise,' Tarzan Cool Guy tried to comfort his new friend. 'You know the Colonel can be a bit vague over detail.'

Major Powderham opened the door of the officers' mess and received the salute of the sergeant with the cyst on his neck. The man was so drunk that he saluted with both hands at once.

'Sir, Sergeant Kovary and Sergeant Fluellen send their greetings and wish to invite you and the Colonel over to our mess, sir, for the show!'

Major Powderham was trying to decide whether he should put the drunken sergeant on a charge when Rembrandt heaved himself out of his chair, putting down his book on make-up.

'What is it, Major?'

'The sergeants' mess have invited us over, sir, some damned show they're putting on. This man is abominably drunk, sir.'

'Ah yes, we can pop over. Always interested in a show. Nothing like live theatre, Powderham, nothing. I've got some ideas up my sleeve for a little show next week myself . . . can't do any harm to have a look at what those two are doing. Except for his inability to cast musicals Humphrey Fluellen has got a lot of interesting things to say about theatre.'

The sergeant ex-sergeant-major limped happily back across the square to the sergeants' mess to announce the arrival of the Colonel. He was conscious of the great African night above him, the stars riding softly on the billowing darkness and a feeling of fulfilled manliness. Touching the cyst on the back of his neck he started laughing. For the first time, Margaret from the Tonga Bar had fastened her eyes elsewhere on his anatomy than that blighted nuisance. Not only had he demanded and got her attention but she had stepped back in surprise, her mouth open. At the top of his voice he had recited the short address to his organ of creation as it lay on the trestle-table, and he repeated it to himself now as he returned to the place of his triumph.

Proud member of the human race
how I wish you had a face
you're proud, upstanding, ambitious, free
and more intelligent than me.

This quatrain had drawn a tremendous ovation from the crowd and Sergeant Fluellen had personally congratulated him while Sergeant Kovary hastily copied it down in his notebook. While everyone else in the sergeants' mess who was interested in the origins of theatre began to unzip their flies and look at the ceiling, working out their poems, the first bard had been asked by Sergeant Fluellen to run over and fetch the Colonel as he was sure that Rembrandt would enjoy this foray into group experimentation on a selected theme.

'You know I've been surprised at the way we've managed to get through to these men,' Colonel Vaal Rembrandt said to Major Powderham as they strolled through the night. 'They've really come together in the last week. There were times when I wanted to give up, I don't mind telling you that. Then, we're there! They've got *esprit de corps*, some semblance of organization.'

Major Powderham nodded and tapped his knee with his rattan cane.

'I think the Tarzan Cool Guy promotion did a lot of good in fact, sir, yes, unexpectedly though, eh? He polarized their resentment for a while, you know, then he won them round because he's such a nice chap don't you know, hmm ... lot of noise coming from the sergeants' mess, sir, must be a jolly good show.'

'Done wonders for the recruitment figures in civvy street, him joining up, you know. That Party feller, Mutale, he rang me today. Coming in droves since Sergeant Pyper published that series of articles in the newspaper. The one about the independence party didn't go down too well with the authorities, nor the fracas with the police they had, but the youngsters seemed to be attracted to Tarzan Cool Guy even more when they read them. More of a hero than ever. They're resigning from the Youth Brigade in their hundreds and joining the Territorials.'

Colonel Vaal Rembrandt's enthusiasm for Pyper's journalistic skill was understandable. He was not Pyper's friend. Nor was

Major Powderham. He hated both of them. Up until recently Sergeant-Major Loudwater had been immune from attack, but since his conversion to humanity Pyper had grown fond of the sharply-pointed soldier and was working on an exposé of the Loudwater Shuffle for world syndication.

'You think they're ready, sir?'

Major Powderham's question touched on a wireless message that had been received earlier in the evening. As befits men of sang-froid, they had not yet discussed the order to move north against the Muntu which had been stamped 'Secret', 'Urgent' and carried Doctor Mulombe's personal authorization through the ministry of Internal Affairs.

'I'm just glad that they're having such a night of it, Paul.' The Colonel blinked rapidly, the sparkling moisture that tripped from his long lashes caught by the moonlight. 'There's hard times ahead.'

'Yes, sir . . . we'll pull through, I think,' Powderham turned his head away.

'I hope the regulars can keep up with us. What's the name of that place where we're meeting up?'

'Chimbusu, sir,' Powderham mounted the first step of the rickety verandah and paused, raising his voice above the din that was coming from inside the sergeants' mess. 'What did the ministry say about our request for an air-strike?'

'We can talk about that later,' the Colonel waved him on. 'Let's join in the fun before it's too late.'

Johnny, his arm firmly round the blushing Marilyn's waist, looked down the length of the trestle-table.

'Well, what d'ya think? I cannae think of a better way of picking sides,' he said, while thoughtfully perusing the display. 'Say what ya like, it will give 'em a sense of identity. It's natural selection I'd say. If I can get the eejits worked up about it, we might get a competition going.'

While Johnny noted down the circumcised on one side of the page and the uncircumcised on the other, it came round to Pyper's turn. He glanced scornfully along the Bucket-Wheel Excavator Gang's presentation – a row of sturdy railway sleepers – and dumped his genitalia on the crowded trestle-table.

'Beat that, you poor bastards!' he crowed, blue eyes ablaze with pride. 'And here's my bit of old original verse.'

If you want to build a future
don't look for bricks and mortar
go round to Mrs Brown's
and show this to her daughter.

Margaret from the Tonga Bar smiled at Pyper's offering as if saying hello to an old friend. As everyone else in the sergeants' mess was either lined up at the trestle-table or critically examining the display, she was the only person who could see the door. When Rembrandt and Powderham came in she realized that newcomers had arrived but such was her enjoyment of the moment – never before had such a cornucopia been laid at her feet – the dizzy whore did not give the alarm. Instead she thought that the Colonel and his aide were going to join in the show.

'What d'you reckon old Margaret from the Tonga Bar. You've never seen a beaut like mine, have you?'

She was at a loss. How could she choose from such a richly varied selection? There were old friends there, passing acquaintances, new boys – what kind of standards could she use?

'Come on then! Give us the prize!' Pyper hammered the table. 'Let's not hang about!'

Pyper was jostled by the men on either side of him. They had been waiting for Margaret's judgement for longer than he had – they had experienced those long, painful minutes of anticipation when a man has given his all, can do no more, and knows that his measure is being taken. Margaret from the Tonga Bar ran her brimming eyes along the row – she did not want to make a choice. Every one of them was a friend, a staff of life, a crutch.

This was the happiest moment of her life.

'Attention!' Loudwater bawled, wrenching at his flies as he sighted the officers standing at the door.

'At ease, Sar'major, at ease. Don't hold anything up for us. We'll just make ourselves at home, eh?' Rembrandt wandered to the centre of the room. 'Sounds as though you're raising the roof tonight. Where's this show then?'

Tarzan Cool Guy, drunk out of his head with Marge hanging on his arm, turned from the table and gave a wavering salute.

'I'm going to be the winner, sir!' he chuckled darkly. 'No matter what that boy Pyper says, this has got the prize. You want to hear my lyric, sir? It will slay you, slay you...'

Powderham stared at the black cannon that was being aimed straight at his heart.

'Lieutenant!'

Powderham's shocked cry brought the Colonel's attention back from the rafters where he had been searching for any tips that Humphrey's lighting effects might provide. He saw before him an obviously intoxicated African lieutenant with his cock out.

'Adjust your dress, sir!' Powderham snapped. 'This is too much!'

'Too much?' Marge expostulated. 'How can it be too much? You need all you can get in this kind of competition!'

'Tell him my poem, Marge, tell the Colonel. He'll love it! Oh, it's a blinder, sir! It just came to me in a flash of inspiration! It'll slay you!'

Rembrandt was at a loss for words. Powderham had paled with rage, his nostrils twitching and the rattan cane vibrating with pent-up indignation against his leg. Before he could stop her, Marge had begun to recite Tarzan Cool Guy's address to his phenomenal *umtondo*. The officers were forced to listen, still threatened by this sable barrel.

Said the Ego to the Id,
See what the *bwanas* did,
They brought us civilization,
So praise Caucasian Man!
Said the Id unto the Ego,
See what hangs upon the negro
For the purpose of creation,
And beat that if you can!

There was a flutter of applause from Margaret from the Tonga Bar who had still not caught up with the situation. She leaned over the trestle-table, her voice husky with emotion.

'What can I say? Every single one has something to recommend it. I don't think I can possibly choose between them.

You've all been so kind, so thoughtful ... excuse me,' she wiped a stray tear away with the back of her finely-boned hand, 'but before I say anything else I'd like to thank you all for putting this show on specially for me. I wouldn't have missed it for the world. I'm sorry to be so hopeless at deciding a winner but I'm a bit overwrought with all the excitement. Next time ... there will be a next time, I hope, then I might have had the opportunity to work out some standard which I can go by, a yardstick I can use to judge the best. Not tonight, though, I'm too overwhelmed by it all. Thanks, thank you all. I think you're all marvellous, really I do.'

Then Margaret from the Tonga Bar cried with happiness, her dark, noble head bowed as the tears flowed.

'Lieutenant! Adjust your dress, damn you!' Powderham eventually managed to splutter.

Tarzan Cool Guy touched his collar.

'Is my tie on crooked?'

Powderham's eyes blazed through menacing slits.

'By God, what kind of example do you think you're setting to the men? You'll be placed on a charge for this disgusting behaviour and I've got plenty of witnesses. You won't get away with it this time, no, by God you'll suffer for this obscene exhibition, yes, yes, you will, sir! Now put that appalling thing away!'

All friendship is a form of love. Love creeps up on people like the 'flu, or as a summer morning slides through the curtains, then up the eiderdown to the face of the sleeper. One day you are alone and without love. It is a cold world and the wind seems to ferret out your heart and blow on it. You are miserable and unhappy because if you dropped dead in the street it would be a stranger who would have to care and he would find that irksome. Then love arrives and you cannot hold it back. You become surrounded by the stuff. It can enter the most crustacean and despairing life and never leave a sign as to the place it entered. The shell remains smooth, the man apparently unchanged except that he has love inside him and he is warm again.

As one, in perfect parade-ground drill, the officers and men of the National Territorial Emergency Force executed an about-turn and saluted their Colonel.

9
Ace High Low Gets

The tower of the cathedral of Myanis Kupela was visible long before the Bengweulu Swamps took over the landscape. Desaix kept his eye on the red column. He was flying on reconnaissance and old habits of mind kept him wary. As the dry bush was transformed beneath him in a sea of tufted green, dark pools and small islands, his ears were pricked. He was crossing Muntu territory.

It was good to be in the air again. He had finally submitted to the indignity of recognizing Squadron-Leader Skidmore as his immediate superior plus Wing-Commander Foley (the only six wings that he commanded were all on the Fokker), and Doctor Mulombe's brother, Eustace, as Air Marshal. Being the only aircraft in the Z.A.F. was not an honour that he had sought, nor did he relish the eminence that it gave him; but it was useful. Having accepted the commission to fly for the government he had insisted upon a complete, thoroughgoing overhaul of his precious plane from tail to propeller. The engine had been stripped down, de-coked, re-bored, new cylinders made, all worn parts replaced, electricals re-done, and all the conversions and adaptations necessary for rendering the Fokker capable of acting as a fighter-bomber carried out at government expense. In addition he had negotiated a huge hire-charge for him, and the plane. Skidmore had been forced to agree to these rapacious demands when Desaix threatened to simply keep on flying once he was outward-bound on his first mission.

'What's there to stop me, Skidmore? I don't owe you anything, you bureaucratic *cochon*,' he had said evenly. 'I might go over to the enemy.'

Skidmore's imagination had played with this idea for ten seconds before he agreed to pursue the case with the Air Marshal. Mulombe could not afford to have the Muntu supreme in the air.

Desaix spotted two reed boats and dived. As he straightened

out, the waters ruffled by the wind of his passing, he saw the Africans sitting cross-legged with their paddles. They raised them in salute as he passed over and he could see the quick flash of their smiles.

He was still the only man in the Bengweulu Swamps who was making a noise. Myanis Kupela was near now. There was no gunfire. Except for the superbly-tuned engine, the high whistling of the slipstream through the ailerons, there was nothing that could break the damp peace of the morass below. Under the sun it shimmered soft, green, mysterious ... but not hostile.

Eustace Mulombe was a very different man from his brother, the President. He was a fatalist. Whereas Doctor Mulombe believed that he was part of the destiny of Africa, Eustace was convinced that his path in life had been signposted by the stars. He had been given a book to read when at an impressionable age, and it told him that because he was born under the sign of Taurus which was very tied-up with Venus, he would be obstinate, slow, like a settled life, love good food and drink and need a lot of loving. By the time his brother made him Air Marshal, Eustace had proved that all this was true.

This was the real reason for the first air-strategy meeting of the Zonkendawon Air Force high command being held in the La Gondola night-club. Eustace had an office but it was not the kind of place that a natural-born Taurean would prefer as a venue. It was cold, impersonal, rigid, inhuman and induced feelings of repression in the Air Marshal. In the La Gondola night-club he could be as slow as he liked, as obstinate as he wanted to be, and do all the loving necessary to keep his unique character intact.

'Air Marshal!'

Eustace had awoken with Foley's nervous hand on his gold-encrusted epaulette.

'What's for breakfast?' he asked through a sumptuous yawn.

Foley smiled wanly through the candle-lit gloom.

'No, sir, it's nearly midnight.'

'Then what's for dinner?'

'We've all had dinner, sir, we had it here.'

Eustace ran his tongue round his mouth and rubbed his balls.

'Where's my hostess?'

'She's dancing with Pilot-Officer Desaix, sir. Shall I call him over? It's time we got down to business. The President wants to know what our contingency plans are first thing in the morning.'

Eustace looked at the dance-floor. Desaix and the hostess were standing on the spot, wrapped in an embrace.

'He's got my hostess?'

'We can get her back, sir.'

'He's got a hand up her dress.'

'That's the lights, sir, these revolving coloured lights are very deceptive. Pilot-Officer Desaix would never stoop so low, sir.'

Eustace thought for a while then fell asleep again. It was a slow dream he was having. In it he was trying to explain to his mother why he had sneaked off to the beer-hall instead of staying with the old lady and her gang of Party-card sellers. In the dream he tried to lay his head on his mother's breast, tears in his eyes. She hit him over the head with her stick.

'Argh!' he cried out and woke up. *'Cha! Mame!'*

He saw Foley, Skidmore and Desaix looking at him. By his side was the unfaithful hostess.

'Who wants a drink?' he murmured, raising a hand for the waiter.

'Can't we get on please, sir?' Foley whined. 'We're well behind on the agenda.'

Eustace nestled into the hostess's shoulder, his round face smiling like a dark saint.

'I need a lot of affection,' he murmured, 'a hell of a lot.'

'You're telling me?' the hostess replied drily. 'Are you taking me home now?'

Eustace raised his head and looked into the hostess's eyes.

'I have never loved like this before,' he sighed. 'Let's go.'

Foley jumped to his feet.

'You can't go yet, sir! Not yet! What about . . . ?'

'Shush!' Skidmore hissed. 'Not in front of her, sir. This is a top-secret meeting.'

'You can talk freely in front of her,' Eustace stroked the hostess's cheek. 'She's in love with me. Aren't you?'

'Of course I am. I've been in love with him every night for the last three months.'

Eustace smiled fondly as he heard her admit to what he had always suspected.

'You see? She loves me, I love her, we trust each other. What else do you want?'

Eustace went down on to the hostess's lap and tried to curl up into a ball.

'What do we do now, sir?' Skidmore said helplessly. 'We can't take any decisions now, can we?'

Eustace came up for air. Winking across at Desaix he held out a hand.

'Hello, Bwana Arse, yoo-hoo! What star were you born under, *chamware*?'

Desaix tightened his lip. Not only was Eustace being presumptuous by using a familiar form of address that he only tolerated from his closest friends, but he was also walking off with a woman who Desaix had planned to take back to his flat and screw.

'Sagittarius,' he answered, 'and watch your lip.'

'Christ! What a mouthful!' Eustace giggled and went back to the breast. 'Hmm! Well, what are we going to do about Myanis Kupela?'

'He remembers!' Skidmore mopped his brow with a serviette. 'Go on, sir! Go on!'

The hostess was quite attached to Eustace. He had kept her in business for some time. Also she understood the life that the Air Marshal liked to live. She bent over and kissed his nose.

'You're a bum,' she whispered.

'Who's a bum?' Eustace chuckled.

Obeying Eustace's order to bomb Myanis Kupela meant finding the wherewithal – namely, a bomb. There were no bombs in the quartermaster's stores, nor were there any bombs in the catalogues that arms firms were sending to the Air Marshal every other day. Eventually a bomb was found by Skidmore who took a trip to Elizabethville in the Congo and bought a 500-pounder from an Irish corporal in the United Nations Peace-Keeping Force.

The bomb was now at Myakajunji airport under guard while Desaix flew out on his first reconnaissance of the target.

As Desaix reached the first of the outlying stockaded villages he braced himself. He had been assured by Skidmore that the Muntu were getting anti-aircraft guns, pom-poms and ground-to-air missiles from the Chinese in Dar-es-Salaam. No flak came up. Leaning over the side of the cockpit he saw people waving to him, children scampering in the Fokker's shadow.

He headed straight for the tower.

Myanis Kupela was the largest of the islands and the stockade was five times larger than the others. If there was going to be any concentration of ground fire it would be from the Muntu capital. Keeping low he flew past the tower, across the square, then climbed. Not a sound. All he had seen was a crowd of Africans waving up at him and twelve ping-pong tables.

'Where did they get that old crate?' Firbank said to himself, as he crouched behind the wall at the top of the tower. 'What a pile of junk.'

'Is it God?' a child tugged at Maud's skirt who was standing in the square with the crowd. 'Is it God coming?'

'Reactionary aircraft overhead!' Bwana Cat's-Eyes hissed into the mouthpiece of the transmitter hidden in the roof of his hut.

Desaix reached 5,000 feet, banked and headed south, back to Myakajunji.

The band at the La Gondola night-club had just finished playing and were packing up their instruments. Eustace looked at Foley from under the sombrero which he had borrowed from the maraccas-player in the band, and yawned.

'Do you want to take her home tonight?'

He nodded at the hostess who was very tired.

'Sir, we must discuss Pilot-Officer Desaix's reconnaissance report,' Foley insisted. 'It changes everything. Myanis Kupela is undefended.'

The hostess fell asleep in her chair. Eustace caught her head as it dropped towards the table.

'Would you like me to put her somewhere more comfortable, Air Marshal?' Foley suggested purposefully. 'Then we can really talk in safety.'

'Just as long as I can find her again,' Eustace warned gravely. 'Love isn't a thing you should lose sight of. I might need her.'

Skidmore and Foley lifted the sleeping hostess.

'Give a hand here, Ace?' Skidmore groaned. 'My truss is twisted.'

Desaix took the hostess's feet and helped his superiors carry her across the dance-floor. The piano's dust-cover was lying behind the instrument so they bundled a pillow up out of it and laid the hostess out.

'Now we can get down to business,' the perspiring Skidmore grinned in the half-light. 'We might even get a decision out of that drunken Kaffir.'

'Quiet!' Foley hissed in the darkness. 'Don't let him hear you talking like that.'

'Well, he makes me sick,' Skidmore muttered under his breath as he got up from his knees. 'It's sheer bloody nepotism him getting that job. What does he know about the aviation business?'

The two senior officers of the Zonkendawon Air Force returned to the table and woke Eustace up. He had been dreaming again. This time his mother was pressing a Molotov cocktail into his hand, the paper stuffed in the neck already alight, and pointing at a doorway. In the doorway stood several young women who were crying. Eustace took the flaming wick out of the Molotov cocktail and drank it.

'Yuk!' he spat. 'Argh!'

'Sir,' Foley leaned forward into the candle-light, 'we must talk about Myanis Kupela. Pilot-Officer Desaix is ready to give his reconnaissance report now.'

Eustace shook himself and looked at his glass.

'Carry on then,' he muttered sorrowfully. 'What a business.'

Foley sat back and nodded to Desaix's chair for him to begin.

The chair was empty.

'Where's Pilot-Officer Desaix?' Foley asked.

In the silence that followed all that could be heard in the darkened, deserted night-club was the sound of laboured breathing. Skidmore put his hands over his eyes.

'Desaix!' Foley shouted. 'Where are you, man? Come out immediately!'

Eustace got unsteadily to his feet and took off the maraccas-player's sombrero. Lurching across to the band-rostrum he placed the sombrero carefully on the cymbals and saw the hostess's feet sticking out from behind the piano.

'Do you still love me?' he inquired softly.

'Of course she does,' Desaix replied breathlessly.

'She's not tired of me? I'm very self-indulgent but that's what all Taureans are like,' Eustace sat down on the drummer's stool and looked into the agitated shadows. 'It's our essential nature to be profligate.'

'Have you found him, sir?' Foley asked tremulously. 'Is that him you're talking to?'

'It is indeed, Wing-Commander,' Eustace replied gravely. 'He is behind the piano.'

'What's he doing there, sir?' Skidmore squeaked. 'Oh God!'

'He is fucking.'

There was a scraping sound as Foley and Skidmore thrust back their chairs and ran across the dance-floor.

'Here, sir, let me handle this!' Foley stood over Desaix. 'I've had about enough!'

'I don't think he has,' Eustace said mildly. 'Sit down.'

Foley bent down and grabbed Desaix by the shirt-collar and tried to lift him up. At the same time as he received a jolting kick in the groin from Desaix, Eustace pulled him back and pointed to the other musicians' stools.

'Sit down, I said. And if I ever see you trying to deliberately wreck the course of true love I'll fire you.'

Foley and Skidmore sat down in the dark, stupefied with bewilderment.

'Now, Bwana Arse,' Eustace addressed the heaving shapes behind the piano, '*kuluma*.'

'Can't it wait?' Desaix gasped.

'Steady up a bit, get into the rhythm section,' Eustace chuckled and kicked the bass drum. 'If you were a Taurean instead of a . . . what was it you said you were?'

'Sagittarius!'

'Yes, well if you were one of us you'd perpetuate the pleasure of perfect love and train yourself to make it last. I make it last, don't I?'

There was a brief discussion behind the piano.

'She says you certainly make it last,' Desaix agreed. 'She says that you have no end and no beginning.'

'I'm all lover,' Eustace feathered the snare-drum. 'Now let's hear this report about the Muntu.'

'Well,' Desaix was breathing more evenly now, 'all that talk about air-defence was so much shit. They've got nothing. No pom-poms, no anti-aircraft guns, no ground-to-air missiles ... they're unarmed.'

Eustace thought for a while and looked across at Skidmore.

'I thought you told me that the C.I.A. were sure that the Chinese had been shipping stuff into the swamps by the truck-load? You said they'd seen launching-pads, gun-emplacements, all that kind of thing.'

Skidmore did not reply.

'I'm talking to you, Squadron-Leader!' Eustace snapped suddenly. 'I want your comments!'

'Sir,' Skidmore said tiredly, 'I can't sit and discuss a serious matter like this under these conditions. I know you don't like red-tape, I know you think this is all a farce.'

'Hush!' Foley whispered. 'For Christ's sake be quiet.'

'No, sir, I've got to speak my mind. How can we sit here talking top-secret business when our only pilot-officer is copulating with the Air Marshal's girl-friend behind the bloody piano?'

'She can be trusted,' Eustace stood up and ran a finger along the keys, 'which is more than I can say for you two.'

Foley went over and stood by Eustace's side.

'He didn't mean that, sir. It's just the drink talking, and the strain of the situation. We are both anxious to get this operation off the ground . . . literally, ha, ha! Yes, quite literally. . . .'

'A couple of cock-sucking careerists!' Eustace thundered on the bass. 'Go to it, Bwana Arse. Change of tempo here!'

'Sir, the Chinese stuff must be still on its way. If we strike now we can be guaranteed a hundred per cent success!' Foley gabbled. 'Think of that! Our first job, whizzo! A hundred per cent!'

'All I saw was a dozen ping-pong tables!' Desaix called up. 'They're undefended! You can't bomb a place like that!'

'What does she say?' Eustace tinkled middle C and a few flats. 'She's an experienced person.'

While the Ace of the Air consulted the hostess Skidmore slid off his stool and started crying in the dark.

'Sir, if the President hears Desaix's reconnaissance report I know he'll want us to move in right away,' Foley rubbed his hands. 'We've got everything on our side.'

'She says what's the point of pushing the Muntu around if they're living in the Bengweulu Swamps? Do you want to live there? Does anybody in their right mind want to live there? They'll all be dead from malaria and black-water fever in two years. Why not leave them alone like they ask?'

Eustace tripped through the treble and crashed the piano-lid shut.

'My thoughts exactly! Exactly! And you, Bwana Arse?'

There was a pause.

'Look, I don't like being called Pilot-Officer particularly, but I prefer it to that . . .'

'Man, I was the one in the Party who stuck up for you. Anyone who believes what John Pyper writes is a mug. Can't you take a joke?'

Desaix was silent for a while, then he spoke up.

'Why waste time and money on what Nature will do for you anyway? Maud Mamuntu won't hurt anyone up there. Africa's big enough for everybody.'

Eustace nodded sagely and looked Foley up and down.

'So you see? Do you? You've heard the wise man speak back there and I agree with him. We can't go dropping bombs on innocent people just because my brother has a swelled head. He was always like that, always bullying. He only gave me this job because he thought he could boss me around. Did you know that?'

Foley's hand twitched. Behind him Skidmore wheezed and coughed, trying to pull himself together.

'No, sir, I don't agree with you. The President has given us our orders and we should carry them out until they're changed.'

'But I'm the Air Marshal. I interpret the order, Wing-Commander!' Eustace peered over the top of the piano. 'Isn't that so, Bwana Arse? That's my function.'

'That's the way it's always been!' Desaix agreed.

'Then we must agree to differ, sir, with respect.'

Eustace frowned at Foley's apologetic smile.

'Oh no, you can't differ, Foley. If I say jump then you just ask "how high?" Isn't that how you like it?'

'I'm trained to obey orders, sir.'

'Right then! How are you getting on down there, Bwana Arse?'

'Working up a storm!'

'Foley! On the drums!' Eustace commanded.

'Sir?'

'This is an order! For once you're going to help with something worthwhile. Give me a two-eight time . . . and you, Skidmore? On your feet you greasy bastard! Grab those maraccas! Take it from me! All right, Bwana Arse? All together now!'

While Foley falteringly dabbed at the pigskin with a solitary drumstick and Skidmore weakly shook his bean-filled canisters, Eustace flung up the piano-lid and ripped off a quick-time version of 'La Vie En Rose'.

Informed sources near to the President were not surprised when his brother Eustace, the Air Marshal, was dismissed from his post and replaced with Mrs Renfrew Mulombe, the President's mother. She had been waiting in the wings for some time, waiting for the right post to fall vacant. It was rumoured that she was the real power behind the President.

Her first order was for the immediate bombing of Myanis Kupela. The Territorials had asked for an air-strike to precede their ground attack.

'Give me four days and an assistant and I'll be ready,' Desaix promised Skidmore. 'Smack on the nose you'll get it, smack!' he crashed a fist into his palm. 'There's a few little repairs need doing to the Fokker, I need a bit of time to train my assistant.'

'Where the hell am I going to get an assistant from? There's no African I know who could give you any help. They're no good on engineering and science.'

Desaix shrugged.

'They've been helping me for long enough. If it wasn't for the Africans I wouldn't be able to keep the Fokker in the air under normal circumstances. They're born technicians, first-class artisans.'

Skidmore looked out of the window and rubbed his stomach.

'This job is upsetting me, Ace, it really is. All this delay. You know what the Air Marshal will say.'

'If she moans about it, tell her to come and fly the mission herself. That'll shut her up.'

'What about this assistant? Where will I find him? Shall we advertise?'

'No, there's no need. I know exactly the man. I can have him down here tomorrow.'

'Where is this rare bird?' Skidmore winced and sat down, his belly thumping on to the desk. 'Ooooh, I'm fed up with this pressure from the top. Why won't they let us get on with the job in our own way?'

Desaix opened the telephone directory and found the number of the Mufunsi Theatre Co-operative.

'He's a stage-carpenter at the moment, a real craftsman.'

'What will he do?'

'Well, I'm going to need a rear-gunner for that pile of junk you've got on the second cockpit, also I'll need a navigator. He's good with his hands and he's done fuselage and wing repairs for me before. He's the perfect man for the job.'

Skidmore picked up the phone and began his twenty-minute wait for the operator to ask him what number he wanted.

'I hope you know what you're doing, Ace. My job's at stake as well as yours.' He grieved, 'It's always the same in a big organization. You never feel secure.'

'Will you allocate me some training space as well, a small room somewhere, a shed, anything will do? I'll need a store for our special equipment that the hangar-staff aren't familiar with, O.K., *bon . . . au revoir*.'

Desaix left the office of the Squadron-Leader and went to the airport bar to think some more.

'So that's where you got to, Maud,' he said to himself. 'I wondered where you'd turn up next.'

10
The Wife of God Marries Again

Desaix L'Ace was an identified flying object. Bwana Cat's-Eyes had sent off a full, detailed description of the plane to Peking via Dar-es-Salaam where a team of experts at the Ministry of Aviation had spent all night poring through pocket reference-books for Chinese boys on how to recognize aircraft by their silhouettes.

'It was a Fokker D.R.1,' Bwana Cat's-Eyes announced to the Muntu Council as they sat on the cathedral floor with the evening light striking down through the windows.

'What is a Fokker?' a member of the Council asked.

The question echoed through the vaulted gloom of the nave. Bwana Cat's-Eyes had always disliked the cathedral. It was distractive. Whenever he gave lectures on rice-planting to the Muntu inside the vast, sentimental building, they always seemed to be thinking about something else. When he sat beneath the sweet-smelling tower – the mud that had been used in its building was full of seeds and odoriferous leaves – and allowed his mind to wander, he often found himself back with his mother and father on the banks of the Yangtse-Kiang. Such nostalgia was a sign of a declining resolve. Homesickness was a luxury that the Chinaman could not afford to cherish.

'It is a fighter-plane designed by a Dutchman, Anthony Herman Fokker, and manufactured in Germany for the Great War of 1914–18. It had an interruptor gear for firing a machine-gun straight through the propeller. This one had an additional cockpit. The original was a single-seater. It was the mount of the ace Baron Manfred von Richtofen.'

Firbank rounded off his display of aeronautical erudition by smiling smugly at Bwana Cat's-Eyes.

'And up yours, you hairless Oriental fink!' he whispered as he sat down. 'There's nothing you can teach the U.S.A. about technology!'

'That is not what flew overhead today,' Maud's voice boomed down the nave. 'Unless I am much mistaken that was Desaix, the man they now call Bwana Arse according to *The Zonkendawon Times*. He is an old friend of mine.'

'You mean you know the guy?' Firbank asked. 'That was a military aircraft carrying national insignia. He was on no joy-ride.'

'What is he doing with a machine-gun?' Bwana Cat's-Eyes inquired meanly. 'Do old friends always bring gifts of that nature to your country?'

'That was no machine-gun, that was his telescope!' Maud chuckled. 'Oh, we had some good times together. He was fun to be with when I knew him. Well, well, old Desaix ... fancy him looking me up after all these years.'

'Telescope? What is he looking for with a telescope?'

Maud squatted down on her hams and her eyes went misty with memories.

'When I knew Bwana Arse he was younger and full of energy and new ideas. There was never a day went past without him thinking up a new scheme. While I was living with him ...'

Firbank's head shot up.

'You lived with him?'

Maud studied the beaten earth of the cathedral floor, her bottom lip hanging slack.

'That was before I met God. Bwana Arse was a good man then, and we called him by his real name, Desaix. It was only recently that I read in The *Zonkendawon Times* of his fall from grace and the terrible name that the people had landed him with. But that was in his nature even then. He was kind to me but his game-spotting safaris were a con from beginning to end. That was where the telescope came in. He would charge tourists a lot of money to fly in his aeroplane and watch the bush for game through the telescope. That was why he put in the extra cockpit.'

'What's so dishonest about that?' Firbank queried. 'People get a kick out of that kind of thing.'

'There was no game. The game had been shot out years ago. He used to send me, his woman and the bearer of his child ...'

'You had a child by him?'

Firbank stalled on his outburst. At the cathedral door, in the square, under the high-altar, everywhere in Myanis Kupela played Maud's offspring. She had had children by the dozen, some of them by God, others by her living and dead husbands. That she should have had a child by the pilot of a Great War triplane should not have been considered extraordinary by any right-thinking individual.

'As I was saying ... he used to send me, this Desaix, off into the bush. When I heard the plane I had to jump out from under the trees and run through open ground while he flew the plane low. Never did he allow me to wear a garment, nothing, he made me run naked through the bush.'

'But he must have had trouble with his customers ...' Firbank started to butt in again.

'He said that he never had any complaints!' Maud said with dignity. 'Men used to come back for a second and third time!'

The Muntu Council murmured their appreciation of Maud's point. They were not quite sure of Firbank's relationship with Maud and they were getting tired of his constant quizzing of their leader's activities. He always had a moral tone, a hint of disapproval.

'So you think he's a friend?' Firbank opened his hands in a gesture of welcome. 'You would trust him?'

Maud got up and rubbed her stupendous thighs.

'I wouldn't trust him with any of my daughters even though he is getting on in years; but I would trust him not to hurt me, or my people. There were many little criticisms I could make of him, shady sides of his character, but he was sick of killing. He was in many wars. He was in Spain when they had their civil war, he was a young man then. He dropped bombs, so he told me. Then he was with the French Air Force in the last white man's big war and he saw much killing. When that was over he went to Indo-China to fight the Communists.'

Bwana Cat's-Eyes tightened his already-tight lips and said nothing.

'By the time he came to Africa he had sworn off killing like he has tried to swear off drink. With the killing he was more successful.'

Firbank took Maud's hand.

'What you're saying is that you like this guy, isn't it?'

'Yes, I like old Desaix, Bwana Arse, call him what you like. I felt sorry for him.'

Firbank and Bwana Cat's-Eyes both spoke at once.

'I'm afraid that I'm going to have to disillusion you,' said Firbank dramatically, as he prepared to deliver his analysis of the threat to Myanis Kupela. 'I think he was on reconnaissance. Mulombe is moving against you.'

'He is only the first of many. Never trust a man who has fought against the legitimate aspirations of the People,' Bwana Cat's-Eyes chimed over the American's drawl. 'You are going to be besieged.'

Maud married Firbank and Bwana Cat's-Eyes that afternoon at an impressive ceremony in the cathedral which she conducted herself. It was her way of showing gratitude to the two men who had shown her the danger that was approaching Myanis Kupela. Both men were overwhelmed by their destiny. For totally different reasons they went through with the marriage and did not try to escape. Bwana Cat's-Eyes had been instructed by his government to exploit the political situation to the full regardless of any indignity to his person, and Firbank had to admit that he felt closer to his personal god than at any time before. The only part of the afternoon that demoralized them both was when Maud decided that Bwana Cat's-Eyes should give Firbank away, as his father wasn't around, and vice versa. There was hardly a dry eye in the crowd as the tall, bronzed American walked up the aisle with the Chinaman on his arm.

'I see him!' Maud hollered from the altar. 'I see the bridegroom as he cometh leaping and skipping upon the hills.'

Fifty drums thundered under the roof as the Muntu answered her.

'He is blessed among men!'

'He is my eyes! He is my ears! He heard the armies coming from afar off so we are ready!'

'Sondela! Sondela!'

Maud was always happy when she was marrying a new husband, and even happier when she was marrying two new husbands. Today she smiled, strutted before the high altar, put feathers and flowers in her hair and wore the finest beaded apron in her collection. Over her vast magnificence she rubbed the oil of the *mufundwelaba* tree until she shone and rippled. In her ears she hung two of Bwana Cat's-Eyes' ping-pong clamps.

But she was not really happy.

Women of warm heart treasure their old loves. Every new lover has in him something of the old, and evocation of youthful ecstasies is as good a stimulant to the cooling passions of the later years as anything else. When a man betrays a woman during the course of their affair then he is either cast out or forgiven – the matter is handled there and then. Once dismissed it might be thought that the man is free of all responsibilities, he can conduct his life in his own fashion and forget whatever strictures were laid on him by his ex-mistress. This is true as long as he does not adversely affect the memories that he has left behind. If an affair breaks up by mutual consent, or in such a way as to leave both parties without bitterness against each other, then the woman's recollection of the sweet times will grow sweeter as the years pass. Maud had always remembered Desaix. Now, if she met him face to face, she would forgive his baldness, forgive his corpulence, forgive his battered features, forgive his heavy drinking...

But not what he had done to her memories. He had raised his hand against their past together. By working for the downfall of Maud and Myanis Kupela he had made an old and cherished love a mockery.

At the wedding breakfast the bride and grooms exchanged gifts. Maud gave Bwana Cat's-Eyes an embroidered waistcoat and received in return a consignment of arms which was parachuted into the square. Firbank watched jealously as his counterpart broke open the padded crates and showed Maud and the Muntu the arms and ammunition that his friends had sent all the way from Peking. There were automatic rifles, machine-pistols, mortars, an anti-tank rocket-launcher, hand-grenades.

'Everything you need,' Bwana Cat's-Eyes bowed, enjoying Firbank's envy from the cover of his red-starred forage cap.

'Everything WE need,' Maud reminded Bwana Cat's-Eyes. 'You're one of the family now.'

'And happy to be so, honourable wife,' the Chinaman curtsied.

Firbank was given a set of well-used wooden dominoes with a chipped double-three.

'Well,' he smiled ruefully, his frank blue eyes lowered, 'I can't match our Oriental friend's munificence here, but I sure want to let you good folks know how I feel about this fabulous gift my wife has given me. You see, I'm a plain man – I have to speak my mind. I haven't got any big Daddy behind me like our friend here, not unless you call our God that – yes, OUR God for I have been sincerely converted to your way of thinking – but I can say that I believe in honestly expressing my own viewpoint and when I look at what Maud has given me in her wonderful innocence, I feel mighty touched. It's a game I don't play, hell, I don't play games! But the symbolism! The aptness! The white spots on a black background, eh? That really somethin'! Isn't that Africa? Isn't that the whites on the dark continent? The pestilence, the plague, the white-spotted fever? Isn't that what this war is all about? Now hear this, folks – your God, the Husband of Maud, the Muntu saviour, is the old god of old Africa as she was – black through to the holy backbone and breathing bloody fire! He hasn't been kitted out in European frills and bows, He's no milky babe in a manger man! He's dynamite! He's the big one! He's a bucket of blood and a spit like a waterspout! He's strong and powerful, He's all elephant! And there's not a white spot on Him, no, sir! Not one speck! He's clean through and through! These simple wooden playthings [here he rattled the dominoes] are the bones of colonial Africa! They're the finger-bones, the toe-bones, the neck-bones, the knee-bones of the old slavish god that the missionaries stuffed down your throats! We're holding that submissive god here, in the palm of my hand! We have him!'

He held the box of dominoes aloft and shook it. The Muntu stared at the American whose face was now radiating a strange fervour.

'With this kind of god you can fight no battles. He wants you to give in to every damned autocrat fascist bastard that comes along and kicks your ass! He'd have you surrender to Mulombe right here and now! He lives on weakness and he'll destroy you good people, he'll have you eaten up by the unholy! But OUR God! He says fight! Fight! And die if need be!'

Firbank threw the dominoes on the ground. The box split and the dominoes were scattered. The Muntu murmured, their eyes on the American. Maud tightened her lip but did not interrupt.

'He's gone! To hell with the old ways and the slave-god! Our God will be saved by a man's sacrifice, by him laying down his life and fighting. We will save God! God has guts! God is guts! He'll stick up for us if we'll stick up for Him! Who's afraid of dying now? Death is our God's friend!'

This speech was all that Firbank gave Maud for a wedding present. The Muntu had listened open-mouthed, many of them stirred and excited by the American's rhetoric. When it was over he marched over to where Maud was sat and stood to attention, making sure that his boots kicked the dust into the face of Bwana Cat's-Eyes who had ingratiated himself into a position curled up at her feet.

'Captain Firbank at your service, ma'am. I request permission to prepare God's people for the defence of their faith.'

Maud rubbed her broad nose with a finger and regarded the buzzing crowd. They were with the American heart and soul. They wanted to fight. She had never seen them this way before.

'One thing,' she reflected, 'one thing you must promise.'

'Anything you want,' Firbank threw open his arms. 'If it is impossible, even then it will be done.'

'You must never take my people from me.'

There was a sadness in Maud's eyes as she listened to Firbank's clipped reply. As the American went back among the crowd and Bwana Cat's-Eyes went down to join him in distributing weapons to the men, she seemed to be far away.

11
Ptyelus Grossus

The move from Balyete Camp up the Great North Road to Chimbusu was held up by all the sergeants, plus Sergeant-Major Loudwater, Second-Lieutenant Tarzan Cool Guy and Doctor Russell, being court-martialled and sentenced to a week's solitary confinement for indecent exposure. Marge, Marilyn and Margaret from the Tonga Bar had been unable to make a contribution to the theatrical experiment and were only adjudged to be accessories after the fact. While Balyete Camp was changed from a basic training establishment to a military prison for the week's duration (Major Powderham altered the board outside and closed the gates), the women had to live in a bell-tent pitched outside the wire fence. Inside the military prison life went on much as usual except that everyone was in single cells. These single cells were just any room unit that could take a man and members of the National Territorial Emergency Force found themselves sitting in coal-bunkers, laundries, pantries and disused baking ovens. As there were no locks on the doors and inadequate supervision, they soon crept out and enjoyed a week's idleness together. It was during this time that Johnny McSilver organized his first football match between the circumcised and the uncircumcised.

Meanwhile Colonel Vaal Rembrandt was having more trouble with the local Party. They could not understand his mania for rigid discipline.

'If it was not for the fact that the air-attack on Myanis Kupela and these treacherous Muntu has had to be postponed for a few days, we would be in serious *mulandu* with Doctor Mulombe. Delay, delay, delay! Is this your famous British Army system? While we wait, they are getting stronger.'

Mr Vapour Mutale sat in his car looking at the gates of the military prison. Beside him sat Colonel Vaal Rembrandt while

Fines Chingola and Major Powderham occupied the back seat. The Regional Secretary was slowly losing his grip on the situation.

'We must maintain discipline at all cost,' Rembrandt replied coolly. 'There's no point in thinking that a man will obey instructions that may lead to his death if he doesn't respect the authority behind those instructions.'

Mr Vapour Mutale watched the football game through the wire fence. It had an unreal air, like a mirage.

'And those are the men who are in prison?' he shook his head. 'To me, an ordinary fellow, they look as though they are playing football.'

'Army orders, sir. Prisoners must be exercised regularly. It's in the manual. And their minds have to be exercised as well. We're having a one-act play competition tonight in the sergeants' mess. Sergeant Kovary has a new work that he wants to try out and I'm doing the first act of *The Boy Friend*. Perhaps you'd like to come?'

Rembrandt's sincere invitation, pleasantly offered, was snubbed by the Party men. They were under the hammer from H.E. and only wanted to achieve one objective – to get Rembrandt and his host out of their territory on to the Great North Road. Then the responsibility for acting as commissar to the Territorials would pass on to another Party group.

'What are you going to do with these women?' Fines pointed at the bell-tent and the three scantily-clad bodies sunbathing on the grass verge.

'They will be working with Doctor Russell in the Medical Unit. We have an ambulance and field hospital,' Major Powderham explained. 'Even though we are not anticipating many casualties we are well prepared.'

Mr Vapour Mutale looked at his watch.

'We have a Party card inspection in twenty minutes and we must go.' He paused, weighing his words carefully. 'Colonel, can I tell the President that you will *definitely* be leaving for Chimbusu tomorrow?'

'Yes, that's right. Tomorrow. We can't see any hold-ups ... can we, Major? Nothing to stop us leaving on schedule is there?'

'No, sir, well, things do have a way of going wrong even in the best of organizations, yes, that's so ... the best-laid plans of mice and men ... but no, sir, not at all.'

'I'm asking for a guarantee, Colonel, a guarantee!' Mr Vapour Mutale seethed. 'Please say you'll be gone in two days! Please!'

Rembrandt turned to Major Powderham.

'Prepared to put your head on a block?'

'They're a good bunch, sir. They'll lend a hand after this little lesson, be more tractable, yes, sure of it. Great team we've got there.'

As this was as near to a commitment as Mr Vapour Mutale could obtain from the officers, he had to be satisfied. Fines took the empty tea-cups back to the bell-tent and thanked the ladies. As he poked his head into the tent, looking for Marge who had just gone inside, the chihuahua sprang from his lair and bit him.

'Are you taking that thing with you?' he managed to say as he stemmed the bleeding with a handkerchief.

'Of course. He'd never stay in kennels. The little darling can get through the holes in the wire-mesh,' Marge cuddled the raging pygmy to her breast. 'We've got to take him with us.'

Fines smiled thankfully.

'Madam,' he said with measured sincerity, 'I am glad that I am not a Muntu.'

The survivors of the campaign against the Muntu still reminisce about the last night at Balyete Camp. If you could track them down in their retirement, catch them in a loquacious, nostalgic mood, and whisper *Fergus Bull* in their ear, they would, for a couple of pints of brandy and orange, roll up their sleeves, show their scars and tell you how they got them on the last night at Balyete Camp when they had the one-act play competition.

Rembrandt's show, the first act of the twenties' musical, *The Boy Friend*, opened the programme. Being men of the world, the sergeants knew that it was a load of sentimental bullshit, that reality wasn't like that, but they gave it a good reception. Rembrandt tended to overact and wouldn't stop playing with his hair – a habit that irritated the audience – and Powderham as the female lead was stiff, awkward and never really got to the heart of the rôle; but there was a lot of sympathy for the officers and the show gave the impression of having much time and effort put into it – so they gave it a standing ovation.

Kovary's new play was a very different kettle of fish. It was certainly the best thing that he had ever written. It was taut, well-made, concise, economical in its use of language, credible, pertinent, avoided sentiment and diversions and was about a Gaelic hero who fucks a cow.

Humphrey had spent two days sitting alone with the script in the officers' billiard-room (his solitary cell) before deciding to do the part. What decided him in favour of the adventure was the fact that people do get emotionally involved with the beasts of the field. It was a real situation. He remembered cases in the outlying farms around Fishguard, and Kovary's work was based on an actual case in Kendal, a newspaper-clipping of the court proceedings having been sent the playwright by his doting mother. Since it was a subject which deployed the human psyche, drew on love, desire, ambition and Man's animal self, then it was obviously a fit subject for theatre, the most social of all art forms.

In *Fergus Bull*, the opening is very much in the genre of sound naturalistic works like Ibsen's *Wild Duck*. The man, a pick-swinging piss-artist, well past his prime, is sitting alone in his lodgings reading a girlie magazine. His wife and children are in Ireland, and have been for twenty years while Dad worked the roads, the Mersey Tunnel, the Victoria line and Ford's foundry at Dagenham. He has provided for them all this time, keeping only enough for his digs and a few pints on a Friday night. Yet he reads in his magazine that he is no longer a man. The world has changed around him.

The wanker's-manual tells him that unless he earns 15,000 dollars a year, is under thirty-five, drives a fast car and is capable of five ejaculations a night, he shouldn't be reading the magazine in the first place, and in the second place he's a second-rate sexual citizen. He goes out and gets drunk, very upset at being emasculated. Tottering along a country road afterwards he sees a cow in a moonlit field. It has a beautiful face, big brown eyes and an udder like the girl in the gate-fold of the girlie magazine. There is a box in the hedge that once held oranges from Israel. The navvy takes it into the field and approaches the cow. The cow smiles at him enigmatically. The navvy tells the cow that he loves it. The cow nods its head and adopts a pose of lubricous invitation, its tongue hanging out and big liquid eyes begging for love. Fergus Bull stands on his box and prepares to fulfil his dream, but before he does so he has a speech to deliver. It was the point in the play which Kovary had taken most time over; it represented his basic interpretation of the human dilemma:

FERGUS BULL: Now, Miss September ... Jesus, Mary and Joseph, what'll become of me immortal soul ... back up now, steady there. Am I above the beasts now? God, we're all Life aren't we? ... Whoa there! Steady, girl ... if only mother could see me now she'd understand ... (he crosses himself) God forgive me for this terrible sin but he made Man to want to stay a man and I'm damned if I'm being left behind by Progress!

Before accepting the part Humphrey had insisted on Kovary allowing him to use a wooden dildo for the actual screwing of the herbivore, also that a cow should be found that had calved a few times so Humphrey wouldn't have too much difficulty with stage-business. The stage-carpenter made a beautiful dildo on his lathe before he went down to join Desaix in Myakajunji and a suitable animal was borrowed off a local cattle-rancher.

Up until this critical stage in the play, Humphrey had kept the audience in the palm of his hand. They were with him all the way. The predicament of Fergus Bull was that of Everyman when faced with the cruel commercial barons of sexual fantasy. Humphrey made his speech, with telling effect, then brought the dildo out of his corduroy trousers. In the half-light he stabbed at the cow's backside. There were tears in many eyes as the navvy poked to find the entrance of his Aladdin's cave. The cow stamped nervously and shifted. Humphrey grabbed its tail to keep it still.

Kovary was in the wings, delighted with the reception that the play had received so far. He was really getting through to the sergeants, building them up, re-creating them as men. Then he heard Humphrey use an unscripted word.

'... steer.'

The cow lowered its head and bawled. The word came again.

'D'you think you're riding a bike?' a wag shouted from the audience.

'It's a steer!' Humphrey said in a loud stage-whisper.

'What's a steer?' Kovary called out as the cow charged off-stage and knocked him into the back-drop.

'It's a bull with no balls!' Humphrey roared, purple in the face. 'You ignorant Jew bastard!'

'You could have made do with its arse!' Kovary complained as the steer reversed over him, desperately trying to find a way out. 'You've ruined the *moment critique*!'

Kovary was a strong man. He had been a P.T. instructor in the Israeli army. Grabbing the steer by the horns he wrestled with it and backed the beast on to the stage where Humphrey was still on top of the box with the dildo. The Welshman was crying, big tears rolling down his face. As the steer's rump came within striking distance he let out a scream of rage and kicked it. The beast bucked and Kovary was tossed to the ground, still holding on to its horns.

The audience had been carefully brought to a peak of excitement by Kovary's skilful word-play. He had exploited their weaknesses, their innermost secrets, tapped the strange places of their subconscious desires. They were left high and dry, completely unsatisfied. One man stood up and gave a strangled, incomprehensible cry before rushing up the aisle, snatching the dildo out of Humphrey's hand and hitting him on the head with it.

'You impotent bastard!' he raged. 'You hopeless idiot!'

Soon the stage was a mass of fighting men. The steer collapsed under the sheer weight of bodies as the sergeants jumped on its back, rugger-tackled its hind-legs. The steer bellowed, threshed around, pissed itself with fright. Kovary wriggled out from beneath the mêlée and ran down into the audience, taking a seat. It was superb. Kovary had at last won through to the inner man. For the first time he had galvanized people into action, not the insincere clapping of the classical-music concert-goer, not the polite toleration of the tourist audience, but the full-blooded response of a mass of screaming, fighting, crazy men who were determined that the play should reach its proper consummation. As Humphrey was dragged over to the pinned steer and forced to screw the heaving animal with his splintered dildo, Kovary made up his mind. He was good enough. The time had come. In later years when he was a successful playwright in London's West End, he looked back to the last night at Balyete Camp as being the turning-point in his career.

To the overwhelming relief of Mr Vapour Mutale, the National Territorial Emergency Force left Balyete Camp at 1400 hours the next day. Their departure had been scheduled for 600 hours but the Medical Unit and field hospital had been employed full-time in treating cuts, bruises, breaks and black eyes all morning, getting the sergeants ready for their 600-mile journey to Chimbusu.

Colonel Vaal Rembrandt travelled with his officers. As the column drove along he briefed them on the strategy that he was going to employ to reduce Myanis Kupela and the Muntu rebellion.

'Basically the terrain is tank-country, great for heavy armour,' he tapped the map with a pencil.

Tarzan Cool Guy was doubtful as to whether he should interrupt his commanding officer on a tiny point of detail. Up until now he had not made much of an impression on Colonel Vaal Rembrandt. He suspected that the Colonel thought of him as a mere political appointment whose presence would have to be tolerated while the professionals got down to the task of achieving the Force's objective. So he did not speak, holding back the essential information he had until an opportunity arose in the future.

'As we have no tanks ... ha! ha! ha! ... it might appear that this isn't much of an advantage, but we have made arrangements with the Open Pit Manager to borrow some of his D8 bulldozers, suitably converted for military use, and with these we'll be able to provide cover and support for our infantry advance and penetrate their defences. These stockades are only wood, you know, we'll go through them like a dose of salts. The Open Pit Manager, Mr Hammerkop, you might know him, knowing the nature of the terrain around Myanis Kupela, has especially requested that we use certain of our Territorials to drive these D8 bulldozers. I believe there's a chap called Matthias and a group of African fellows who used to work with the Bucket-Wheel Excavator ... they're familiar with this heavy earth-moving equipment ... so they'll be responsible for manning our armoured division, eh? Good, now we come to the problem of ...'

'Sir,' Tarzan Cool Guy said hesitantly, 'I don't want to interrupt ...'

'Then don't ... ha! ha! ... that's the best way,' Rembrandt crackled sarcastically. 'We've got a lot to get through, Lieutenant.'

'I know the area round Bengweulu, sir.'

'Even better. You can be the first patrol ... what about that? Earn your keep, eh?'

Tarzan Cool Guy wrestled with his conscience. He would have preferred to keep quiet but the thought of the tactical errors that were about to be made gave him the necessary courage.

'It's swamp, sir, miles and miles of swamp. There's a few islands and that's all. A bulldozer will never get across.'

Major Powderham snorted and looked at his colonel.

'He knows better than we do, sir. After all, he's a native ... yes, he's a native all right. Lieutenant! What do you take us for? These maps were drawn up by the cartographical section of the colonial survey office and each section of the country was covered inch by inch – on foot! Have you walked through Bengweulu?'

'I couldn't even if I wanted to, sir, I'd drown!' Tarzan Cool Guy expostulated. 'The map's wrong, sir.'

'Lieutenant,' Rembrandt folded up the map, his face pale with anger, 'I suggest that you speak when you're spoken to in future. You've got a lot to learn about soldiering.'

Chimbusu was a hot, dry valley lying between a range of low hills and the Great North Road. There was no particular reason to give the place a name as there was nothing there but thorn scrub, a dried-up stream and a few tattered, shadeless trees. When Rembrandt's column arrived, the National Army was already encamped. Rembrandt consulted with the senior officer and suggested that his force deploy themselves a little way distant from the regular soldiers.

'I'm not saying that your chaps would corrupt my fellows, far from it, but we've managed to get a real sense of regimental pride into these part-timers and I don't want that being adversely affected. You know what regulars are like.'

The sad Colonel of the National Army regulars did know what regulars were like. They were not like National Army regulars. For two years he had been on loan from the British Pioneer Corps, originally sent out to Central Africa to train a cadre of officers in simple construction work such as digging mass latrines. One by one his colleagues had been sent home with nervous breakdowns as they tried to teach the African soldiery the rudiments of the art of war. The sad Colonel did not have a nervous breakdown because he had a friend, and he was too unimaginative to admit defeat. He poured Rembrandt a glass of his friend.

'We've been told to hold on here a while. Did they tell you?'

Rembrandt studied his drink.

'What's this stuff?'

'Zonkendawon whisky. It's terrible.'

Rembrandt put the glass down with a shudder.

'Why have we got to wait?' he asked, staring at the bright yellow liquid.

'Somebody has snitched on Mulombe to the United Nations. I think it was his brother, you know him, the one who used to be Air Marshal before the President's mother. He trotted over to Elizabethville and told them U.N. boys there what we were going to do to Myanis Kupela. With the trouble they've got in the Congo next door they'll probably just throw us in with the rest and billet a few battalions of Irishmen here.'

The sad Colonel drank his whisky and grimaced.

'I don't know why I drink this stuff,' he murmured glumly. 'I'm sure it's not good for one.'

'Have you seen any bulldozers?'

The sad Colonel grinned momentarily. He had seen some bulldozers. They were being transported up the Great North Road by a Mr Hammerkop who seemed to be in the best of spirits as he led the giant transporters up the dirt highways towards Myanis Kupela. He had stopped for a drink with the sad Colonel.

'Where's he leaving the bulldozers?'

'On the edge of the hostile territory. He says it will only be one hour's drive from there to Myaṇis Kupela. Those big things will do fifteen miles an hour, you know.'

Rembrandt poured his whisky on to the floor under the table and bade the sad Colonel good-night. Except for the delay, everything was going to plan.

By noon the next day the temperature in the shade at Chimbusu was 102°. The sun hung in the sky like a flame-thrower, burning up the air. Under canvas, the Territorials sat, waited and sweated. There was nothing to do.

The only person who was not wasting his life away was Dennis. As soon as they had arrived at Chimbusu he had recognized it as a place with the correct environmental conditions for his leaf-eating beetle. As there were so few leaves in the valley it would reduce the work necessary to locate them. Leaving his companions to their thoughts and curses he slipped away from the camp with his killing-bottle and started to scrutinize the tattered trees for his prize. By the time night fell he was seven miles away and still going strong. Sergeant-Major Loudwater discovered that he was missing at roll-call before the evening meal.

'Where's Sergeant Dennis?'

There was a silence.

'Well, where is he?'

'He's gone looking for beetles.'

It was Doctor Russell who had spoken. Dennis had borrowed some ether from his medical supplies before setting out on his hunt.

'Will he be back soon?' Loudwater's eyes sagged, 'I'll have to fiddle the register for him.'

'He didn't say when he'd be back,' Doctor Russell replied.

Loudwater fiddled the register and reported Dennis as present. The same evening the United Nations Fact-Finding Mission arrived from Elizabethville in the Congo by helicopter. After an hour with the sad Colonel and Rembrandt they flew on to Myakajunji to see Molumbe and entered into negotiations with him over the safety of the Muntu. When the negotiations started the Fact-Finding Mission had found enough facts to convince them that the Muntu were an oppressed minority group struggling to protect their beliefs against an autocratic Party organization. By the time they left the capital in their helicopter they had turned up additional facts, mainly in discussion with Doctor Mulombe and the cabinet, that had proved to them that the Muntu were mere puppets of the People's Republic of China, a dangerous group of suicidal activists, Communist to a man, who were trying to undermine the democratic and humane government of an enlightened freedom-fighter. They asked Doctor Mulombe to delay his campaign against Myanis Kupela for a further two days to give them time to cable the United Nations headquarters in New York and get a committee to agree to ignore the forthcoming attack. Doctor Mulombe concurred. With world opinion on his side he was more than pleased with the outcome of his brush with the guardians of peace.

By the time Sergeant-Major Loudwater took the morning roll-call Dennis had still not returned. Marge and Tarzan Cool Guy were worried sick and had not slept all night.

'You don't think he's skipped, done a bunk, do you?' Loudwater felt the top of his pointed head. 'I hope to Christ the silly little bugger hasn't gone awol. That's desertion when you're on active service and that's what we're on – no matter what it looks like.'

'He'd never leave me,' Marge's mascara was running and her eyes were red with weeping. 'He's just got lost somewhere. Can't we go and look for him?'

'If we do that then we've got to tell those two,' Loudwater jerked his head at Rembrandt's tent, 'and you know what they'll do to him.'

Dennis was lost. When darkness fell he had examined his last tree by the light of a match, then walked on until he found a patch of soft earth. Tired with his exertions he had fallen asleep almost immediately, unconscious of the fretting of his friends back at Chimbusu. He had not found his beetle but his day alone in the bush had been full of rewards. He had encountered old comrades in science; plants, fungi, small animals, birds, all the well-known, comprehensible part of Africa's pattern of life. After his spell at Balyete Camp it was like going home to people whom he knew and loved. The bush was sane, full of unexplored mysteries but even those had the attraction of being knowable. His beetle was there, he could find it, pin it down, study it – which was more than he could do with Marge and Tarzan Cool Guy.

During the night it rained – not on the rest of mankind but on Dennis only. He was sleeping beneath the Rain Tree, *mufundwelamba*. In its leaves sat Dennis's beetle, a species of froghopper now called *Ptyelus grossus*, belonging to the order Hemiptera, and it was his dream that was showering him with cooling moisture. The beetles, when immature, cover themselves with a light froth for protection. They obtain this, and their nourishment, by piercing the wood and leaves of the tree with their stylets, a prehensile mouthpart, and sucking up sap at great speed, ejecting the pure water equally fast. This causes the rain.

'Here is the man who has been looking for us,' they sang, as they squirted their capillary jets on to the sleeping man. 'He has come a long way. Is it wise for a man to pursue a beetle like us – are we exceptional? Or should he go after his own sort, those he can understand? What does he want us for? To stick us in his killing-bottle.'

All night long *Ptyelus grossus* worked on Dennis until he was soaked to the skin and the ground about him pitted with the impact of their rain. In his dreams Dennis smiled and clutched his killing-bottle close to his chest, not aware that he was being pissed on by what he held most dear.

Sergeant-Major Loudwater was forced to report Dennis missing on the third day because he heard on the radio that the United Nations had rejected the U.S.S.R.'s demand for armed intervention in the Muntu dispute and accused the Russians of acting as a mouthpiece for the Red Chinese. Doctor Mulombe had a free hand.

'He's been gone a while, sir. I didn't like to bother you.'

'Have you gone mad, Loudwater? Mad! A soldier deserts his post and you don't bother to tell me? You're mad, sir, mad!'

A search-party was raised and while Sergeant-Major Loudwater was being court-martialled for neglect of duty and reduced to the ranks, they set out to look for the missing biologist. They found him only a few miles from Chimbusu, striding vigorously along with a healthy tan and a twinkle in his eye. When he was brought back to camp he met Private Loudwater (now the only private in the National Territorial Emergency Force), who was doing clean-up work in the prisoner's compound which had been hurriedly erected for Dennis's arrival. Without more ado Colonel Vaal Rembrandt and Major Powderham mounted a drum-head court-martial and opened the case for the prosecution.

'You expect us to accept as a valid reason for desertion, that you went out looking for beetles? We are waiting here, Sergeant, waiting here for an order that will send us into battle. Human life, sir, is at stake, and you go off looking for beetles?'

Rembrandt played with his long hair.

'This is the worst case I've ever tried, eh, Powderham?'

'No doubt, sir, yes, ridiculous. I don't believe him anyway. He's been somewhere where he's had good care taken of him. He's looking better than ever I've seen him, yes, he's hitched a lift somewhere.'

'And did you find your damned beetle?' Rembrandt asked sarcastically.

'Yes, sir!' Dennis replied gaily. 'I did.'

'Well, I'd like to have a look at it ... eh, Powderham? Let's have a look at this damned nuisance, eh?'

'I haven't brought one back with me, sir. They asked me not to.'

Rembrandt studied the prisoner warily.

'Sergeant, you're not a drinking companion of the Colonel who commands the regulars, are you? That's not where you've been? You haven't been on that stuff he drinks, have you?'

'I don't drink often, sir, only to keep company.'

'So the beetles asked you to leave them where they were then?' Rembrandt scoffed. 'That's what you want me to believe?'

'Yes, sir. They said they were perfectly happy on the Tree of Life.'

'The Tree of Life, eh? Who wouldn't be happy there?' Powderham sniggered. 'Some people have all the damned luck.'

'Oh, they know how lucky they are,' Dennis said eagerly. 'They know that they're fortunate insects. Not that I found them at all exclusive or jealous, far from it, but just aware of the honour that had been done to their particular species of frog-hopper. They seemed to be very generous and asked me to bring some of my friends round the next time I paid them a visit.'

Colonel Vaal Rembrandt sentenced Dennis to be shot.

When Madge heard the news she grabbed Tarzan Cool Guy and made him demand an interview with Rembrandt to plead for Dennis's life.

'It's not fair, sir!' Tarzan Cool Guy said firmly. 'It's a travesty.'

'Spell it, Lieutenant,' Powderham sneered.

'F-A-R-E.'

'I meant "travesty", Lieutenant.'

Tarzan Cool Guy could not spell 'travesty'.

When the wrestler confessed his failure to Marge she had a fit of temper and ran off into the bush crying. She was not to know how determined Rembrandt and Powderham were to maintain discipline at all cost, nor how they resented being made to look foolish by Dennis's account of his conversation with *Ptyelus grossus*.

'You just want to get rid of him like they do!' she screamed at her confused lover when he came to find her, guided by her sobbing.

'Why should I want to get rid of old Dennis?'

'So you won't have to mow the lawn, your heartless bastard!'

Marge beat frenziedly at Tarzan Cool Guy's chest and cried on until she was in hysterics.

'I love him, poor Dennis ... oh, you brute! You calculating *inja*! You had this all worked out!'

'I wouldn't hurt Dennis!' Tarzan Cool Guy protested. 'He's done nothing to me. We get along all right for God's sake!'

'Then save him!'

'How?'

'I didn't ask you how to do it when I saved you, did I? It's about time you Africans started thinking for yourselves!' Marge snapped, suddenly composed. 'And if you don't save him then I want nothing more to do with you!'

Tarzan Cool Guy returned to the camp and went straight to Rembrandt's tent to try and get him to be merciful. When he reached the entrance he heard Matthias's voice. Peeping through a flap he saw the Bucket-Wheel Excavator Gang drawn up in front of the Colonel.

'You want us to shoot Dennis?'

Matthias was echoing the sentiment of all the Bucket-Wheel Excavator Gang. Shock, horror, rage, insult was written all over their faces.

'I'm ordering you to shoot him,' Rembrandt made the nice distinction. 'It's not on offer.'

'But he's our friend. How can we shoot him?'

'Because if you don't I'll shoot you.'

'But that is barbaric.'

'You are barbarians.'

'Why not ask somebody else?' Matthias pleaded.

'An execution of this sort has to be done by the prisoner's comrades-in-arms. It's an old British Army tradition.'

'This isn't the British Army, sir.'

'You're telling me!'

The saving of life is the only true grace that war has; a grace that would not be necessary if war never happened. It brings out the best in people; all their courage, ingenuity and audacity. All the medals for valour are given to those who save life; they are awards for grace and not brutality. When Tarzan Cool Guy walked away from the tent, his mind entered into a state that was recognizably gracious – he had had an idea that would keep his patron, friend and provider alive.

Gathering the Black and White Minstrel Show together some distance from the camp he explained his plan.

He had noticed that both Rembrandt and Powderham were heavy smokers. He got Humphrey and Kovary to roll two full twenty-packets of joints using the best grass in their fumidor, modelling the cigarettes on the brands used by the officers. They were instructed to swop them for their mild Virginia originals while lunch was on.

'I've told the sergeants running the kitchens to make a really hot vindaloo curry for tomorrow. That'll get their jackets off. Make the switch then, they won't notice,' he said, then turned to the Bucket-Wheel Excavator Gang. 'Now we come to you.'

'We cannot shoot our friend yet we don't want to be shot.

We are in a quandary,' a member of the gang said thoughtfully. 'We could shoot the Colonel, I suppose.'

Tarzan Cool Guy dismissed this suggestion and told the Bucket-Wheel Excavator Gang that the best way they could miss a stationary target would be for them to aim straight at it.

'If you keep him in your sights, with your past record at the rifle range, he'll be all right,' he told them.

The Bucket-Wheel Excavator Gang scratched their heads.

'We once clipped the edge of the outer ring,' one of them said in worried tones.

'Yes, but it wasn't the man's target. He was shooting at the one next to it. There's nothing to be nervous about. Dennis will be at least ten feet away and none of you have a cat in Hell's chance of hitting him.'

'Perhaps if we shut our eyes?' came the helpful suggestion. 'Private Loudwater instructed us to close one eye and squint down the barrel – why not shut the other?'

Tarzan Cool Guy held up his hands to stem the flow of imaginative ideas. They were complicating the issue.

'No! We don't want any unknown factors in this business. With your eyes shut you might hit him by chance. With them open he's as safe as houses.'

Doctor Russell was agog with excitement when he heard about Dennis's statement at the court-martial and he readily agreed to pronounce the doomed man dead after he had not been shot.

'I will be allowed to talk to him before we don't bury him, won't I?'

'There'll be plenty of time for talk afterwards,' Tarzan Cool Guy said heavily, 'but just make it look good for the Colonel. First things first.'

Doctor Russell tickled the insides of his nostrils with the tip of his beard.

'Livingstone mentioned these beetles, too, you know? He probably met them as well. Maybe that's why he was delirious in the final stages of that last journey – not malaria at all . . . a vision.' Doctor Russell continued enthusiastically, his brown eyes shining. 'Holy God, this is exciting, isn't it?'

'Handle him like he's a dead man. You must have handled corpses before, Doctor?'

'Oh, hundreds, hundreds. You've got no worries there.'

'And no whispering questions at him while you're at it, eh? Promise?'

'But he said the Tree of Life! The Tree of Life! I told you it was here somewhere. When can I talk to him? When can we discuss it in detail?'

'After he's dead,' Tarzan Cool Guy said in a low voice.

At three o'clock the following afternoon Dennis was blindfolded and led out of the prisoner's enclosure by four of the sergeant ex-sergeant-majors. They marched beside the stumbling man, tight-lipped, their eyes fixed straight ahead.

'I didn't know I had to wear this blindfold before I got to the place of execution,' Dennis chuckled indulgently. 'Bit silly, isn't it?'

'We're just obeying orders,' a member of the escort whispered. 'The Colonel just said you had to be blindfolded. He didn't tell us when so we thought we'd better make sure and do it from the start.'

Dennis laughed aloud, his fine teeth bared.

'What's he trying to prove?'

'He said it was customary. The condemned man isn't supposed to see what is happening.'

Dennis's shoulders shook as he guffawed.

'Isn't that typical? Is he saying that I'm not being executed because I can't see? I've got to be executed. It's justice!'

The escort halted, nonplussed, their faces miserable with bewilderment.

'Do you agree that justice must be seen to be done?' Dennis raised his eyebrows behind the blindfold. 'Isn't that a basic principle of the Law in any country?'

'Yes, that's right,' one of the escort answered hesitantly. 'I've heard that.'

'Well, if I can't see the justice that is being done to me, can it be justice?'

'Of course it can't!' the escort replied.

'Now,' Dennis paused, turning his head from side to side, 'do you think that it's right that I'm being shot?'

'No! It's a bloody shame!' the four men declared fervently.

'So you don't think it's justice?'

'No!' they chorused. 'Who do they think they are? Shit, it's not fair.'

'Then you mustn't watch it being done, must you?' Dennis smiled knowledgeably. 'If you do then you'll be admitting that it's justice.'

One of the sergeants in the escort was more mentally alert than his companions and immediately saw what had to be done. Taking the blindfold off Dennis's eyes he tied it over his own. The other three followed his lead, using handkerchiefs and shirt-tails for the purpose. Then they each put a hand on Dennis's shoulder and he slowly led them through the ranks of the Territorials towards the stake.

'Good afternoon!' Dennis shouted boisterously. 'I'm the one-eyed man in the country of the blind!'

This sally raised a murmur of nervous laughter. Rembrandt and Powderham who were sitting in two deck-chairs to one side, smoking their fourth cigarette since lunch, raised their heads and gazed at the strange little procession.

'We were right to sentence him to death, Pow-wow, listen to that. All his comrades laughing at him. By God, he must have been unpopular. Look at those four chaps pushing him forward there! They can't get him shot quick enough! It's nice to know that our decision meets with everyone's approval.'

The Colonel nodded genially, the pupils of his eyes lambent, wide and deep. With a strangely winsome smile he bent over, untied his laces, stripped them out of his shoes, knotted them together, and made a cat's-cradle, holding it out at the penultimate stage for Powderham to bring the strings over his thumbs.

'Where's mine then?' Powderham demanded. 'It's all very well expecting me to help with the difficult bits, but what do I do for fun?'

'Make your own!' the Colonel advised dreamily. 'Didn't that take an awfully long time?'

Powderham laboriously undid the cat's-cradle out of Rembrandt's fingers, put one end of the tied laces between his lips and started sucking it into his mouth like a piece of spaghetti.

Rembrandt waved his cane round his head.

'Where's the officers' mess orderly?' he shouted.

'Sir!' a sergeant ex-sergeant-major stood to attention.

'Be a good chap and fetch the Major some Parmesan cheese, will you?'

As the orderly ran off, rage and disgust in every step he took, Rembrandt and Powderham played three quick games of Pat-a-Cake, their hands a blur of speed. As they smacked their palms together Rembrandt sang:

Pat-a-cake, pat-a-cake, baker's man,
Bake me a cake as fast as you can,
Pat it and prick it and mark it with T,
Then put it in the oven for Pow-wow and me!

The escort were in tears as they groped their way back to their places in the ranks.

'Listen to those cold-hearted bastards!'

'Fucking hell! What kind of men are we? Dennis is one of us, isn't he?'

'Those two think they're a race apart.'

'One day they'll get their come-uppance and I only hope I'm around to see it!'

'Firing-squad! Attention!' Tarzan Cool Guy shouted above the indignant buzz from the parade. 'Shoulder arms!'

'Everything all right?' Dennis yelled at the top of his voice. 'Everything all right? You've forgotten to tie me to the post you know!'

Marge burst into tears, Margaret from the Tonga Bar ululated sadly, Marilyn prayed. Tarzan Cool Guy stood the firing-squad at ease again and marched smartly over to the prisoner.

'Take it easy, Dennis,' he whispered, as he tied his hands together behind the stake. 'Don't overdo it.'

'Ho! Ho!' Dennis bellowed. 'Come on! Let's get on with it! Oh, why are we waiting? Why-eye-are-we-wai-ting? Why are we wai-ai-ti-ng? Why do we wait?'

'By God, there's a brave man Pow-wow!' Rembrandt averred. 'He's got guts.'

'I bet you never had a green bakelite potty like mine,' Powderham mumbled through the shoe-laces in his mouth.

Tarzan Cool Guy brought the Bucket-Wheel Excavator Gang up to the ready. They aimed their rifles straight between Dennis's eyes.

'Lower down!' Dennis honked. 'Try the heart! Plenty of room there.'

Tarzan Cool Guy tightened his lip, cast a quick glance at Marge who was now having hysterics, and raised his sword in the air. As he did so the orderly returned from the kitchen tent with a canister of Parmesan cheese and gave it to Powderham. The Major undid his belt, pulled out his trousers, and shook a considerable amount into his crutch.

'That's cured my Dhobie's Itch!' he smiled happily. 'I can feel an improvement already.'

The Colonel noticed the sword held high in the air.

'Lieutenant!' he called.

'Sir?'

'Have you asked the prisoner if he has a last wish?'

'No, sir.'

'That's rather inhuman, isn't it?' Rembrandt leered.

Tarzan Cool Guy lowered his sword, misery inscribed all over his face. Marching over to Dennis he looked straight into his eyes.

'Please keep quiet until it's all over. Will you do that for me?'

'What d'you expect me to do? Just stand around here all afternoon?' Dennis barked.

Lieutenant Tarzan Cool Guy straightened up and marched over to the Colonel.

'He says he just wants to get it over, sir. He says it's very hot stuck out here in the sun.'

Rembrandt slapped his knee and chucked Powderham under the chin.

'Hear that, Pow-wow? What a cool customer, eh? We've got a real soldier out there. I don't know what we're doing getting rid of him. By God I'll remember this, oh I shall. What do you say, Pow-wow?'

But Pow-wow had fallen asleep under the influence of the

benevolent herb and lay curled up on the ground, sucking his thumb. He did not hear the resentful murmurings of his troops, the shouts of bile, hatred and remorse, the command 'Fire!', the crash of rifles, the honks of surprise as a flight of spurwing geese lost one of their outriders, shot clean through the head by a bullet aimed straight between Dennis's eyes. Nor did he see Doctor Russell gallop across to the slumped body, apply his stethoscope to its chest, pronounce it dead with a broad conspiratorial smile, then start hissing questions into its ear as it was loaded on to a stretcher and carried off, followed by the frenzied wailings of Marge.

For Pow-wow was with the gods while Dennis remained behind, earth-bound.

The order to move northwards against Myanis Kupela came through that evening. As both Rembrandt and Powderham were fast asleep, dreaming away the gentle influence of their after-lunch cigarettes, Tarzan Cool Guy received the message from the wireless-operator. He announced the news to the rest of the National Territorial Emergency Force as they sat round a bonfire celebrating Dennis's resurrection and his discovery of his leaf-eating beetle. It aroused little interest, especially from Marge who was sitting with her husband, holding his hand and begging his forgiveness for all the terrible things that she had done to him in the past.

'And you'll let him work in the garden?' Dennis asked. 'I don't mean just stand around but work, cut the grass, do some weeding.'

'Why shouldn't he? He's big enough!' Marge glanced up at Tarzan Cool Guy. 'He'll be glad to do something around the place, won't you?'

The wrestler nodded humbly and sat down on a fallen tree.

'Whatever you say.'

Doctor Russell butted in, his buck-teeth gnawing at his beard.

'We must get together to talk about the tree! They actually told you the Tree of Life? Those very words?'

Dennis nodded behind his disguise, a Pancho Villa moustache and a pair of polaroid sun-glasses.

'Yes, though it has other names. It's also called the Rain Tree, or *mufundwelamba*. But it's the Tree of Life to the beetles. They could hardly be wrong now, could they?'

Doctor Russell scribbled excitedly in his notebook.

'Not at all. They sound reliable enough to me. Now did you notice any details?'

'So you think this might be the old cure for death, eh, Doc?' Pyper interrupted with feigned nonchalance. 'I could do with some of that according to you and that bastard medicine man in Myakajunji.'

'Of course I do! I've always known that it was here. The conditions in this part of Africa are absolutely perfect.'

'Well, you'd better be quick about finding it. We might need a dose or two of what it's got to offer once we get going tomorrow. Old Maud Mamuntu is a tough nut I've heard.'

Pyper's reminder of what the morrow promised dampened the high spirits around the fire. They were all still in Chimbusu, still in the National Territorial Emergency Force, still lumbered with Rembrandt and Powderham, still moving against an unknown enemy with a reputation for savagery. Doctor Mulombe had mounted an acrimonious propaganda campaign against the Muntu, which claimed that they were cannibals, Communists, homosexuals, disciples of the Black Art and no better than vermin. To the soldiers who were being pitted against the giant prophetess and her people, the Muntu had got no nearer as enemies, nor further away as friends. They were a mystery and every man in the Force would have preferred to keep them that way. They were a name in the darkness; a darkness haunted by talking beetles, the risen dead and the Tree of Life.

12
Ace of Spades

Having given his solemn promise that the bombing-raid on Myanis Kupela would take place as scheduled, Desaix L'Ace and the stage-carpenter from the Mufunsi Theatre Co-operative worked around the clock to get the Fokker ready for action. Skidmore had allocated them a small hangar in a deserted corner of the airfield and the bomb was moved there, still under heavy guard. Day and night echoed with hammering, sawing, the whine of electric drills and lathes, the thumping of mechanical punches. Only the bored sentries gave the scene any sign of exterior life, everything of any significance was going on in the humped-back corrugated-iron shed. The doors were firmly locked. No unauthorized person was allowed within half a mile of the place. When Desaix sent the sentries to the nearest illicit shebeen for cane-for-pain and some female company, the messages were intercepted and destroyed. Foley and Skidmore were determined that he should keep his word. The mission would fly out of Myakajunji on time.

Mrs Renfrew Mulombe, the new Air Marshal, paid the hangar a surprise visit one afternoon. She had been studying Skidmore's expenses claim for his visit to Elizabethville and had noticed the item:

> Bomb, h.e., 500 lb., 1 (one) purchased from Cpl.
> McCafferty £15,000.

For the last ten years Mrs Renfrew Mulombe had been interested in bombs. She had managed a factory on the outskirts of Myakajunji which supplied the whole of the Progress Party with Molotov cocktails for the struggle. The reek of petrol was a perfume to her. But she had never been able to aspire to this summit of technical achievement. A bomb which weighed five times more than herself! A thunderbolt!

'Open that door!' she commanded the sentry.

'*Ikona*, madam!' the sentry shook his head. 'I have the orders.'

'If you don't open that door I'll set fire to you!'

The sentry eyed the small aspirin bottle in the old woman's hand. It contained a clear pink fluid, had a paper wick stuffed in its neck and there was a lighted match being held perilously close, steady as a rock in the hand of the new Air Marshal. As he was about to succumb, Foley and Skidmore drove up. Unwillingly they agreed to get Desaix to open the door. As soon as the two aviators stood blinking in the strong sunlight, Desaix made a bee-line for the female shape of Mrs Renfrew Mulombe, unable to pick out detail because of his long sojourn in the hangar. Hustling her into the hangar he started undoing the buttons of her blouse. Desaix had got to the third button before Mrs Mulombe fetched him a terrific blow across the head with her stick. He sat down on the floor.

'You decadent *musungu* dog!' the Air Marshal screamed.

'I think I can explain,' Foley intervened, a ghastly smile on his blanched face.

Mrs Mulombe slashed at him with her stick.

'I hope you can! There's too many randy *musungus* who think they can just give the big hello to any decent African girl and she'll come running. Well, I'm not one of them! *Cha!* I wouldn't have this tub of lard if you paid me!'

Desaix was holding his injured head in his hands. Through the fingers he saw Mrs Mulombe for the first time as she was.

'*Merde!* Oh holy Christ!' he moaned. 'What a blue!'

'Pilot-Officer Desaix was searching you, Madame Marshal,' Foley fixed an eye on Desaix and tapped the fallen man's foot. 'Weren't you?'

Desaix nodded rapidly.

'You could have been an enemy agent,' he mumbled sourly.

Mrs Mulombe sniffed and buttoned up her blouse, pausing at the last one to study Desaix closer.

'He knows who I am. Everybody knows who I am.'

'Oh, yes, we all know who you are, madam,' Foley wagged his head enthusiastically. 'You're the President's mother.'

'And the power behind him ... don't forget that. I'm no namby-pamby like Eustace was.'

The stage-carpenter was still hiding behind the stack of timber, his teeth chattering. He had recognized Mrs Mulombe. She had been the leader of the gang of Party supporters which had sold him his seventh Party card. The sales-talk employed by the old lady had not been as sophisticated as those used by vacuum-cleaner salesmen or encyclopaedia sellers, but it had been very effective. Taking the stage-carpenter, his wife, his brother and four children outside their house, she had supervised a series of dynamic, persuasive sales tactics that had left the stage-carpenter in no doubt as to where his last month's wages were going.

Desaix rooted him out.

'What are you shaking for?' he asked. 'You can't have the eleven o'clock horrors. It's half-past four in the afternoon.'

'No, Bwana Arse, it is that old woman. She is very strong.'

Mrs Mulombe came up behind Desaix and saw the stage-carpenter. Her eyes closed and the ancient lady racked her memory.

'*Hau!*' she exclaimed suddenly. 'I remember! You were an obstinate case. Where is it?'

The stage-carpenter drew his Party card faster than any gun-slinger ever flashed his forty-five.

'You know this expires in eleven months' time,' Mrs Mulombe frowned unpleasantly. 'Don't forget to renew it, will you, comrade?'

'No, madam, I will renew it promptly.'

The stage-carpenter replaced his card in his pocket and faded into the background as Mrs Mulombe looked at the Fokker.

'What is all this secret hush-hush work for? You have a plane and the bomb and a man to fly it,' she demanded cantankerously. 'What's all the messing about for?'

Desaix, a red weal across his cheek and ear, explained smoothly:

'The Fokker is a fighter, madam. We have had to adapt it to carry the bomb. It's a heavier load than she's used to and there's changes needed to the engine to get more thrust.'

He pointed to the bomb-carrying grabs that had been installed under the cockpits.

'Where's the bomb?' Mrs Mulombe's eyes gleamed. 'I'd love to see it.'

Desaix took Mrs Mulombe across the hangar to a wooden crate and opened the side. The bomb lay there, supported on two wooden yokes.

'There it is . . . can I touch it?' Mrs Mulombe grinned.

'Very gently,' Desaix replied stiffly, his eyes on the bony claw that was already outstretched.

'I'll just stroke it.'

Desaix stepped back and watched Mrs Mulombe stroking the bomb. He looked at the faces of his squadron-leader and wing-commander. They were smiling happily.

'That's cheered the old bag up anyway,' Foley whispered. 'Now we might be able to get some work done.'

When Mrs Mulombe finally left the hangar with her escort, Desaix and the stage-carpenter shut and bolted the door and got back to work. The mission was scheduled to start at 800 hours the following morning and there was still a lot more to do. All through the night they slaved over their tasks, snatching a cold beer out of the antique refrigerator and a few bites off a stick of biltong, driving themselves to the limits. From across the runways Skidmore and Foley saw the lights in the hangar and heard the distant hammering and whine of electric drills.

'People are funny you know, Skidmore, damn funny. I'll never understand them. I mean that fellow Desaix is an odd character, one on his own. He gave me the impression at first that he hated the sight of us but look at him now – really pulling his weight. He's compromised, you see? We all have to compromise if we want to survive. I would have thought him uncontrollable as far as service life is concerned, but we seem to have got him licked. He's been almost well-behaved lately apart from that business with the Air Marshal this afternoon . . . and that was a genuine mistake I think.'

Skidmore looked at his watch.

'Only three hours to go, sir. The sun will be up shortly.'

They poured themselves a last drink, turned their chairs to the window, and watched for the morning. It came with African suddenness, a short prelude of simmering red, then the sun climbing over the eastern fringe of the bush. The windows of the hangar still carried their artificial lighting where the industrious, sawdust-filled atmosphere of the Zonkendawon Air Force secret workshop rocked and reverberated with the energetic clatter of Desaix and his assistant. By half-past six they had finished and went outside to sit in the cool air and smoke a cigarette.

'It is done, Bwana Arse,' the stage-carpenter stretched his legs. 'We have finished.'

'A beautiful job, *chamware*,' Desaix shook his head and ran fingers through his curls to get all the sawdust out. 'You should feel proud of your handiwork.'

'It is a good piece of work, as good as the space-machine that I did for the pantomime.'

Foley and Skidmore drove up to the hangar.

'Everything set, Ace?' Skidmore said breezily. 'No hold-ups?'

Desaix shook his head.

'No problems. We'll load the bomb on the tarmac after I've got the Fokker into position on runway six.'

'Why not load her while she's in the hangar?' Foley interrupted. 'Get it all tied up in there.'

Desaix got to his feet and put his hands where his hips had once been.

'Listen, Foley, I'm not taking any more crap from you. The plane's going to be overloaded as it is. I don't want her jeopardized any more than is necessary. The ground is uneven round here. I don't want that bomb jogged.'

'All right, all right, we'll overlook the impertinence, Desaix. Don't get ruffled. I know you've been working extremely hard ... I'll get a squad over to move the bomb for you.'

'No! We'll do it all ourselves. It's our mission and we want to see that everything goes to plan.'

'But that's a five-hundred-pounder, two men will never lift it into the grabs!' Skidmore barged in on the conversation. 'That's only just a bit heavier than me. I bet you can't lift me up!'

Desaix cast Skidmore a pitying look.

'With one finger, Skidmore, with one finger.'

'You sure your assistant knows how to fire the machine-gun?'

'He can shoot the pips off your shoulders ... can't you?'

The stage-carpenter blew a lazy cloud of smoke into the crisp air.

'Man, I could pick the eyes out of a King Edward potato.'

Foley scrutinized the stage-carpenter closely. Having only two flying personnel in the air force was bad enough, but why they had to be Desaix L'Ace and this smoke-blowing, goofy, spindle-shanked creature he did not know.

'When you get back I'll want a full report immediately. Good luck.'

Foley turned on his heel, having saluted and received no responding gesture.

'Pin their ears back, eh, Ace, just like old times,' Skidmore chuckled as he squeezed his bulk into the back seat of the car. 'Remember Guernica, Dresden, Coventry ... Dien Bien Phu.'

'We lost at Dien Bien Phu ... didn't we?' Foley inquired under his breath.

'We weren't fighting, sir. It was the French and the Commies, sir. I'm never sure which side Desaix was on.'

When the car had driven off Desaix and the stage-carpenter hauled the Fokker out on to the runway.

The old war-plane slid into the sunlight, a coloured plate out of an aviational history. It looked much as it must have done when it was first built in Germany fifty years before this momentous day. As Desaix clambered into the cockpit he was not too tired to appreciate the importance of the occasion and he sat quietly looking at his instruments for a while before taxi-ing over to runway six. Then he walked back to the hangar and helped the stage-carpenter load the bomb on to a trolley fitted with two special cradles that were supported on two hydraulic jacks. Slowly they pulled their load across the airfield.

'We must get another bomb,' Mrs Mulombe licked her lips as she looked through Foley's binoculars. 'We must have more than one.'

'They're very expensive, madam,' Foley reminded her.

'Hang the expense!'

'It will need a budget revision, madam. The Air Force vote won't stand more than one bomb per annum at the moment.'

'I'll get that revised. My boys can get to work on some of

those members of the legislature who understand my kind of thinking.'

The bomb was beautiful. It gleamed black and round in the morning, a gorged mamba sleeping with its prey deep inside its bowels. As Desaix and the stage-carpenter jacked the cradles up so the projectile could be slipped into the hold of the grabs, Mrs Mulombe seized her stick and headed for the door.

'Where are you going, madam?' Foley gasped, racing after her across the tarmac towards the Fokker. 'Please don't interfere.'

'I want to have a last look!' Mrs Mulombe jabbered, saliva flying from her toothless gums.

Desaix L'Ace saw Mrs Mulombe coming, a witch-like figure scudding across the tarmac with her clothes streaming behind her, stick flailing at the air. Climbing into the cockpit he helped the stage-carpenter up and kicked over the engine.

'O.K.? *Etes-vous prêt?*' he shouted over his shoulder. 'The bomb's safe. Stand by!'

'*Mina funa hamba!*' the stage-carpenter choked as he saw Mrs Mulombe approaching. 'Let's get out of here, Bwana Arse!'

Heavily laden, the Fokker moved forward, the bomb barely a foot from the ground. Mrs Mulombe was running with incredible speed for one so advanced in years. The stage-carpenter was terrified as he saw her catching up with the slowly-moving aircraft and swung the barrel of the machine-gun round.

'Bwana Arse!' he yelled above the engine. 'Should I shoot the President's mother?'

But Desaix was not listening. The Fokker had collected all the weight aboard it and was gathering speed, skimming across the airfield. The stage-carpenter felt the acceleration, the wind in his face, then saw Mrs Mulombe falling behind. Leaning over the machine-gun barrel he tried to forget the bumping of his frantic heart.

The Fokker soared into the air and headed north.

Maud stood on the cathedral steps and watched the Muntu drilling. At the whistle they ran from their huts to their positions at the stockade or on the cathedral. Firbank had converted the anti-tank rocket launcher into a ground-to-air missile, erected machine-guns at all vantage points that could command a wide view of the sky to the south, dug anti-aircraft shelters and established an early-warning system. Myanis Kupela was ready for Bwana Arse, whenever he should come.

'God is pleased with you, my daughter,' Maud said to the hostess from the La Gondola night-club who had trekked up from Myakajunji. 'It is ironic that it should be your own father we are waiting for. If you had not been able to give us this tip-off, the animal might have murdered us all in our beds. Now we will beat him off.'

The hostess was plainly upset by the news that the sturdy, bald-headed man who had lain with her behind the piano had been her progenitor. Although she had considered it her duty to resign from La Gondola and get to Myanis Kupela as fast as possible in order to warn her mother of the impending air-attack, she had not forgotten the husky tenderness of Desaix. She had hoped to see him again and by the look of the bristling preparations around her this was going to be unlikely.

'Must you shoot him down?'

'Daughter, he is coming to kill us for Mulombe. He is a hired assassin. Since I knew him, he must have changed. The man I knew would never have had the meanness in him to do this thing. *Ufunani?* We should let your father destroy his own daughter? Would he want such madness on his head?'

Firbank blew his whistle again and the Muntu left their posts.

'Okay, you guys, take five!' he shouted. 'But don't go far away!'

Maud took the hostess's face between her hands and looked deep into her daughter's troubled eyes.

'You were right to leave Myakajunji. It is a place of despair. Here you can be safe and be close to God.'

'But I don't believe in God, *Mame*!' the hostess sobbed. 'I don't! I can't help it!'

Maud laughed indulgently, cuddling the hostess to her bosom.

'Don't be silly, dear. How can you not believe in your own stepfather?'

'I've never seen Him, have I?' the hostess blubbered. 'How can you expect me to believe in Him?'

'That is like saying that you do not believe in Mount Everest because you have never climbed it!' Maud chuckled deeply.

'Oh, what a girl for questions you always were. Ah well, you youngsters always grow up to criticize your parents. I suppose we have to expect it. Hmmm, what a life it is for us mothers. Have you washed your neck this morning?'

Three shots sounded over the swamp. Firbank blew on his whistle. The Muntu ran to their posts. Bwana Cat's-Eyes scuttled into the cathedral and wound the handle of a primitive siren, sending its wail out to the other stockades.

'Get into the shelter, Maud!' Firbank grabbed his wife's gigantic arm. 'He's on his way.'

Maud shook off the American and clutched her daughter closer.

'I haven't seen Desaix for a long time. If he is coming to kill me and his daughter here, his own flesh and blood, then we will look into his eyes as he does it. He will have to live with that all his life.'

'For God's sake, Maud, you're a perfect target for him! You'll be killed if he hits the cathedral.'

'It is for God's sake that I stand here. I will live and die for God's sake. Don't you lift your voice to me again! I know what I am doing, husband!' Maud frowned with annoyance. 'If my old lover wants to kill me then perhaps it is time for me to die.'

Firbank shook his head in despair and ran up the tower-ladders to the anti-tank rocket-launcher. Maud craned forward, her eyes scanning the empty sky. She could hear a powerful but distant roar. It was the sound of the Fokker approaching.

Desaix sighted the two columns driving up the Great North Road. He was tempted to lose height and buzz them as he knew that his friends were there, but he resisted it and flew on towards the Bengweulu Swamps. As he crossed the first patches of reeds and the ground colours started to change from the parched ochres, browns and reds to the green of the watered terrain he saw three yellow blocks grouped near a clump of trees. Intrigued, he banked and lost height to take a closer look. He saw three D8 bulldozers. While he was wondering what the machines were doing on what could be an insecure footing, he caught sight of two figures toiling through the shallow periphery of the swamp towards Myanis Kupela. Unable to identify them from the height he was flying at, Desaix climbed the Fokker back up to 3,000 feet and continued on his mission.

'That's Des!' Marilyn shouted excitedly, up to her golden thighs in mud. 'He's had his plane smartened up, hasn't he? It looks really *distingué*.'

'Never mind him, woman!' Johnny grunted as he floundered on. 'Keep ya mind on the project in hand. We've got to get to these eejit Muntu and get the match arranged. Will ya take things seriously, just this once? If we can get to this Myanis Kupela before the shit hits the fan we can prove our point to the world that Football Conquers All.'

On the day of Dennis's execution Johnny had been very upset. He liked Dennis, admired his learning and quiet ways and understood his problem with Tarzan Cool Guy. With the whole of the Bucket-Wheel Excavator Gang always trying to lay his wife he perpetually stood in danger of ending up with the same kind of deal as Dennis had had to endure with everything to the power of ten. The only man at Chimbusu with any whisky had been the sad Colonel so it had been to his tent that Johnny had wandered. By the time Dennis had not been shot, Johnny and the sad Colonel had drunk several bottles of the saffron potion. The sad Colonel had taken himself to bed complaining about how dreadful he was sure to feel in the morning, leaving Johnny alone. It was then that Johnny had seen his vision. Doctor Mulombe and Maud Mamuntu were dressed in full football strip, standing at the centre-spot with a football at their feet waiting for the whistle. The football had been the world with Africa clearly visible. Fired by this hallucination Johnny had collected Marilyn and immediately set off northwards, in his heart the identical spirit to that of Doctor Livingstone when he travelled round and round the Bengweulu Swamps in circles for months on end searching for the source of the Nile.

The McSilvers waded on.

Three shots sounded over the swamps.

'Come on, ma wee wife!' Johnny gasped. 'The hostilities have started. We'll have to do better than this. Take ma hand!'

Grabbing hold of Marilyn's hand Johnny plunged on, his brows knotted, the black water spouting gouts of foul-smelling gas beneath his flailing boots. Come what may he would get through to the Muntu. The radical alternative to war would happen or he would perish in the attempt.

Desaix heard the shots, banked and flew west. So the situation had changed. If there were patrols out in the swamps and they were armed, then there was sure to be a fiery reception waiting for him at Myanis Kupela.

Behind him the stage-carpenter was trying to find somebody to pray to. He'd never been fired at before. It was one experience that had evaded him. The Party card-sellers had clubbed him, kicked him, tried to strangle him, hung him by the braces of his overalls from the roof-timbers of his own house, thrown him into thorn bushes, stamped on his fingers ... but they had never shot him. Now here he was, inexperienced and exposed, stuck in the sky with nothing between him and the earth but a piece of fabric. Closing his eyes he wished that he was back at the Mufunsi Theatre Co-operative bar discussing the finer points of a double-take with Bwana Humphrey Fluellen and the *avant-garde* playwright Bwana Kovary. So, as the stage-carpenter did not believe in God, he prayed to Bwana Humphrey Fluellen for forgiveness. He had said that Humphrey had fucked like an arthritic elephant purely for effect. It was a turn of phrase that he had been proud of and he had only been waiting for an opportunity to use it tellingly. The stage-carpenter had become theatrical and he was now ashamed.

A flash of scarlet leapt from the top of the tower. The stage-carpenter cried out as he saw a blur and felt a hot wind fan his cheek.

Desaix crossed Myanis Kupela at 5,000 feet and looked down. The island was pricked with fire and the cathedral tower gobbed flame repeatedly. The din of small-arms rose up to him. At that height he would be safe but never sure of being on target with the bomb. Banking, he lost height and flew northwards.

The Muntu cheered as the Fokker flew away over the swamp, even though their triumph had been spoiled by a tragic accident. Firbank had trained them in the use of all the equipment contained in the wedding present of Bwana Cat's-Eyes, all except the hand-grenades. There simply had not been the time to explain how to use them. While the machine-guns, rifles and the anti-tank gun were beating off the Fokker, a youth ran out into the square with one of the small bombs and threw it at the Fokker. As the Fokker was at 5,000 feet and directly overhead, the hand-grenade fell back to earth at the youth's feet and blew him to pieces.

The first blood had been drawn.

Unaware of this accident, Desaix hedge-hopped over the swamp, his deadly load nearly touching the trees. While the Muntu were picking up the bits of their first casualty he roared over the square, narrowly missed the tower, and dropped the bomb smack into the middle of the surprised crowd which was still on its hands and knees. The only man who was still at his post, scanning the horizons for the possible return of the Fokker, was Firbank. As the plane swept through Myanis Kupela he had managed to get a sight on the retreating tailplane and blow it off with a brilliant snapshot from his anti-tank rocket-launcher.

The Fokker shuddered, turned on one side, then plunged into the swamp. Moments later an explosion erupted from where it had landed, then a column of oily smoke billowed heavily into the air.

Maud looked at the bomb and held Desaix's daughter closer.

'God is looking after us. Your father has failed,' she whispered shakily. 'Poor old Desaix.'

Firbank tried to shepherd Maud away from the huge black cylinder that had buried itself to a third of its length in the square.

'Keep away now,' he said importantly. 'Keep away from it! It will have to be defused.'

The hostess looked from under Maud's arm and saw the pall of black smoke on the swamp. Maud saw her staring at the ugly cloud and clutched her closer to shut out the sight.

'If he'd only kept going, the old fool! No wonder they call him Bwana Arse nowadays. It must be where he keeps his brains!'

While Firbank helped Maud and the sobbing hostess into the cathedral he explained about the precautions that would be necessary before he could dispose of the bomb. Maud lurched along the nave, not heeding his chatter. Out in the swamp one of her old lovers was lying dead, just as her parcel of husbands had been burned by the Party on the night when she had loved God in the tree. He had suffered and even in her rage against him, she thought of his suffering, of the pain of death. Fire again, and smoke. Even in the swamps where water lay at the root of everything, there was damned fire and smoke.

Firbank realized that he was not getting through to Maud and left her by the altar with the hostess. Running back down the nave he went into the square and drove the curious Muntu away from the unexploded bomb. Within minutes he had them building a high wall of earth around it with enough room for him to get inside and tinker with the firing mechanism. When the wall was finished he sent the helpers away with instructions to take cover and re-entered the cathedral.

'Maud,' he called down the rose-coloured nave, 'I will say good-bye just in case it doesn't come off. I'm not an expert in these things though I have some idea.'

'Leave it,' Maud sighed tiredly, 'leave it. We will build a new Myanis Kupela somewhere else.'

'No! We are fighting for our lives! For our freedom!' Firbank's eyes glowed fanatically. 'We will save God here! In this place or nowhere! Your people have built you this place...'

'They will build me other places. Mud-bricks are easily made and we can always steal corrugated-iron off the mines.'

Firbank hesitated.

'Maud, you must not give up.'

'I am not giving up. I am thinking.'

Firbank left them where they were, seated on the ground, and went across the square to his hut, emerging a moment later with a screwdriver. Striding across to the earthen barrier thrown up by the Muntu he climbed inside and found Bwana Cat's-Eyes with a stethoscope clamped to the bomb.

'Are you trying to be a hero?' he snarled, as he picked up the Chinaman and hurled him over the wall. 'This is a man's job you goddamned yellow coolie! Get the hell outa here!'

Then Firbank was alone with his God. He turned and faced the bomb, the screwdriver held in his hand like a short stabbing sword. The gladiator was at last in the arena, facing his final test.

'Right,' Firbank breathed, his eyes fixed on the shining black cylinder of the bomb. 'Let's go.'

Its smooth shell was divided up into sections only just visible to the naked eye. With a lover's tender finger-tip he explored the lines, picking out four screw-heads. He had seen enough bad movies about bomb-disposal squads working against time to know the way into the abdomen of his lord. With a surgeon's flinty calm he approached the casing, the steel implement steady in his hand. He knew that the first touch might trigger off the device – that the bomb might have been put on a time-fuse to dupe the Muntu who could be trusted to gather round it in ingenuous curiosity – even as the blade touched the cleft head of the screw he knew that the mighty ticking from inside the bomb's belly was his death-knell. Dying in this way was more than he ever could have wished for; it had all the bloody beauty of the most spectacular martyrdoms.

He had no idea how to defuse any explosive device, not the faintest inkling of how to even get past the first stage. When he had left Maud in the cathedral, having seen the defeat in her eyes, he had caught sight of the bomb at the same time as he became aware of the long-suppressed death-wish breaking into his consciousness. God was Death, he was Death. God was sitting in the square, an idol that had plunged from the heavens. By embracing the black body of the bomb, tampering with its iron tripes, he could achieve a wonderfully catastrophic extinction. He would go down with God screaming in his arms.

The first screw came out easily, then the second. The ticking continued, steady, unflustered by his interference.

His blood pounded with delicious anticipation. The world was already clouded with thunderous gore. In his ears thudded a distant mighty heart. Was it his, or God's? The third screw was withdrawn. Now the section moved, held on by the final screw.

This was the moment he had come so far to experience. As he took the remaining screw out, he asked himself an oft-repeated question. Did he really want to die, or just know what it was to die? A click. A second click. The section fell away. God's heart was opened up.

The wooden bomb played 'La Vie En Rose'.

13
An Attack of Peace

Rembrandt and the sad Colonel had agreed a plan of attack. When the two columns arrived at the parked D8 bulldozers, the troops were deployed into their battle stations. Rembrandt's force was to attack due north with the armoured vehicles leading the way and breaking through the island's defences, while the regulars circled round to the east and attacked simultaneously in a pincer-movement.

The Bucket-Wheel Excavator Gang received their instructions from Major Powderham.

'Major,' Matthias patiently tried to explain, 'it will never work. Not in the swamps. The D8s will sink.'

'What swamps? Eh? What damned swamps? Have you been talking to that idiot Lieutenant Tarzan Cool Guy? Eh? Is that what it is? Talking to that silly fellow? Look here,' he spread the map out on the ground. 'There's none of those funny little signs you get when it's marshy.'

'Sir, if you'll come with me I'll take you to the swamp!' Matthias said desperately. 'It's not far from here. I'll show you!'

He started marching purposefully into the bush looking over his shoulder at Major Powderham.

'If you don't come back here, Sergeant, I'll shoot you!'

Matthias glanced at the unbuttoned holster and the cold, angry stare of his superior officer, and returned.

'It is Hammerkop who has done this to us. He is seeking our deaths. This is the way he has planned to get rid of us!' Matthias raved suddenly. 'That man is a cold-blooded racist murderer!'

'Frank Hammerkop is a personal friend of mine!' Powderham's eyes glittered dangerously. 'And he thinks more of you black people, yes, of you especially, than you deserve. Put you in a fix and what do you start screaming, eh? Well? You know as well as I do. It's because of your colour. That's your excuse, isn't it?'

'We will go because we have to,' Matthias declared in a martyred tone, 'but let him watch out. We curse him, you tell your friend that, we will come back and haunt him. We will haunt his house, his wife's womb and his green Dodge. We will haunt our Bucket-Wheel Excavator. I have spoken.'

'*Hau! Hau!*' the Bucket-Wheel Excavator Gang chanted angrily. 'We will come back to *tshaya* Hammerkop!'

'What are you talking about, eh? Hm? Without Frank and his sort you'd be out of a job and this hole you call a country wouldn't be more than a desert, yes, a wasteland. Trouble is with you, Sergeant, you don't know the meaning of gratitude!'

Matthias abruptly turned his back on Powderham and ordered his unit into action. As the yellow monsters rolled forward, engines rumbling, their giant tracks flattening trees and bushes, the Bucket-Wheel Excavator Gang raised their voices in song, hurling a proud defiance at the hated Hammerkop and their inevitable fate.

> We are going forward
> But we will not be coming back!
> Backwards and forwards! *Upi?*
> *Upi? Upi? Upi?*
> *Upi? Upi? Upi?*
> Forwards and backwards! *Upi?*
> We will not be coming back
> Because of the way we are going forward!

Powderham watched them until the bush swallowed up the last primrose-coloured bulk then walked back to headquarters to find out if the infantry attacks had been launched on time.

Colonel Vaal Rembrandt had chosen a pleasant site for his command centre. The trees cast a cool shade and the view from the southern-facing entrance was of a gently-undulating land tempered by thousands of long summers. On the horizon was a suggestion of haziness as though the curved earth and the sky had no precise division and merged one into the other.

'So Lieutenant Tarzan Cool Guy did not return from his patrol?' Powderham heard Rembrandt saying above a woman's sobbing. 'Well, he may be missing but there's no point in hoping

. . . sorry, thinking that he's caught it. We couldn't hold up the attack any longer. Yes, that is a bit grim for you, dear. Lost both your fellows, eh? Well, never mind. There's always other pebbles on the beach.'

'All right if I come in, sir?' Powderham stuck his head under the cheerfully striped awning.

'Ah, Powderham . . . that will be all for the moment, Nurse, we'll do our best to find him.'

Marge left the tent and went over to the ambulance where Doctor Russell and Dennis were discussing the Tree of Life.

'The leaves are compound, imparipinnate, alternate and deciduous with a one- to two-inch petiole, lightly grey tomentose,' Dennis was explaining. 'You can't miss it.'

'They've heard nothing,' Marge flopped down beside them. 'I'm sure that brute has gone off somewhere and left me.'

Dennis patted her hand and smiled reassuringly.

'You'll be all right with me. I'm twice the man Tarzan ever was. The way I'm feeling right now, I reckon I could tie that idle bastard in knots. Forget him. Now, Doctor, another feature that I noticed was a caducous, intrapetiolar, lanceolate stipule about a quarter of an inch long. . .'

Dennis was so absorbed in his conversation with Doctor Russell that he did not see Major Powderham come out of Rembrandt's tent and stroll over to the ambulance. Marge was crying again, her head in her hands, and Doctor Russell's eyes were on the shining, intelligent, healthful face of the man who had set eyes on the Tree of Life.

Major Powderham stared at Dennis who had forgotten to put on his disguise. Dennis raised his eyes and smiled brilliantly, his bold eyes latching on to Powderham's like the talons of an eagle. Powderham's jaw sagged, the colour sped from his face. He tried to call out to Rembrandt but speech had left him. Dennis turned back to Doctor Russell.

'Well, on one I examined it was a good half-inch but there must be a reason for that,' he continued.

'You're dead!' Powderham whispered thickly, his tongue numb. 'You're dead!'

As Powderham fainted and crashed to the ground at Doctor Russell's feet, Dennis jumped up nimbly and took his leave.

'Someone to see you, Doctor,' he said in a ringing, clear voice. 'I'll be back later when you're less busy.'

Johnny McSilver and Marilyn stood before Maud. They had been captured while trying to pull Desaix and the stage-carpenter out of the blazing Fokker. It had been a hopeless task as both men were dead but they had struggled on through the flames until both of them had dropped, badly-burned and exhausted, into the arms of a Muntu patrol.

'So you want me to play football with Mulombe?'

Marilyn summoned up her last reserves of strength to flash a radiant smile through the muck that plastered her lovely face.

'May we sit down? We're very tired,' she begged politely.

'Keep them on their feet, Maud!' Firbank advised coldly. 'We want no tricks. They might have an ulterior motive.'

Maud gestured to Marilyn that she and her husband should sit down. Marilyn took Johnny's weight and slid to the ground, conscious of the hatred in Firbank's eyes and the suspicion of the Muntu. Only Maud, towering above them with her great rosy cathedral behind her, was not hostile.

Marilyn smiled again, weaker but still with sunshine.

'My husband . . .' she began.

'They're spies!' Firbank shouted suddenly. 'They're army spies! You can't have mercy on them, Maud, not at this stage! They'll have to be shot!'

Maud beckoned Firbank to be quiet and leant forward to listen to Marilyn. Firbank refused to be counselled and cocked his automatic rifle, aiming it at Marilyn's beautiful, mud-caked head.

'You're jeopardizing our defences!' Firbank screamed. 'They'll have to die! They'll have to!'

As he took first pressure on the trigger, hoping for Maud's nod, a look-out on top of the tower shouted down that the enemy was approaching from the south. Firbank rushed to the stockade, blowing his whistle. The Muntu manned their posts. Maud was left alone with Marilyn and Johnny.

'What is the point of playing football with Mulombe?' she reasoned. 'He will cheat, he will foul, he will bribe the referee.'

'See you, God plays football,' Johnny murmured through cracked lips. 'Woman, He's the best centre-forward there is, He can kick with both feet, and He's never had His name taken yet.'

'I know what God does with His spare time!' Maud bridled. 'I've been married to Him for long enough.'

'Ya cannae be with Him all the time, He must be of a proud and independent nature!' Johnny tried to straighten up, his eyes blazing. 'You're not keeping Him in on Saturday afternoons, are ya?'

Marilyn's eyes closed. She was going to stop shining soon.

'Don't be rude, John,' she sighed. 'Oh, I'm cold. Why is it going dark?'

'If ya'll play a game against Mulombe, if ya'll both abide by the rules ...' Johnny paused, a tremor passing through his body. 'Oh, that would be great.' He slumped forward, then crawled on his belly until he was staring at Maud's enormous feet.

'By God!' he croaked admiringly. 'Ya'd make a terrific full-back!'

Maud picked Johnny up and put him in Marilyn's arms. She had seen men and women dying before, husbands watching wives, wives watching husbands, but these two were going together which was one up to them.

Marilyn raised a final glimmer of a smile, a dawn under a grey cloud, a sunset in the rain.

'John ... O John, I can't see.'

Johnny glared up at Maud, his fierce eyes glittering a nordic blue beneath his mud-covered brows.

'I'll train ya! I'll put in the time! I'll work out tactics for ya! I'll even play for ya mesel'! Christ, ya Old Man can play if He likes! He'd make a good inside-right! What d'ya say?'

As the McSilvers went down like a sun into a brown sea, Tarzan Cool Guy's patrol reached the stockade and was promptly seized. Firbank hustled the captives over to where Maud was shaking her head over Johnny McSilver's unusual proposal, and closing his eyes with her thumbs, shutting out their last gleams of fanaticism. Grabbing hold of Tarzan Cool Guy's hair, Firbank yanked back the wrestler's head and stuck the muzzle of his FN under his ear.

'Say the word, Maud! More goddamned spies! Let's get it over with!' he screamed. 'We can't let them live!'

Maud studied the tall, well-proportioned African male before her. He was strikingly handsome in a strange, but familiar way, even with an expression of amazed recognition in his rolling eyes. The build was right, the age, yes, the nose was just like his father's, number fourteen.

With a mighty cuff she sent Firbank crashing to the ground.

'Oswald!' she cried joyfully. 'Oswald, my son!'

'*Mame!*' Tarzan Cool Guy choked in Maud's crushing embrace. 'After all these years!'

'I didn't know he was called Oswald,' Humphrey Fluellen whispered to Kovary out of the side of an ooze-filled mouth. 'No wonder he changed it. Looks a bit like his old lady, doesn't he? Same build and all that. Lovely pair of knockers the old girl's got, Christ! You wouldn't get many of them in the pound, would you?'

While Tarzan Cool Guy and his old Mum hugged each other, Inspectors Kwango and Grutchfield were arguing between themselves. They had been critical of Lieutenant Tarzan Cool Guy's idea that the patrol should ignore its instruction to reconnoitre Myanis Kupela and instead make a direct approach to the Muntu to try and arrange a peaceful settlement of the war, but once they had been out-voted, and were in the presence of wanted criminals, the situation had entered a new phase.

'According to the police manual, we should arrest them all,' Kwango said heatedly. 'That's in the paragraph about our function in society.'

'Not now, not now,' Grutchfield squeeezed Kwango's hand. 'We've got other things to think about. Look at that one ... he's our man!'

Grutchfield nodded at Firbank. The American was screaming at Maud in a strange, high-keyed voice and waving his FN rifle in the air. Grutchfield recognized the classic symptoms of a homicidal maniac on the loose.

'Well?' Kwango whispered. 'We can do him for illegal possession of arms or threatening behaviour.'

Grutchfield closed his eyes, took a firmer grip on Kwango's hand, and they stepped forward together.

'Put that gun down!' they commanded in sharp, clear voices. 'You haven't got a chance!'

All the sergeants and sergeant ex-sargeant-majors made an orderly advance through the bush behind the D8 bulldozers. Their instructions were to follow the armoured division at a distance of a quarter of a mile and to await fresh orders if the situation was drastically changed.

Pyper, a rifle in his hand and his typewriter in his knapsack, marched along behind Margaret from the Tonga Bar who was going up with the troops as First Aid Orderly.

'You know, I've never seen an arse as nice as yours,' he said reflectively, 'and I've been around. I reckon if you were in London you'd be sitting on a fortune.'

Margaret flung a grateful smile over her shoulder.

'Where's the old din of battle then, Private?' Pyper nudged Loudwater with his rifle-butt. 'Must be just like old times for an old war-horse like you. So this is what all the bullshit's about, is it? I'd rather be sitting in the park playing with myself under the Sunday newspaper. Where's the excitement?'

Loudwater shook his pointed head until his beret span round like a record on a turntable.

'This isn't the real thing, son, not the big stuff. This is a daft little business compared to the fuck-ups I've been in. There's only a few thousand of these Muntu, lad, a mere handful. It will all be over by tonight and we can go home and forget it.'

Loudwater slipped a friendly arm round Margaret from the Tonga Bar's waist.

'Have you thought about what I asked you?'

His drooping eyes lifted momentarily, roaming over the dark whore's handsome face.

'I'm not going back into this lark, lady, never. I've seen the light,' he pressed on, riding his bulky hip with hers, 'and we get along like a house on fire.'

'Everyone says that to me,' Margaret from the Tonga Bar lowered her eyes and smiled shyly. 'What's so different about you?'

'I can offer you plenty. I've got a pension coming and a brother who runs a little club in London who would give you a job.'

'What kind of job?'

'Strip-tease, you know . . .'

Margaret sighed and felt at her chest.

'I don't think so somehow.'

Loudwater strengthened his clasp and stole a kiss on the delicate ebony ear.

'I'll let you into a secret. You know I was a piles-sufferer. Doctor Russell cured me with this herbal remedy from a tree. Now I heard him talking to Dennis back at the camp, and there's one for you.'

'For me?' Margaret faltered in mid-stride. 'You mean ...'

'That's right! You just rub it on your boobs and it makes 'em bigger. Called the *mulombwa* tree it is, I think that's the name ... yes, we'll make a bloody fortune!'

The three D8 bulldozers were up to the tops of their tracks in the swamp. Ahead of them the Bucket-Wheel Excavator Gang could see Myanis Kupela.

'It won't be long now,' Matthias said calmly. 'We will shortly disappear from the face of the earth. Hammerkop lives, but then so do many other tyrants. I only wish we could take them all with us into the depths of this stinking bog.'

The Bucket-Wheel Excavator Gang shouted their agreement. None of them was prepared for death, their minds even now were full of idle licentiousness, as though not believing that their destruction was possible would be sufficient protection against it. As the black water crept up the sides of the D8s they shifted themselves higher on to the engine-casing.

'But one thing you bastards are going to do for me – you're going to die like men! For years I've taken care of you, cleared up your mess, got you out of trouble, but now I want something in return. If I'm going to die I'm doing it with dignity! And so are you, you scum!'

Matthias was now standing up on the driving-seat on the middle D8, his fierce eye roaming over the Bucket-Wheel Excavator Gang.

'How do you think this country is going to survive if its people are like you? What kind of future can it look forward to? You have lived your lives in bars, shebeens, brothels, *dagga*-smoking dens, beer-halls. Your families have been neglected, your children run wild in the townships like animals. Your women are fed up, never get any of your wages, and you never take them out anywhere. Is that the way for a full-grown man to behave? It is irresponsibility that will ruin Zonkendawo! *Hau!* You are nothing but leeches on your native land, contributing nothing! Do you know what self-control means? Sacrifice? Nobility? Honesty?'

The Bucket-Wheel Excavator Gang had lapsed into a subdued silence. None of them could look their leader in the eye. Each man hung his head in shame.

'So, having lived a low-down life, you're going to climb up to the heights of human greatness for one brief moment! You're going to die like heroes!'

The Bucket-Wheel Excavator Gang began clapping and singing their praise-song.

'I don't want your flattery!' Matthias bawled furiously. 'You think that kind of thing makes me feel any better? You've used me! That's all you've done! Used me! I've been very convenient to have around, haven't I? Whenever there was *mulandu* it was so easy, eh? Get Matthias. Matthias will fix it. Matthias will help us out. Always Matthias, Matthias!'

Crestfallen, their eyes running with tears, the Bucket-Wheel Excavator Gang begged him to stop.

'We have heard you, chief, we have heard you speak the truth. It is as you have said. We are wasters, drunks, loafers, we are *bolile*...' A spokesman got to his feet on top of the engine. 'We will die with you and you will be proud of us, for once!'

With a hoarse cry of support for this declaration, the rest of the gang got into the same position.

Show us the way to die,
Ukazala, ukufa, it is there
We will stop together.

'What would you have us do?' the adolescent whose voice had not yet broken cried out after the song. 'We are men, we are ready!'

Matthias stuck out his jaw. His men were now standing on top of the bulldozers, their heads held high, chests stuck out. For the first time he felt proud to be the supervisor of the Bucket-Wheel Excavator Gang.

'You have seen how the *bwanas* do it? In their hundreds of

years of experience they have worked out a way of dying that fulfils a man's need to die well in the sight of his countrymen. I have passed British Constitution and know these things.'

'It is so, Matthias!' the Bucket-Wheel Excavator Gang chorused loudly. 'We have heard it. The *bwanas* have a way!' Matthias steadied himself as the D8 heaved beneath his feet.

'When the *bwanas* were in their ships and they were finished, then they saluted like we have been taught to do by Private Loudwater, and went down with their vessels. They did not cry like women, they did not flounder like the fallen fish-eagle, our national bird, they stood to attention, like this,' he drew himself erect, 'and died so!'

His ten subordinates braced themselves, stood to attention, narrowed their eyes, filled their lungs with air, and saluted as the three D8 bulldozers crashed through the stockades of Myanis Kupela and ran over Firbank.

Bwana Cat's-Eyes had watched the progress of the three D8s for some time from his perch on the top of the tower. When Firbank had finally gone berserk and riddled Inspectors Kwango and Grutchfield with bullets, the nimble Chinaman had skipped up the ladders to be out of the way. He knew that Firbank had no love for him. Also the American was making himself unpopular with Maud. While Firbank, wild-eyed and breathless with his first killing, turned the gun on Johnny McSilver and Marilyn and blasted out what little life was left in them, Bwana Cat's-Eyes was studying the three churning yellow monsters that were coming up out of the swamp on to the island, their passengers standing upright on top of the rumbling engines, right hands rigidly at the salute.

Bwana Cat's-Eyes was interested in the question of how the huge machines had traversed the swamp. If they could find firm bottom then there was no reason for his rice-planting experiment to be disbanded. The area of swamp crossed by the bulldozers must have a strata of hard rock beneath the surface and this could be used as a foundation for the first paddy-fields. With Firbank out of the way he could push ahead with his project to make the Muntu self-sufficient.

Below the tower Maud was surveying the carnage.

'That's one husband I can do without,' she stared at Firbank's mangled corpse as the bulldozer was reversed off it by a dazed Matthias. 'He knew nothing about God. Would God behave in this way?'

Maud pointed to the Inspectors Grutchfield and Kwango, still holding hands but horribly shot up. Beside them lay Johnny McSilver and Marilyn, now surrounded by a stunned, grieving Bucket-Wheel Excavator Gang.

'The sun is gone!' one man mourned softly. 'He is quite put out.'

'The gold has gone, it has been squandered!'

'Ah, Marilyn, *umafazi* above all *umfazis, mbaimbai* we will see you sunny, smiling one. We will have you perhaps in Heaven?'

'What does she do here, lying in the mud?' a man wiped Marilyn's face with the sleeve of his overalls. 'She should be nearer *langa*, she was *Ihlobo*, our summer, our *empumalanga*. Lift her, my brothers!'

The Bucket-Wheel Excavator Gang lifted Marilyn's body on to their shoulders and walked to the tower. The Muntu made way for them, equally shocked by the bloody events of the last few minutes. As they passed Maud she tapped one of them on the shoulder.

'Where are you taking that *musungu* woman?'

'To where she came from!' the adolescent replied, his voice breaking at last. 'We are taking her home.'

Bwana Cat's-Eyes was in a quandary. He could see the National Territorial Emergency Force wading through the swamps in the wake of the bulldozers, but he could also see the Bucket-Wheel Excavator Gang climbing the ladders up the tower with their precious burden. He judged their mood to be unfriendly.

'Maud! Number One wife!' he yelled from the tower. 'What's going on?'

Maud shielded her eyes from the sun and looked up at the gesticulating Chinaman.

'Who's that?' Tarzan Cool Guy asked.

'He's your stepfather, dear,' Maud said thoughtfully, 'but I'm not sure whether he really loves me for myself. Since I married him he hasn't laid a finger on me. Do you think that's normal? I know the Chinese are very fastidious and think they're more civilized than anybody else, but every husband has responsibilities. I've tried coaxing him with a little cuddle here and there but he struggles and says he can't breathe.'

When the Bucket-Wheel Excavator Gang reached the last ladder-way they were confronted by Bwana Cat's-Eyes waving a revolver. Trained in the art of the propagandist, the infiltrator, the agent provocateur, he had forgotten the power of human grief. These grimy, dissipated Africans hanging on to a bloody cadaver might just as well have been cannibals for all Bwana Cat's-Eyes had learnt from his stay in Myanis Kupela. Hunger was a state that he understood and could calculate. Grief was beyond him.

'*Hamba!*' the panting Africans shouted at him. 'Move away.'

'Rice is far more nutritious!' Bwana Cat's-Eyes argued, still pointing the revolver at the climbing marauders. 'We'll give you food!'

'Husband!' Maud thundered up at the tower. 'Come down here! It's time we had a chat about our sex-life!'

As Bwana Cat's-Eyes looked away for a split-second, distracted by Maud's lusty shout, a hand reached up from the ladder-way and grabbed his ankle. Struggling to get free, the Chinaman tried to wrench himself round into a position where he could shoot his attacker. The man saw the revolver coming round, released his grip and ducked. Bwana Cat's-Eyes lost his balance and fell off the tower, the impact of his 300-foot drop driving his shin-bones through the top of his skull as he landed at Maud's feet.

'Hmmm!' she said thoughtfully. 'He was obviously more interested than I thought.'

Colonel Vaal Rembrandt watched Bwana Cat's-Eyes fall off the tower through his high-powered field-glasses.

'They're all committing suicide,' he said smugly. 'Now that will make our job a lot easier.'

Rembrandt needed a lucky break after the way things had been going. His first setback had been the nervous breakdown suffered by his second-in-command Major Powderham who had come into the command centre with staring eyes and dreadful pallor claiming to have seen the resurrection of the dead. After five minutes of earnest conversation with the demented fellow, Rembrandt had called over Doctor Russell and his assistants to remove him. When the stretcher was brought in by Lieutenant Tarzan Cool Guy's mistress and her husband, Rembrandt had asked them to take good care of Powderham.

'He's a valuable officer. Except for him there's only that bone-headed political appointee that I've been lumbered with and he's no use to man or beast, and now he's disappeared. I really don't know how I'll manage.'

'I had hoped that he might make a good garden-boy,' Dennis reflected as he grabbed the horrified, shrinking, quaking Powderham by the lapels and dragged him on to the stretcher. 'We'd have had to have worked out something because I was getting fed up with him drinking my beer, screwing my wife and just lying around the place.'

'Very understandable,' Rembrandt fingered a lock of silky blond hair. 'Haven't I seen you before somewhere?'

'Of course you have! I've been with you since Balyete Camp. You know me!' Dennis laughed deep-chestedly. 'Everyone knows me round here! You know me, don't you, Marge, eh? Knows me well. And she's getting to know me a damn sight better now that muscle-bound freeloader has left her in the lurch.'

With this remark and an emphatic shake of the loaded stretcher, Dennis and Marge trotted out of the tent and took Powderham to Doctor Russell who gave him a sedative, put him in a strait-jacket and tied him to a tree.

The second thing to go wrong was the swamp. It should not have been there but it was. Miles of it. He had watched the bulldozers ploughing into the morass while the infantry hung back awaiting instructions. By the time Rembrandt had noticed that the D8s had found hard bottom and were making progress towards Myanis Kupela, the infantry sections were a long way behind. He had tried to signal to Matthias to wait but had only received a salute from him in return as the bulldozers crashed through the stockade. The military advantage of the surprise attack had been lost. Now he was having to attack Myanis

Kupela from the swamp, his troops chest-deep in muddy water, each man a sitting-duck for snipers.

The third disappointment had been the discovery of the burnt-out plane. Zonkendawon air power had come to an incendiary end. Rembrandt would not be able to call for more air-strikes against his target. If Myanis Kupela was going to be taken it would have to be an amphibious operation.

Pyper balanced his typewriter on top of his knapsack on a clump of reeds. He could see the gap in the stockades of Myanis Kupela and the yellow hulks of the bulldozers inside. He had heard the shooting. His sharp ice-blue eyes had picked out the tumbling figure of Bwana Cat's-Eyes as he fell from the tower. He had been there when the Fokker had been discovered with its grisly occupants. Now he could see the Bucket-Wheel Excavator Gang on top of the tower dancing in a ring and chanting. He could wait no longer. The story would have to be written now, while it struggled to get out of his brain.

Carefully he picked out the words while trying to keep the paper dry on the roller.

A British Army private now in service with the Territorial Emergency Force is planning to re-start the slave trade from Central Africa, exporting local girls to Britain where they will be used in dens of vice in London's notorious Soho district. In order to groom his victims for their future role as prostitutes Private Loudwater, who was until recently a sergeant-major, is working with Doctor Russell of the Mufunsi Mine Hospital on a breast-developing lotion that will enhance the market value of his human merchandise...

Maud stood at the high altar of her cathedral and conducted the funeral service. On the altar was the bomb, its side open. At the points in the ceremony when Maud talked to God directly, an acolyte would reach into the bomb's belly and rewind the clockwork mechanism so it played again.

'My people, sons and daughters, you see here before you a woman of no sense! God has tried to teach me to trust love, and I did not trust that old lover of mine, Bwana Arse. I did not remember what had been between us! Only the Party was in my head! Only Mulombe! I forgot love! The Wife of God forgot love! *Cha!* That is disgusting! [Here Maud clasped her hands together and wrung them between her huge knees, tears pouring down her face.] I should have known better! Oh, forgive me, Husband! For the first time I ask you to forgive me! I will never forget the man who has loved me again. All my lovers and husbands will be safe in my good opinions! *Mosha! Mosha!* What a waste! What rubbish I have done! This has been a *mubi* day!'

The Muntu groaned and beat their heads on the floor. They had never seen Maud so upset. Her plump cheeks trembled, her stomach shook, the tears streamed down her chin and showered like rain. Suddenly she snorted, wiped an arm across her eyes and took a deep breath.

'This is enough weeping for now! God has spoken to me. In the breaking of my heart for poor old Desaix, he has poured his wisdom. The dead have no worries, they are *pela, pela,* but we have plenty. God says we must go out and find Him another home. So let us go! We will leave the swamps to Mulombe and I hope he catches pneumonia!'

Tarzan Cool Guy shook his head violently.

'You can't, *Mame*, they're waiting for you out there! They'll cut you to pieces!'

'Don't be so melodramatic, Oswald,' Maud reproved her son with a sad smile. 'God will find a way. He's got imagination and vision which is more than you can say for the Army.'

'But there's no time!' Tarzan Cool Guy insisted.

'There's always time, Son,' Maud said gently. 'We will win out. If the Muntu cannot survive then the rest of the world might as well give up.'

Maud left Tarzan Cool Guy with his thoughts and wandered up and down the aisle, looking at her people. They were not frightened, not even the children. Their trust in Maud was complete, admitting no doubt. As her great feet scuffed up motes of sparkling dust and her breasts swayed in rhythm like two giant wine-skins on a stiffly-sprung cart, the Muntu started to hum a tune. Maud nodded, clapped her hands, and began to sing.

Fisiga maningi futi mastin!
Bring a lot more bricks!
Tina zo qala aka ngomso!
We will start building tomorrow!

The gods of Ancient Greece had the power to turn themselves into animals in order to play tricks on their human servants. If a god wanted to lay a woman then he changed himself into a swan, or a bull. This was the kind of morons that the gods of ancient Greece were. They didn't know their arse from their elbow. But Maud's husband, the true God, knew what creature He should change Himself into. He entered the tiny, lion-hearted frame of the chihuahua, inspired the petite creature to gnaw through its steel chain in the back of the half-submerged ambulance, break a window with its pointed nose, then jump into the swamp and go in search of Tarzan Cool Guy. As Maud finished her building-song, it streaked up the aisle and hurled itself into the wrestler's arms.

Colonel Vaal Rembrandt gave the order to commence firing. It was exactly 1600 hours. From the other side of Myanis Kupela came the sound of more firing. The regulars were in position and the Muntu were pinned down. Looking through his field-glasses he scanned the tower and saw the naked, mud-covered corpse of Private Marilyn McSilver.

'So that's the way they treat prisoners, eh?' he said bitterly. 'Even a damned deserter gets a decent burial in this outfit.'

He got through to the sad Colonel on a radio transmitter that was being carried on the head of one of the sergeant ex-sergeant-majors.

'Hell, better take it steady I think. They're obviously in a very nasty mood. You've seen it? Yes, terrible ... what can you do with the bloody barbarians? They're still in the Attila the Hun stage round here, old chap. Yes, we can soften the place up for a while and see what happens. I don't fancy ending up like her, eh? Some curtain-call!'

The chihuahua swam past him towards the rear, a note tied to its collar.

'Crocodiles!' Rembrandt shrieked, slamming the receiver down on the sergeant ex-sergeant-major's lower dentures. 'Let's get out of here!'

While the National Territorial Emergency Force retreated, the chihuahua reached the ambulance and jumped on to the radiator. Marge saw the mud-covered creature leering at her through the windscreen and climbed out to retrieve it. When she got back inside Doctor Russell took the note off the animal's collar. Having glanced through it he waded over to Rembrandt and gave it to him.

MAUD MAMUNTU IS MY LONG-LOST MOTHER. SHE HAS DECIDED TO LEAVE MYANIS KUPELA. I AM TRYING TO PERSUADE HER TO GO INTO THE CONGO. PLEASE GIVE HER SAFE-CONDUCT OR SHE WILL MERCILESSLY EXECUTE ALL PRISONERS WHICH INCLUDES ME, HER VERY OWN SON. SHE IS THAT MEAN. SEND THE DOG BACK WITH YOUR REPLY. TELL MARGE I AM SAFE. LOVE LT TARZAN COOL GUY.

Rembrandt perused the message and looked at the sun.

'Not much daylight left. If we try to get in there now we'll be done for,' he thought aloud. 'Hm, and they'll be in the swamps by the time night falls. Pick 'em up the next morning by their tracks.'

'There's no tracks on water, sir,' the wireless transmitter-porter mumbled from beneath the instrument.

'Yes, that's the way to do it. Then we can get out of the swamp for the night, eh? Nasty scare that gave me. Here, Nurse, here's a return note for Lieutenant Tarzan Cool Guy. By the way are you going to marry him now your husband is dead?'

'I'm thinking about it, sir,' Marge snatched the note and tied it to the chihuahua's collar. 'After a reasonable period of mourning.'

As soon as he had seen the message despatched, Rembrandt contacted the sad Colonel on the transmitter. A minute later all firing stopped and peace descended on the Bengweulu Swamps.

14
The Tree of Life

Maud lugged the bomb down off the altar, put it over her shoulder, and walked down the nave of her cathedral for the last time. She had bowed to the inevitable, and the wisdom of her son Oswald. He knew the world outside the swamps better than did his mother – she had fought against it whereas Oswald had fought within it. Tarzan Cool Guy was a name born of the Zonkendawo that she had rejected. With Humphrey and Kovary at his back he had managed to persuade Maud that her faith was doomed if she stayed at Myanis Kupela.

'Where can we go?' Maud had argued. 'Nobody wants troublemakers.'

'The Congo, *Mame*, go into the Katanga, it's only the other side of the swamp.'

'But there's a war on there and it's full of Irishmen!' Maud rubbed at her brow as if cudgelling her brains. 'That's jumping out of the frying pan into the fire.'

'*Mame*, there's so much confusion, chaos and mayhem over there that nobody will notice a few thousand people coming through. All you have to do is find yourself a corner somewhere, build another cathedral, and you're away!'

'My Husband doesn't speak French,' Maud said obstinately. 'Neither do I or any of my people.'

'Then don't talk to anyone. Just keep walking if anyone talks to you. There's room enough in the Congo.'

'What about you, son? You're coming with us, I hope. Your stepfather will be very disappointed if you don't.'

Tarzan Cool Guy wanted to say no. He wanted to get back to Marge and the house in Field-Marshal Montgomery Crescent. After his experiences at Myanis Kupela he had decided to accept Dennis's offer and be his garden-boy. If he had refused to go with his mother, the chances were that she would have changed her mind and stayed in the besieged village. Humphrey and Kovary had said that they would come too, and return to Mufunsi when the Muntu had found a new home. When the chihuahua had returned with Rembrandt's note tied to its collar, the flight into the Congo had been agreed. They would wait until darkness, take only what they needed for the journey, and set fire to Myanis Kupela.

Matthias and the Bucket-Wheel Excavator Gang had decided to drive the D8 bulldozers back to Mufunsi. They had a score to settle with the Open Pit Manager. They knew of the difficulties facing them, the lack of fuel, sustenance, navigational aids.

'We will come with you to the place where the Congo Katanga border with Zonkendawo turns south, then we will go on our own,' Matthias promised. 'It will be a long journey for both of us.'

'You'll never make it!' Tarzan Cool Guy protested. 'Not with three bulldozers.'

'That's what Hammerkop thought when he sent us into the swamp,' Matthias grinned. 'We're going to *bulala* the enemy of our race once and for all!'

When darkness fell over the swamp the Bucket-Wheel Excavator Gang manned the D8s and drove them to the edge of the island. The Muntu had gathered their few possessions and fired their huts. Only the cathedral remained.

'He won't like it,' Maud looked up the tower that was now illuminated by the blazing huts and stockade. 'He was very comfortable here.'

'There's always somewhere else, *Mame*. Do you want me to do it for you?'

Maud shook her head and gripped the torch.

'I made the fire, son, and I must light it. If we didn't love each other so much, God and me, then there'd be times when I'd feel like giving up. Do you know the feeling?'

'Everybody does ... sometimes. But it goes away. Look at me! I'm going to have to accept a menial job.'

Maud turned the torch towards him.

'But you're coming with us, aren't you, Oswald? You promised. If you're thinking of letting your very own mother down!'

'No, *Mame*,' Tarzan Cool Guy explained hurriedly. 'I'm going to see you settled. But there's a woman . . .'

'Oh, Oswald, I never thought you had it in you. Bring her too!' Maud's face softened. 'Poor *piccanin* Oswald, have you got it bad?'

'She's out there in the swamp somewhere. I sent the dog back with a message for her to wait for me. I think she'll do that... I hope so. Her husband can take care of her while I'm away.'

Maud paused on her way up the steps.

'You mean she's married?' she asked, perplexed.

'Yes, you'd like old Dennis.'

'You seem to have led a very complicated life.'

Shaking her head, Maud walked up the steps, her massive figure outlined in flame. Entering the cathedral she crossed to a pile of chopped-up ping-pong tables and thrust the torch into its centre. The flames caught the dry timber immediately. She watched it burn for a moment then turned on her heel, tucked Desaix's bomb under her arm, and went to the west of the island to join her people in flight. As she strode among them in a fire-lit sadness she was full of memories of what lay behind her, but she did not look back at the huge column of flame. Was this how it always had to be? Was the fire always there, waiting to break out of the African earth? Was Fire and Man the same pitiless, greedy element? She stamped on through the mud, her mind bursting with unutterable sorrow.

Rembrandt clapped his hands as he sat in a deck-chair watching the conflagration.

'That's the way to go, eh? By God, that's a wonderful sight. Those people have got guts. Just like that fellow we shot the other day.'

Dennis nodded and shuffled the cards.

'I suppose that means the end of Lieutenant Tarzan Cool Guy.'

Rembrandt nodded vigorously.

'Yes, he'll be in there. Done to a turn. And Humphrey Fluellen and that damned pornographer friend of his who wrote that terrible play. Can't help thinking that there's a mite of poetic justice in it, eh? Look at it go!'

Major Powderham struggled inside the strait-jacket. He saw the dead man rising out of a great cloud of flame, a devil approaching through the blood-thickened night. He had never seen anything so horrible. Now Satan was playing three-card Brag with his commanding officer in Hell. Everywhere was smoky with gore, the trees dripped blood.

The Doctor joined them at the table. Powderham saw his red chewed beard, his fiendish buck-teeth stained with green bile, eyes brown as the flesh of the decaying dead.

'Excuse me interrupting, sir ... I just want a quick word with your companion here,' the ghoul croaked. 'Dennis, this tree, didn't you say that the flower was typically papilionate, calyx green pubescent with light violet colour?'

'That's right,' Dennis slapped down the Ace of Spades and Powderham shuddered, dragging at the ropes that bound him. As he pulled, the drops of blood that were showering from the tree came down with increasing force.

'I wish that lunatic would keep still!' the immature beetles said amongst themselves. 'It's difficult enough to get to sleep as it is with that inferno blazing over the way. Poor old God, he'll be house-hunting again.'

Powderham screamed aloud, his eyes brimming with the tree's blood.

Rembrandt looked across at the writhing officer.

'Keep quiet, old chap. You're getting a little tiresome with all this gibbering. The Doctor here has tried everything he knows and it's no good. You're off your head. That's a good hand you've got there, eh, Dennis?'

The beetles, *Ptyelus grossus*, kept their stylets jammed into the Tree of Life and sucked out the generous sap. As they ejected the pure water over Powderham they sighed amongst themselves. It was a waste. The man did not see the baptismal water, he saw only blood, horror and death whereas he was being bathed in the purest water of the spirit.

Rembrandt wiped his eye.

'Did you spit at me then, Powderham?' he said in amazement.

'Argh!' Powderham gurgled desperately, 'ooooh! argh! I can't stand it! Take me away!'

'Damn cheek!' Rembrandt glared across at the flame-illumined, writhing bundle that was his second-in-command. 'You're getting as bad as the rest of them!'

A beetle chuckled and vibrated its wings on a perch over the card-table.

'What a shot, eh? And from this angle ... not bad.'

'Holy Christ!' Doctor Russell shouted, his face inflamed with wonder. 'I've done it! I've found it! Right under our noses!'

The beetles clicked and whirred among themselves.

'Doesn't he mean under *our* noses?'

'Why didn't he ask? After all we're residents, aren't we?'

'What a lot of excitement! Look at them running!'

Doctor Russell pulled Dennis out of his chair and dragged him over to the tree. The Territorials had heard his cry and were coming over.

'This is it!' his Irish brogue blazed with joy. 'Look at the flowers! The violet flowers!'

The beetles preened, polished and buffed up their fawny, dull backs.

'What about us? What about us?' they buzzed.

'I've found it! The Tree of Life! I've found it!' Doctor Russell wept with happiness. 'Oh God, I've found it! Now they'll have to listen to me! Come here, you marvellous man!'

He clutched Dennis to his breast and danced under the tree, his flying boots kicking water and mud over Powderham. As he danced and wept he sang all the great songs that he knew, snatches of Gaelic melancholy, tripping airs of joy, stirring marches, all his Irish soul burst forth in his mad capering. The rest of the National Territorial Emergency Force rushed out of the reddened dark and crowded under the Rain Tree, each one anxious not to miss Doctor Russell's moment of discovery. Rembrandt was drawn from the card-table, Pyper from his typewriter, Loudwater from Margaret from the Tonga Bar under a bush, all the sergeants and sergeant ex-sergeant-majors, Marge ... they all jammed themselves under *mufundwelamba* and danced, jostling, singing, crying, raising their faces to the cooling rain of the beetles. As the crowd jigged, the beetles dug deeper into the bark of the Tree of Life and sucked harder, squirted faster, their wing-casings gold and fire like scarab-jewels, their tiny articulated legs fastened on the tree like fish-hook anchors. They pumped and pumped the life-giving rain on to the swirling mass of humanity below, breathless, radiant, uproarious.

Powderham sank lower into the mud which had been churned up under the tree. People danced on his head, on his chest, jumped on his groin. Above the joyous din his cries of horror and despair went unheeded until Dennis reached down and pulled the demented officer to his feet. Powderham saw who it was that had helped him and immediately tried to sink back into the mud.

'Oh, let me die!' Powderham pleaded with the dead man. 'Let me die!'

'Who said that?' the beetles grunted. 'Who passed that remark? Where does he think he is?'

Dennis undid Powderham's strait-jacket and threw it on the ground. Powderham scrabbled at the garment, trying to retrieve it but he was too late. Pounding feet squashed it under the mud. Then he tried to run, break out of the stamping, hilarious crowd that swept round and round *mufundwelamba* singing at the tops of their voices. Dennis pulled him back, clasped him around the waist and made him dance.

'No! No!' Powderham moaned. 'Don't...'

'You'll miss out if you run away now. You'll kick yourself afterwards!' the dead man shouted jovially. 'Come on! Let's see it, Pow-wow! Shake a leg!'

As they danced, the crowd rubbed the pure water into their cheeks and temples, opened their mouths while singing and drank of it, sniffed its sweetness up their nostrils, trickled it into their ears. Margaret from the Tonga Bar tore off her blouse and massaged her chest with it, Rembrandt washed his long blond hair in it, Pyper guzzled it hopefully. Above them the beetles hung on to the tree and worked even faster, sending jets of the pure fluid hurtling down under high pressure so it stung the skin of the reeling worshippers below. They stabbed, sucked, heaved, strained, squeezed until their miniscular muscles ached, their thoraxes buckled with exhaustion, and their feeder-tubes steamed with friction. When they could do no more they lay back and watched the crowd slowly come to a halt, holding on to each other, laughing, kissing, panting, drenched with the beetles' rain. There was a silence. Across the swamp Myanis

Kupela still burned, the tower a fiery coupling between earth and sky. The reeds stirred, bats dived away to avoid a mighty homeless presence. There was a single thunderous sniff.

'Well,' said a gentle, melancholy voice, 'what do we do next?'

The following morning a runner from the National Army regulars came over to see why nobody was answering the sad Colonel's wireless signals. He found the camp abandoned, weapons, equipment, everything left behind. There was a pool beneath a tree with a strait-jacket and a blouse floating in it.

Shaking with fear, the runner contacted the Colonel on the transmitter.

'No one here, sir, *ikona, takuli*! They have gone! Witch-doctor's things though, sir, oh, I see it!'

'Put that doctor on, will you. Got a terrible hang-over this morning with that awful stuff I've been drinking,' bleated the instrument.

'Sir, they are gone. All their *imphale* is here, sir, they haven't taken it with them at all!'

'Have you been drinking my whisky?' the sad Colonel asked suspiciously.

The runner pelted back to his unit and warned his comrades. What were they against such power as Maud had? The sad Colonel sat in the reeds while his army melted away, throwing their weapons aside, ripping up their Party cards. As they passed through villages and settlements on their way home, they told the story of Maud's witching of the armies in the Bengweulu Swamps. They had seen a terrible wonder. God had revealed Himself in Africa at last. Up until then He had only shown His face in places like Jerusalem, Mecca and India. Now He was coming to Africa with a vengeance. Maud was His wife and not to be tampered with, or underrated.

15
The Crossing

As the three D8s rolled south again, following their outward journey, their drivers only had a meagre starlight to guide them. The bulldozers were crammed with the aged, the sick and small children, the Bucket-Wheel Excavator Gang electing to walk with the Muntu except for two drivers and Matthias. Behind them roared the flaming tower, ahead stood the vast darkness and the unknown position of Colonel Rembrandt and the National Territorial Emergency Force. As the bulldozers crawled along, crushing reed-islands, ripping up the swamp bottom, the flies and mosquitoes poured from their hiding-places, the crocodiles left their lairs.

Many were taken, many choked with the flies, many sank into the oily murk, many gave up, too tired to wade on behind the grumbling motors. Maud plodded on, helping those she could, gripped by many hands. She knew that many would die that night in the swamp, from the young and the old, from those already on the point of death to those still unborn. Her people would suffer but there was no staying on the island. Myanis Kupela had to be moved.

In the water around her swam the fire. Over her head hung the great tower of God, burning, burning. Brick by brick she had watched it rise until it was done and her lover had His sign. Now God's house was a pillar of fire and it was on her back. He lay on her in his rage and frustration like a disappointed man burns in the bed of a cold wife. She had let him down. She had answered love with suspicion.

Maud clutched the bomb closer to her bosom and thought about God and Desaix. Both men sat in her dream and supported her as the Muntu dragged themselves through the mud, their strength ebbing, their faith their only boldness.

*

The first light spread across the Bengweulu Swamps. Over the still surface of dark water and reeds animals slowly struggled, dragging themselves step by step through the ooze like the original amphibians. Indiscernible from the murk they waded through, the Muntu followed the three D8s on to the dry ground. They flopped down, snakes, lizards, turtles, anything but men and women. The crossing was over but the cost had been heavy. Maud remained on her feet long enough to find a safe place to stand the musical bomb. The place she selected was a little way from the rest of the Muntu in a small grove of trees.

'*Hau!*' she moaned as she saw the National Territorial Emergency Force drawn up facing her people, their presence hidden by a fringe of bush.

'What is it, *Mame?*' Tarzan Cool Guy shouted tiredly.

'Your friends are here!' Maud replied bitterly. 'We have crossed the swamp for nothing.'

The Muntu stared at the advancing lines of soldiers, unable to offer any resistance. A few women ululated softly, then turned their heads away. Men hid their faces in the earth. There was no strength left for fighting. They were as helpless as landed fish.

'Colonel!' Tarzan Cool Guy staggered towards his commanding officer, his hands outstretched. 'Please! You can't! They'll surrender! You'll surrender, won't you, *Mame?*'

Maud nodded, her great head hung on to her chest, the bomb still between her knees.

The vanguard of the National Territorial Emergency Force reached the grove. Tarzan Cool Guy fell on his knees at Rembrandt's feet, clutched Powderham's hand. He gabbled. He pleaded. He wept. In the shade of the trees he grovelled in the dust and dried earth aud turned himself inside-out with begging.

'That's enough, Lieutenant!' Rembrandt ordered, taking off his cap. 'Hogging the scene again, eh?'

Maud looked into the face of the man who had brought an army to destroy her. She saw the magnificent head of blond hair. She saw the flash of fabulous rings on his fingers. She saw his eyes, grave and deep. She saw the light in those eyes and her heart was lifted up.

'Maud Mamuntu,' Rembrandt and Powderham said together, 'will you marry me?'

Doctor Mulombe drove along the line of Canberra bombers which the British Government had loaned him. As a defence against Chinese infiltration they would be most effective and he would have no trouble with hostile neighbours. He was pleased with the way that the defence agreement with the old colonial master was operating. They had kept their word. Mulombe would be protected against alien creeds.

And that included the Muntu.

Beside him in the Rolls-Royce sat his mother. She had been very upset when the initial air strike against Myanis Kupela had failed but besides the desertion of the entire National Territorial Emergency Force and the rout of the Zonkendawon Army, the loss of the ancient Fokker and its pilot were a drop in the ocean. Now the old lady was happy. She had a full squadron of jet bombers to run, plus a magazine crammed with bombs.

'All right now, *Mame*?' Doctor Mulombe squeezed her gnarled hand. 'Now we can really rule the roost. We'll catch Maud wherever she is.'

Mrs Renfrew Mulombe was breathless with delight. One by one the beautiful silver planes slid past, their handsome, white pilots standing rigidly to attention beneath the wings. It was a fairy-tale vision for the old woman, a dream come true.

'We'll keep the Press embargo up until you can get stuck in with this lot, then we can release the news that Maud has been annihilated. She can't get away now. We'll soon be able to forget all the humiliation that Red-inspired bitch has caused us.' Mulombe smiled fondly at his mother.

Mrs Mulombe clutched at her son's hand, her rheumy eyes brightening.

'When we've finished Maud and the Muntu off, then we can use the squadron to sell Party cards. All we have to do is fly over with a bomb or two and the Kaffirs will be queueing to join.'

For three months the Canberra bombers roamed the skies of Zonkendawo. They trespassed on the air-space of neighbouring territories. They caused international incidents. Every inch of the country was explored from the air. There was no sign of Maud and her people, or the National Territorial Emergency Force. They had disappeared.

Doctor Mulombe sent out spies, groups of Party men; he contacted embassies, sent legations, offered rewards, but all to no avail. The only clues which he ever found were the three D8s. They were found parked in a village, deep in the Congo Katanga pedicle. When Mulombe sent an agent to investigate, he received this telegraphic message a few days later.

Mpukane Vill. Haut-Katanga. Time: 1600 21 4
Agent DX67.
LOCAL PEOPLE REPORT A PARTY FROM THE EAST. TEN MEN CALLED LO BW GANG, A PERSON MATTHIAS, A MUSUNGU PYPER OR GREAT WRITER OF LIES WHO WROTE IN A BOOK AND ONE UMFAZI WHOSE AMABELE WERE GROWING BY THE HOUR. LO BW GANG VERY TALKATIVE AND SPOKE OF A GREAT WEDDING FEAST THEY HAD ATTENDED. ALSO THESE MEN TRADED THEIR TRANSPORT OF 3 BULLDOZERS FOR GOURDS OF SWEET BEER AND AUTHORITY TO HALANGANANA YOUNG WOMEN. MATTHIAS ARGUE WITH THIS TRANSACTION AND SAY – I WISH I HAD GONE WITH MOTHER SIXPENNY CASSAVA ROOT REPEAT SIXPENNY CASSAVA ROOT – HE ALSO SIT IN HUT DOORWAY AND CRY. LO BW GANG SAY THEY HAVE UNFINISHED BUSINESS IN MUFUNSI. FROM TALK HERE THEY MUST BE ONLY SURVIVORS OF ATTACK ON MYANIS KUPELA RETURNING HOME SHELL-SHOCKED ALTHOUGH LO BW GANG HAD MANINGI ENERGY SO SAY LOCAL YOUNG GIRLS, WHEN PARTY LEFT MPUKANE MATTHIAS TOO SAD TO WALK SO LO BW GANG CARRY HIM IN LITTER OF CREEPERS SINGING O-O-O-LEVELS.

The Muntu, their numbers increased by the mass conversion of the National Territorial Emergency Force, wandered through the Congo for the next two months. Through jungle, rain-forest, desert and savanna they trekked in search of God's new home, their spirits kept up by the tinkling melody of 'La Vie En Rose'. Over 600 miles of hostile territory, hiding from Simba rebels, Irishmen, Danes, immigration officers, United Nations observers, fact-finders, peace-keepers, tax-collectors, government agents, policemen, insurance salesmen, bandits, and Mrs Mulombe's trespassing Canberra bombers, they wandered, looking for a site to build their new capital.

16
The Ntlokohlaza Mountains

High in the Ntlokohlaza Mountains of the eastern Congo, there is a valley. It is bounded by a great range of sheer crags which tower over the surrounding forests and river-basins, their summits hazy and blue with distance and sometimes crowned with snow. Even the high-ranging eagles do not attempt to ride the equatorial winds up to these lofty peaks. The valley is a secure, fast place, well protected from the outside world, having an earth and sky of its own.

Only one pass enters the valley, from the south. It is a hard and dangerous climb through rocks and streams, cataracts and scree. Occasionally a stray traveller stumbles across it. One or two have ventured to climb into the valley and they have never returned. Most of the time it is bypassed, even by the beasts – the elephant in its migrations, the genial gorilla looking for a lining for its nest, the fluttering carmine bee-eater, even the inquisitive wild dogs trot past showing the whites of their eyes. They know that to go up the pass means entering a mysterious country, an unfamiliar land.

The tribes which inhabit the lowlands around the Ntlokohlaza Mountains cannot see how life could be supportable in the centre of that vast volcanic pile, its blue-edged craters shouldering the clouds. Although aware of the valley's existence, they never go near it and advise the hunters and seekers who pass through their villages to do the same thing. It is not that they believe the rumours that are current in the neighbourhood, but being a superstitious people they have no wish to offend whatever power might have made the valley its home. They give the stories credence as a sign of respect, rather than accepting them as truth.

They tell of a giant woman, the mistress of God and Man, and her embrace is mightier than Death. Anyone who has suffered it must leave all lesser loves and stay in the cold climes of the valley. What will keep him warm will not be the sun as it rides along the Equator, nor the winds that blow down from the mountains, it will be the perpetual love of this woman, a love that never tires or ceases, a love that has no end and no beginning, a love that has built its own world.

To go up to this valley and meet this monster needs a courage beyond the summons of most men : not the courage to face an enemy but to face the biggest friend imaginable. This enormous concubine of the old earth demands, and will have, all.

Also the stories tell of a city with a great tower.

Of a tinkling song that is always being whistled and sung.

Of an orchard of Rain Trees.

Of a host of fawny beetles making the purest of water.

But it is the last story that the lowland tribes cannot believe.

It tells of a people who are black and white and live as one.

More About Penguins and Pelicans

Penguinews, which appears every month, contains details of all the new books issued by Penguins as they are published. From time to time it is supplemented by *Penguins in Print*, which is our complete list of almost 5,000 titles.

A specimen copy of *Penguinews* will be sent to you free on request. Please write to Dept EP, Penguin Books Ltd, Harmondsworth, Middlesex, for your copy.

In the U.S.A.: For a complete list of books available from Penguins in the United States write to Dept CS, Penguin Books, 625 Madison Avenue, New York, New York 10022.

In Canada: For a complete list of books available from Penguins in Canada write to Penguin Books Canada Ltd, 2801 John Street, Markham, Ontario L3R 1B4.